Love is
a time of enchantment:
in it all days are fair and all fields
green. Youth is blest by it,
old age made benign:
the eyes of love see
roses blooming in December,
and sunshine through rain. Verily
is the time of true-love
a time of enchantment — and
Oh! how eager is woman
to be bewitched!

MERLAKE TOWERS

Merlake Towers dominates the remote island off the rugged Cornish coast, and it is here, early in the reign of Victoria, that Jade-Anna escapes to from the memories of a lost love. But no escape awaits her at Merlake Towers, not even when she becomes the bride of Ivan Sterne, owner of Merlake. Mystery and brooding pervade the island, and Jade-Anna is determined to solve it.

MARY WILLIAMS

◆

MERLAKE TOWERS

Complete and Unabridged

ULVERSCROFT
Leicester

First published in Great Britain in 1984

First Large Print Edition
published March 1993

British Library CIP Data

Williams, Mary
    Merlake towers.—Large print ed.—
Ulverscroft large print series: romance
I. Title
823.914 [F]

ISBN 0–7089–2834–X

Published by
F. A. Thorpe (Publishing) Ltd.
Anstey, Leicestershire

Set by Words & Graphics Ltd.
Anstey, Leicestershire
Printed and bound in Great Britain by
T. J. Press (Padstow) Ltd., Padstow, Cornwall

Many the wonders I this day have
    seen;
The sun, when first kist away the
    tears
That fill'd the eyes of morn; — the
    laurel'd peers
Who from the feathery gold of evening
    lean; —
The ocean with its vastness, its blue-
    green,
Its ships, its rocks, its caves, its hopes,
    its fears; —
Its voice mysterious, which whoso
    hears
Must think on what will be and what
    has been.

               JOHN KEATS

1

1840

ACROSS the room I saw Ivan Sterne staring over the heads of the wedding guests, as though no one in the room interested him. That of course was quite untrue. His thoughts just then must have been very much upon the bride, my cousin Evadne. That he had come at all to the reception surprised me. I suppose it was a matter of pride, of trying to show he didn't care. He certainly appeared not to. But everyone must know, surely, that his aloofness was merely a façade — a pose.

During the last year he had made it his business to call at Mounterrith, my uncle's home, on any possible excuse. Neither family nor servants could have been blind to his infatuation. It wasn't surprising. Evadne was strikingly beautiful, violet-eyed under her mass of red-gold hair, with the art of entrancing any eligible male who crossed her path.

She was also a flirt and a coquette, and had never seemed content until she'd proved herself irresistible to her string of courtiers — Ivan Sterne, in particular. Then, when she'd successfully ensnared him, she'd confided to me secretly that he'd asked her to be his wife, and she'd refused.

"Fancy!" she'd exclaimed. "As if I'd dream of it? Can you imagine it for one moment — me married to such a stern-looking joyless prig? And that island of his! — it would be like prison. Oh, no, thank you." She'd paused, eyeing me a trifle slyly. "I think he was hurt, though. He'd no reason to be. Far too old anyway."

Something about her manner had irritated me. She'd been so clearly enjoying the situation, savouring once more another conquest.

"I was told he was thirty-eight exactly," I'd said, "very rich, and certainly not a prig. I would have thought you might jump at the chance. Lots of women have been after him."

"Don't be an idiot. I'm not 'lots of

women'. And anyway, I don't love him. I love Chris."

Her last statement had shaken me. So did I. Christopher, the son of Sir Bruce Ferris, had been the one person I really cared about since I'd come to Mounterrith ten years before to live with Sir Humphrey Ellan, my uncle, his wife Clarissa and Evadne, at their stately Cornish mansion. I'd been almost eight years old then; my father Bertrand — Humphrey's wild younger brother — had been disowned by the family when he married my mother, Marietta, a half-Spanish, half-French dancer in a theatre company on the continent. She had died when I was three, and my early childhood had been a medley of good luck and bad — of never staying long in one place — luxurious periods when Bertie had won at the gaming tables — followed by exciting but frightening days of insecurity haunted by debts that couldn't be paid, and posing as tramps, artists, or vagabonds until my father struck rich again — generally through contact with some impressionable landlady, or ageing courtesan.

The nicest times for me had been when we travelled with fairs to country places. Bertie had done sketches then of people in the crowds. He was clever with brush and pen, and the sweet earth-smell of nights spent in the open air with the heady perfume of bluebells and May blossom hanging over lush ditches and fields, had driven away briefly all memories of smoke and ugly city streets and taverns. I'd longed to be a gipsy for ever, or a strolling player performing from a cart in village squares.

It hadn't happened though. My father had met Mrs Price — Mrs Lucy Price — the widow of a rich inn-keeper. She was stout and rosy with fierce black eyes, and she hadn't wanted me in her life; she'd wanted Bertie and marriage as well. That's what she'd got. I'd been packed off one day by coach for Mounterrith in Cornwall to be properly cared for in the 'family bosom'.

The journey west had taken nine days of rough travelling over roads full of holes and pools, with nights spent at various small inns and kiddleywinks often infested with fleas. Sometimes we travellers had been lucky and found clean lodgings, where mouth-watering country tarts had been served. The air in the carts we'd journeyed in, following the crossing by ferry of the Tamar, had been close and thick with human body-smells mingled with smoke. Men and women — even children — smoked those days. Frequently the driver had complained. Once, when a huge lump of a man refused to put out his pipe, there'd been a fight. He'd been left on the road clutching a brandy bottle and shouting curses. I'd drawn my cloak round me instinctively, but a kindly, stout, black-eyed woman had laughed, put an arm about my shoulders, and said, "Doan' 'ee fret, luv — no greedy foot-pad Johnny's goin' to waste time on us lot. An' no-one'll get the better o' Nick Pender neither. You'm safe wi' Nick, m'dear." Nick was the driver, and to me he'd looked more ferocious than the man he'd sent flying.

I'd had the feeling of being in some kind of weird dream, a sensation accentuated by tiredness and the constant clip-clop of hooves and rattle of wheels over stones. What sun there'd been

5

that day had already faded behind a belt of cloud hugging the moorland ridge. Ancient menhirs stood sentinel-like through the rising mist, as guardians of burial grounds where long-forgotten chieftains lay. The queer half-light sent contorted clawing shadows looming over the track. Twisted trees, boulders and tangled undergrowth had assumed a threatening atavistic identity when the sudden squawk of a bird rising broke the eerie monotony of our journey.

Once there'd been a shrill neighing, followed by the dark shape of a wild pony with flying mane and hooves galloping past. The cart had lurched and the horses reared; then we'd gone on again. When the driver stopped to get the cart's lamps lighted, I'd heard the barking of a fox, and a moment later seen its lithe form streaking across the lane.

But at last we'd arrived at Bodmin, where my uncle's coach was waiting to take me to Mounterrith.

How different, and what a relief it had been to lie back in a comfortably padded seat, away from the smells and cursing of the packed cart. I'd been far too tired then to envisage any clear picture of what life might be like in my new home, or anticipate the type of welcome I'd receive from Aunt Clarissa or my cousin Evadne, but I'd tried to believe there'd be kindness, even some sort of affection waiting.

How wrong I'd been.

From the very beginning of my days there, I'd been made to feel an intruder, an unwanted responsibility and dependant. Not by my uncle, who was too concerned with himself and his own affairs to bother, but by his wife, Aunt Clarissa, and in a condescending way by Evadne.

I had been treated outwardly well of course, sharing lessons from Miss Carndale, my cousin's governess, and accepted apparently as one of the family. But with a difference — oh what a difference. Hardly a day had passed without some sly or subtle allusion to my unfortunate state — my personal penury, and the disgrace it had been to be born my mother's daughter. Any hint of vanity on my part had been ruthlessly dispelled at the outset, either with the cane, or some other humiliating punishment. To have been beautiful, like Evadne, would have been a help. But I wasn't. Therefore I'd needed to make an impression in some other way, by being either extremely striking in appearance or clever. Actually my mind and imagination were brighter than my cousin's, but I was given no chance to prove it. And being constantly reminded how plain I was in contrast to Evadne had gradually made me feel there was no point in bothering with my appearance.

My hair, which was dark chestnut brown, was drawn severely to a high knot from my wide forehead. My mouth, which was too wide for beauty, with a rather full underlip, had a sullen look above a pointed cleft chin, and my cheekbones were too high — 'like a cat's' — Evadne said, when she wanted to be nasty. My eyes were cat-like, too, sometimes. But they were so strange in colour — dark, deepest jade, fringed by black lashes, which was why, of course, my mother had named me Jade. Evadne had been outwardly a little contemptuous.

"You can never wear blue or pink — not even violet, with eyes like yours," she said. "You'd look just silly. I suppose it's because you're foreign."

"I'm not foreign," I'd said. "My father's your father's brother."

"Your mother was, though. Your mother was — "

"Shut up," I'd said, before any unpleasant word left her lips, and I'd smacked her face hard.

For that I'd been beaten.

What she'd said — the part about not wearing pink or pretty colours was true, of course. Green, luscious dark rose, orange or gold would have suited me. But although I'd done my best to get Aunt Clarissa to agree, she never did. It was always dull grey or fawn for me — some quiet shade that subdued my own colour to drabness, and my personality to truculent shyness. Even my own name, Jade, she would not allow me to keep.

"Quite ridiculous," she said. "From today you will be known as Anna."

And so it had been. I had grown used to the sound of it, but the role enforced on me with it had remained distasteful and humiliating. To have shown rebellion would have been useless, as I'd learned, when I reached my teens. But beneath my enforced mouse-like exterior — that's how I'd overheard Ivan Sterne refer to me one afternoon when he was visiting Evadne — the real me — Jade — still lurked. However dull and submissive Anna might appear — however despised a member of the 'family bosom' — wretched words — Jade would one day shock them all and take her rightful colourful place in society. Of course, Aunt Clarissa never guessed my bitter resentment, least of all on that momentous occasion of my cousin's marriage. I doubt if she was even conscious of my presence at all. I felt insignificant and trapped, and hated the jokes and laughter, the toasting and celebrating — the wine, the fashionable guests in their splendid clothes — the silks and scents, and silly meaningless chatter.

Most of all I hated Evadne for stealing Christopher Ferris, and destroying the only true friendship I'd ever had. Chris had been so different from Evadne's other admirers. Of all the visitors who ever came to Mounterrith, he alone had made me feel I mattered. However severely I dressed he'd seemed to see beneath the surface, had even flattered me at times by warm glances and remarks that had sent me into a whirl of excitement. I'd even imagined he was beginning to fall in love with me.

Now it was all over. Evadne had made her choice, and he'd fallen at her feet like all the rest. She had been aware of my feelings, too. Sly digs when we were alone together and amused glances from her incredibly beautiful violet eyes had proved the smug satisfaction she'd felt in reducing me again to mere insignificance. The poor relation. Uncle Humphrey's drab mouse of a dependant! I felt a kind of Cinderella.

And yet I wasn't really drab. If I'd had just the chance, for once, of wearing a lovely gown for the wedding reception, I might have softened and restrained the violence of my feelings. But Aunt Clarissa, under a veneer of interest and concern, had insisted on the grey silk, which was quite high on the shoulders and neck, severely cut, with white starched cuffs, and without embellishment of flower or lace.

"Oh no, Anna," she'd protested when I'd suggested satin of a golden shade. "It wouldn't be suitable — with your colouring. You're really not the type. You could so easily look — flamboyant. Your hair is too dense, and when you're excited you flush so. Grey is the most tasteful choice. I mean it, my dear."

She may have really thought so, I don't want to misjudge her. It had certainly been an expensive gown. But if only she had considered my feelings for once, I could have felt kinder.

"Is it so important to be tasteful?" I'd asked sharply. "Everyone knows I'm a throw-back — that's the idea, isn't it? No one expects me to be a lady, I'm sure, not with my background. You've made very certain of that."

The moment the hot words were out, I realised my mistake.

"How dare you speak to me like that, you ungrateful chit? After all we've done for you. You should be whipped; you're not too old, after all. Now no more arguments. You will wear what I choose or not appear at all."

"Perhaps that would be better."

"Try and put me in the wrong? Is that what you want to do? Make out to all our friends that I treat you differently from my own child?" She'd been breathing heavily. I'd felt momentarily triumphant.

"No I don't care what your friends think."

I'd walked out of the room with my head held high, leaving her speechless.

But I'd worn the grey.

And I was hating it — feeling very like the mousy creature referred to by Ivan Sterne as I noticed his aloof stance following the auspicious event of my cousin's marriage to Christopher. He was not, strictly speaking, a handsome man, but impressive, with a panther-like grace setting him apart from most of the other male guests who were inclined to be either on the portly side or giving promise of it — all meticulously attired in velvet cut-away tailed coats, long drainpipe trousers, silk embroidered waistcoats and high neckcloths. Cheeks were flushed, hair elegantly curled, with sideburns, moustaches and beards were carefully trimmed and waxed. Ivan Sterne was quite different. He wore a dark grey velvet jacket, simply cut, and trousers of the same shade. His gold-coloured waistcoat was plain below the white collar of his shirt. An elegant figure, yet forbidding somehow. But then that was to be expected.

The Sterne family, who for generations had owned and lived at the remote towered mansion of Merlake Island, five miles off Land's End, had an impressive and fearsome history behind them. Though nobly born and accepted by society, their enormous wealth was known, from past records, to have been largely accrued in earlier days through dark means, including slaving and wrecking. Such unpalatable facts were now conveniently glossed over. Power in local projects on the mainland, concerned with shipping, and county prosperity, mining, had bred a veneer of respect from natives, only faintly shadowed by an undercurrent of lingering suspicion. Apart from that, the Sternes

14

had shown tremendous bravery during wars with France and Spain. Adventurers they might have been, but colourful figures to be ignored at their peril. Now Ivan, the only surviving son of a proud line, had been dealt a blow which I knew he must find hard to endure.

I watched him for some moments nod politely, as Evadne, in her cream pearl-studden gown, wove her way between the elegant crowd of well-wishers and paused briefly giving him one of her arch, yet so innocent-looking smiles. Very graciously he took her hand, raising it briefly to his lips. But the gesture was mechanical, his face impassive. I wondered if his hurt was as painful as mine was when a few minutes later Christopher Ferris made a point of bringing me a glass of wine.

"Well, Anna," he said, handing it to me, "aren't you going to wish me happiness, and luck?" The latter, certainly, I thought, but I did not say so.

"Of course, Christopher," I answered, adding quickly, "Evadne looks very beautiful."

"You too," he lied gallantly.

"Oh, don't be ridiculous."

I put the wine down, turned, lifted my head, and walked to the door of the great hall. It was really too much — having to watch Evadne queening it with her new husband — the man I'd secretly been in love with for so long — and on top of this being forced to endure his false flattery and pity.

Pity.

The knowledge suddenly stung me to quick action, and before anyone had time to miss me — in any case, no one would have cared — I rushed from the assembly, along the hall and up the vast staircase, bumping into a maid unceremoniously, on the landing leading to my own room. Once there, I stood in front of the mirror staring at the prim grey-clad reflection with mounting defiance flooding my whole being. In a fit of temper, I wrenched the bodice open at the neck, and pulled my thick hair free of its constricting pins. Then, recklessly, but in full command of my senses and quite aware of my intentions, I hurried on light feet to Evadne's room which was nearby. I stared for a second or two at the fancy boxes, numerous clothes and frilly etceteras scattered about the canopied bed and on chairs and chaise-longue, before pulling the wardrobe door wide open.

I knew I had to hurry. At any time a maid might appear to tidy up. But there was so much — so much of all I'd never had — to bewilder and confuse me into envy, my heart was pounding, my skin glowed from excitement, and my head swam as I blinked, trying to make a quick decision. It did not take long.

The green, I thought — the green satin that was the colour of my eyes. As far as I recalled, Evadne had never worn it — to her it was just another gown hidden away among a conglomeration of other lovely unwanted clothes.

I pulled it from its hanging, and after making sure no one was about, hurried back to my own more unimpressive domain, with the dress held close against my side. Nobody saw me. Obviously my absence downstairs had not been noticed. There was no sound of hurrying footsteps — no imperious echoes of Aunt Clarissa's voice calling, "Where are you, Anna?

Come down immediately — "

Just silence holding only muted undertones of the clock ticking, and from far below the faint rise and ebb of conversation and hushed laughter.

The despised grey silk was soon an abandoned heap on the floor. I stepped out of it, gave it a quick kick aside, and took an extra underskirt from a drawer. I redressed with mechanical impatience, locating as best I could the numerous fastenings of the exotic green. The bodice was pointed; with a narrow waist, from which the drapes puffed to a wide hem line, revealing a further skirt of green and gold brocade beneath. The gown was cut low across the bosom, bordered with rich lace that fell almost to the elbows above the full sleeves. My amber necklace lay by the mirror. I picked it up and put it round my neck, where it lay enticingly close to the hollow of my throat, somehow enhancing the shadowed recess between breasts under the tight corsage.

Then I adjusted my hair, parting it in the centre so it could fall in ringlets round my face. After that I secured a portion with a sparkling band, and placed a single yellow rose from a vase near my ear. There were pots of cream and coloured salve in a drawer that had once been used for theatricals at Christmas. Without any conscience at all, I touched my cheeks with palest pink, and darkened my lips. At the last minute, before going downstairs, I took a patch and put it carefully between cheek and chin, just above the upper lip.

Triumph filled me when I faced myself through the mirror.

I knew at that moment I looked spectacular, and the knowledge filled me with a strange sense of exhilaration and confidence. There would naturally be an angry scene later, when I had to face my aunt. But by then it would be too late to spoil the effect. Everyone present at the reception would have seen Jade for the first time, instead of Anna.

Including Ivan Sterne.

So holding my head high, and grasping a fan in my hand — a gift condescendingly given to me by Evadne in a generous mood — I left the bedroom and made my way downstairs.

Whether my appearance, at first, caused much attention, I don't know. Probably not — everyone was so involved in the flippant chatter of celebration. But by the time I reached Ivan Sterne's side I was aware, through my own tensed-up excitement, of little gasps and nearby heads turning.

I lifted my chin an inch or two higher, and said softly, but clearly enough for him to hear, "Mr Sterne — sir — "

As though broken from some unpleasant dream his head turned. He looked down sharply from his six feet two, into my eyes. For one dreadful moment I thought I was about to be snubbed — I was quite certain, at first, that he didn't recognise me. Then a puzzled look of astonishment, holding a flicker of interest, lit his cold grey eyes to kindling life.

"Madam — " he said. "Mademoiselle — "

"Jade — " I said, very quietly. "Jade Ellan."

He took my hand and raised it gallantly to his lips.

"I'm enchanted," he said, adding

quickly, "but you have no glass in your hand."

"Neither have you," I remarked pointedly.

"Ah. So we are — "

"Two of a kind," I interrupted rashly, "in very much the same situation, I think."

I waited with bated breath for his reaction, knowing that I was being extremely forward.

He paused for only a second before saying in cool polite tones, "A state of affairs easily remedied, I'm sure."

What I said then, or whether, even, I spoke at all, I don't remember. All I recall is of accompanying him through the crowd towards the long glittering side-board, where a liveried footman hurriedly produced a tray of sparkling champagne and vintage wines.

When we both had glasses he raised one to his lips, saying politely, "Your good health, Miss Ellan." He gave a slight bow. There was no flicker of an expression on his face, his tones were bland, polite, impersonal.

I inclined my head faintly; then he said

21

in subdued, though quite clear tones, "May I escort you to the conservatory?"

I gave a gesture of acknowledgement.

Who overheard the remark I don't know, but someone must have. With my arm held by his, and a soft rustle of the green draperies, we made our way from the room, across the hall into the large glass annexe. It was warm and steamy, and filled with the heady scent of flowering plants — geraniums mostly — mingled with the perfume of guests who had dallied there earlier. A couple I did not know got up from a wrought iron seat ambling away over-casually when we appeared. They were young, and obviously in love. Ivan Sterne stretched out a hand — "Are you tired? Do you care to rest?"

I faced him, with my colour rising, still possessed by the exhilarating sense of reckless bravado.

"No, thank you. I am not at all tired. I'm just — "

"Grateful to be away from the crowds?" he supplemented before I could finish.

"Yes."

"I wouldn't have thought a young lady

of your looks and bearing would have found parties so odious. Or is it that this one in particular annoys you?"

"You're quite right," I answered.

"And the reason? But perhaps I shouldn't ask."

"I don't think you need to," I replied shortly. "Neither need you comment on my looks and bearing, Mr Sterne. At any moment now, my aunt's likely to storm in chiding me for my unspeakable behaviour in appearing as I am."

"As you are?"

"The 'grey mouse' as you always thought me — appearing in borrowed plumes as a duchess."

I fancied he flushed slightly. There was a pause before he remarked, "I admit I didn't recognise you at first. Though why you should deem yourself a grey mouse — "

I smiled mechanically.

"I don't, Mr Sterne, and I'm not. It was your description, which you've used more than once, if you remember — in conversation with my cousin."

"If I did, it was in jest," he said stiffly. "I don't recall any particular reason for making such a remark."

"Of course not. Why should you? You were naturally far too enamoured and concerned with my beautiful cousin." I lifted a hand and fanned my face languidly, amazed at my own effrontery, yet with my heart beating so wildly I could hardly breathe.

"Indeed!" The word was clipped and icy cold.

"Yes. I don't blame you, of course. Everyone was, and is."

"Everyone was what?"

Not looking at him I answered recklessly, "In love with her. It's the same with all men." I shrugged, and gave a short bitter laugh. "She's always had everything — looks, charm, wealth and all the fine clothes she wanted. Even this dress is hers. I stole it a few minutes ago, to make an impression." A sense of contempt for myself and the soft luxurious satin, seized me briefly, then quickly died again into defiance. When he didn't speak, I continued, "Just for one evening I determined to be myself — Jade. To show them — Christopher — that I didn't care."

"Why Christopher?"

"Because I was in love with him; as you were — with Evadne," I replied.

He didn't deny it, just stared at me with nothing on his face at all to tell me what he was feeling — no indication even of surprise, shock, irritation or despair; merely static, wooden, indifference.

Then he said calmly, "I see."

"Of course, there'll be a dreadful fuss about it," I went on, with the words tumbling quickly out, one after the other. "But I shan't care — a damn!" There! it was out. I could feel my clenched hands, dampen with perspiration.

"I'm sure you're extremely courageous," he said, after a pause. "And what will you do when the 'dreadful fuss' is over? Run away?"

"Probably."

"Where to?"

"I don't know yet," I told him abruptly. "In any case, there's no need to worry about me."

"I don't intend to," he said curtly. "You seem a young lady possessing a remarkable capacity for involving others in your personal affairs, and with an eagle eye — shall we say — for the main chance — " The faint amusement in his cold eyes stung me.

"I'm sorry I intruded. Do you mind escorting me back to the drawing room?"

"Yes, I do mind. Let us get things clear first."

"What things?"

"Your sudden interest in my company. We both know it's not personal. There's no attraction between us — no particular liking. What is it you want then? To save your face for this one evening only? — or revenge? Is that it? I believe it is. Jealousy of your cousin's beauty. Tit-for-tat. You think I somehow have power and can give you sufficient to throw it in her face? What a ridiculous notion."

"How dare you," I said in a furious undertone.

For the first time he really smiled; a cold self-confident gesture that turned my indignation to acute hatred. But like a pricked balloon it evaporated when he continued, "Oh, don't get me wrongly. As you pointed out — in a way we're both in the same boat so I'll be glad to help, if I can."

"Help?"

"Isn't that what you want?"

"I suppose so. Although I don't see — "

"What I can do? No. Well, I'll be brief, or the fussy old hens and their dressed-up odious daughters will scent a scandal." He glanced momentarily towards the door where a few curious eyes were already upon us.

Touching a fern, and pretending indifference to my presence under a veneer of casual politeness, he said quietly, "Suppose you inform your lady aunt that I have offered you a position — at Merlake?"

"At — " I broke off breathlessly, putting a hand to my lips as he said, "Control yourself, just listen and try not to show surprise. Use your fan, and appear to be bored and ready to leave — "

I did my best. But I could hardly believe my own ears as he continued, "Your role would be quite respectable. Feminine company's needed on the island, for my ward and his aunt. You would have a moderate salary, and help with a few light duties domestically. Does it appeal to you?"

"A companion, do you mean? House-keeper or something?"

Still purporting to be examining the plants, he resumed, "Certainly not a housekeeper. I have quite an efficient one, and it's not at all likely you'd be competent. However — " he sniffed a flower "it's entirely up to you. And you need have no fears concerning my intentions. As you so aptly pointed out, my interest lies — or did lie — in quite a different direction. You're no more my type, Miss Ellan, than I am yours, which should provide the basis for a reasonable business arrangement."

"It's all so sudden," I said. "You hardly know me."

"I don't know you at all. But you appear healthy, strong, and with a mind of your own. I think you'd fit in with our life at Merlake. You'd have to, if you decide to come. But, of course, if it's too much of a challenge — "

"It isn't," I interrupted suddenly, realising in one quick moment that this was a chance at last of breaking away from Mounterrith. "All right." I lifted my chin, and could feel my cheeks flush again, and my eyes blaze with decision. "I'll accept your offer, Mr Sterne."

He gave a little bow, took my arm once more, and said, "Then let us go and inform your aunt, shall we? The sooner the matter is settled, the better."

So it was that my immediate future was decided.

The next week I sailed, with Ivan Sterne, for Merlake Island.

2

THE Autumn day was quiet, ruffled only by a slight breeze when Ivan Sterne and myself set off from Mounterrith for our remote destination. We travelled by post-chaise to Penzance, stopping at Truro for refreshments. Aunt Clarissa had been extremely cordial at the parting. I knew she was gratified to have me off her hands, expressing pleasure that I was to join such an illustrious household. That I was also to fill the role of merely servant in some sphere or other, added to her sense of superiority and rightness of things, although her keen eyes told me as well that she was perhaps a trifle jealous of the nonchalant — 'insolent', she would have termed it — manner in which I had so readily accepted the offer.

"I am exceeding pleased for *your* sake — " she had said, after dutifully kissing my cheek at Mounterrith's grand front door before we left. "Your Uncle

and I will miss you, of course — "
hypocritically " — as I *hope* you will
us, just a little. We've tried to do our
best for you during your stay. Try and
remember that in the days to come."

"I shan't ever forget it," I'd said
truthfully, which was quite true, though
not in the way she'd intended.

My Uncle Humphrey had been a little
warmer and more forthcoming.

"Take care of yourself, m'dear," he'd
whispered gruffly in my ear. "It won't
be quite the same here when you've
gone. Here, take this." Unseen to his
wife he'd pushed a small velvet wallet
of coins into my hand, and for the first
time I'd realised there was someone at
Mounterrith who had a shred of genuine
feeling for me.

★ ★ ★

For the first part of the journey to
Truro, where there was to be an hour's
rest for refreshments and for the horses
to be changed, Ivan Sterne said little,
and then it was merely to comment
on the weather, the poor state of the

roads, and some equally mundane topic. Four other passengers of nondescript appearance were travelling — a portly ruddy-cheeked man looking like a farmer, a middle-aged couple, and a thin youth, very correctly clad, who could easily have been a clerk in some shipping office or other business concern.

However, during the meal which was served in the high-ceilinged dining room of an established coaching-house, the stern face relaxed a little as he unfolded a few details of what my life might be on Merlake Island.

"I hope you won't be lonely," he said at one point. "We don't have many visitors, and as the Island's so cut off, visits to the mainland are rare. In fact, except for myself, I prefer the household to be a unit on its own."

"You mean, no one's allowed to leave?"

"I didn't say so. The staff — which incidentally is small for such a large place — are content with their duties on the estate, and it's better for a young child to have a settled background rather than be pushed between Merlake and the mainland. That also applies to my Great-Aunt Augusta. She has her own quarters at the house."

"I understand."

He smiled. "You can hardly do that yet. The prospect must sound a little formidable, but there'll be times of escape for you — occasionally — when I may wish you to act as hostess at my Penzance establishment."

I was surprised.

"*Penzance?*"

He nodded. "I have offices there, with a small house adjoining — Mrs Brand, who usually arranges things when I'm forced to entertain my important business acquaintances, is shortly retiring. So your presence could be useful. Also perhaps for doing a little secretarial work."

"I'm not trained for either, as you pointed out before," I told him, abruptly.

"I'm sure you'll soon learn. And as such occasions will be so very rare, you won't find them too arduous."

When I didn't answer he continued, "Is the meal to your satisfaction? This hostelry is noted for its good food. Simple, but well served generally."

"I'm sure it's excellent," I answered in similar polite tones, "although I find it rather — overmuch."

Actually, I was feeling slightly queasy from the jolting of the journey and excitement; also boiled mutton with dumplings had never been a favourite meal of mine; too reminiscent of the schoolroom where I'd had to eat in disgrace when Evadne was downstairs sharing more delicately sumptuous fare with her parents.

"H'm? Have a little more wine," I heard Ivan saying, as he reached for the bottle and poured more into my glass. "It may lift your spirits." I accepted, and found he was right.

When we rejoined the coach my head was too light to think clearly; any faint foreboding had faded with the memory of the odious dumplings, and I even felt exhilaration as the wooded moorland landscape changed to wind-swept hills overlooking Penzance.

The town was busy when we alighted at the Square, taking a cab down to the harbour. Crowds wandered about the quay. A vessel had just berthed, and merchandise was being unloaded, including brandy, lace, and other much coveted goods. French sailors and Spaniards were among the jostling assembly. A rather rough-looking individual pushed through eager to earn something as carrier for any rich-looking top-hatted gentleman on the scene. Ivan nodded, handed his luggage over, but insisted himself on carrying the valise which contained my only few personal possessions. The air was salty, pungent with the odours of fish, oil, and human beings. When we reached the water's edge, a burly figure in seaman's attire, raised a hand to his forehead respectfully, and Mr Sterne's hand closed on my arm.

"Come along. We shall soon be away."

He paid the carrier, leaving the bags to be handled by the stranger who was not at all a pleasant-looking character. His burly figure was clad in seaman's clothes. He was tall, towering to more than six feet, with a woollen cap pushed sideways over a crop of red hair. His face was broad with small piggy eyes peering from under thick brows. I didn't like him.

My first instinct was that he resented me, but I determined not to be intimidated and to curb a faint stirring of fear.

"Miss Ellan is joining our household," Mr Sterne told the man; then turning to me he added, "Jed Marryat and his son Marte have charge of the boats and any journeys I take to the mainland."

I inclined my head, Jed touched his brow, but there was no servility in it.

Presently we were boarding the barque. I had expected something a little larger and more spectacular. It was small, with two masts for sails, and could obviously be used for rowing by oars, or sailing. 'The lugger', I heard Jed refer to it later, although from a book I studied during following weeks, this strange craft did not exactly fit the description. I'd been surprised when Ivan didn't wait an hour or so in Penzance to visit his offices there, but when we were settled and sailing away from the shore he explained that he would be returning, alone, in a week's time for a short stay, and that he thought it best to get to Merlake before the bad weather set in.

I was surprised. "Bad?" I enquired.

"But everything's so calm and clear now."

"Too clear," he told me. "When the water's glassy and the horizon hard you can take it a storm is on the way."

And this happened.

As evening approached, a chill wind rose and rippled the sea. Jed and his son, Marte, pulled at the oars with increasing vigour. "Come down to the cabin," Ivan said. I followed him, but when I saw the confined space, a wave of claustrophobia over took me.

"If you don't mind I'd rather be on deck," I said. "I don't mind the wind."

He shrugged. "Just as you like. In the end you may be forced down."

So I clambered up again; the tide, in the space of a few minutes, had strengthened, and was lashing and beating against the sides of the boat. At intervals great waves rose furiously, sending swirls of water overboard. Salt stung my eyes and face. I clung to a rail and almost fell. Ivan took my arm.

"This time I insist," he shouted, "come along. Do as you're told." He pushed me below and said coldly, wiping the wet hair from his forehead, "Courage is one thing, stupidity quite another. I hope you're not going to turn into a rebel, Miss Ellan. My word is law on Merlake. Try and remember that or there'll be trouble. Another thing — " his eyes narrowed slightly — "don't flaunt any airs before Jed or Marte. I want no trouble with those in my employ. Jed has serious responsibilities on the island, which he undertakes to my satisfaction. So take care not to defy him."

Feeling like a chastened child and resenting it, I said, "And Marte?" If possible, I had found Marte even more repellent than his father. He was smaller and thinner, spotty-faced, with hair brighter red than Jed's, and light grey eyes appearing shifty looking, and avaricious, especially when they'd rested briefly on me. During that quick moment I'd decided to be very wary indeed of Marte.

"Marte?" I heard Ivan echo. "He, too, does what I say, and what his father tells him."

"I understand," I said recklessly. "Sort of watch-dogs, is that it?"

"Exactly. Although you could have put it differently."

Deciding to change the topic I asked, "Have you decided what place I'm to fill exactly at Merlake? I mean, will the house-keeper tell me what to do? Or shall I be more concerned with your work? You said — "

"All you have to do is to be co-operative," was the cold reply; "in the last resort it's my word that counts. I'm master, remember."

"Of everything and everyone, I suppose." The edge of sarcasm in my voice must have startled him, and perhaps I shouldn't have spoken in such a way. He stared at me sharply, then replied curtly:

"Yes. Including you."

I could feel the colour staining my cheeks.

"Thank you for warning me. And is that what I'm to call you? Master?"

"It would save any uncomfortable speculations. But — " a quirk of humour touched his lips, making him suddenly appear younger and more human. "I don't think that's necessary. 'Mr Sterne' will do for the time being, and when we're away from the island something less formal perhaps. However, we needn't discuss such a situation yet. There's no likelihood of your accompanying me in the foreseeable future."

During the rest of that uncomfortable sea-trip only odd remarks were passed between us. Apart from my ruffled temper I was tired and longing for a bed to lie on. In any case the booming of waves, moaning of wind, creaking timber, and lurching of the small vessel would have made sustained conversation impossible. I tried not to be apprehensive, but for a wild second, when the boat ground to shore and Jed, after dropping anchor, jumped out at the foot of a small granite promontory, I would have done almost anything to be safely back at Mounterrith in Aunt Clarissa's mean care.

The fading sky was deepening to shrouded twilight as Ivan assisted me up the granite steps to the short curving arm of Merlake's private pier. A mist was rising, which with the breaking spray obscured everything into blurred uniformity. When we reached level ground, he took my arm, guiding me along a path that curved abruptly to the right, and then turned upwards. The two men followed with the luggage. As we climbed, the wind sharpened, flapping my face with its salty sting. At one point my cloak blew over my head.

"Sorry about this," Ivan shouted, "there's no other way to get to the house unless you're a mountaineer. Be careful you don't bruise a foot. The ground's tricky." We paused for a moment then went on again. Gulls, disturbed, wheeled and screamed above. I became aware of something black and dark looming ahead — something that could have been a monstrous thunder cloud, but wasn't. As the sky cleared for a few seconds a solid mass of granite wall was visible, rising it seemed, out of the earth itself. I looked up, and had a fleeting vision of turret shapes resembling giant witches' hats towering to the sky. Then cloud and mist thickened, giving the impression of some nightmare hinterland between illusion and reality, in which human beings could be swallowed up and lost for ever.

Perhaps I sagged on Ivan's arm, gave

a cry or stopped again for a moment. He gripped my waist and I was thankful for his support. "Come along, Jade-Anna," he said. "I'm sure you're not the wilting kind."

The remark revived me, and the fact that someone had called me by my full name.

"Of course not," I said, forcing myself to shout against the wind. "Don't worry. I'm all right."

The climb had at moments seemed endless, although the next day I discovered it was not so bad as I'd thought.

When at last we reached steps cutting upwards between terraces to the building, a glow of light zig-zagged from an arched window to meet us. Almost immediately, this was followed by a door opening, revealing a broad figure of a woman holding an oil lamp in an outstretched hand.

"Mrs Traille," Ivan said, "my housekeeper."

Through the flickering glow of the lamp's bobbing and swinging in the wind, it was impossible to discern any features or what age she was, but I had an instinctive feeling she would not like me. I tried to suppress the idea, telling myself I was just tired, and possibly a little frightened. I must not be. I had undertaken a post, a position in Mr Sterne's isolated home, Merlake. Whatever duties he wished me to undertake I would do to the best of my ability — provided he didn't ask too much.

When I look back now, my first introduction to Merlake is impressed on my memory like a fantastic illustration from some far-off fairytale in childhood. The interior of the house appeared vast and bewildering, filled by shadows, cornered recesses, narrow gothic windows and numerous passages leading from wider corridors. The hall was flagged with rugs stirring at intervals from draughts of chill wind, and always, in the background, was the moaning of wind and distant booming and breaking of sea against rocks outside. Odd lights flickered wanly in alcoves, throwing distorted elongated shadows across the floor — shadows that danced and quivered like skeleton shapes resurrected from the past. The glint of ancient coats of armour, swords and other weapons against one wall indicated that Merlake must have endured for countless centuries.

Our footsteps had a hollow ring as Ivan, still holding my arm, followed the two servants and Mrs Traille up a wide spiralling flight of stairs. At each bend the woman paused, holding the lantern to light the way. In spite of the weird surroundings, I thought it odd that Ivan himself did not lead the little procession, recalling with a jerk of practicality that etiquette demanded no gentleman should follow a lady upstairs, in case he saw something he was not supposed to. 'Always go last,' Aunt Clarissa had commanded when she was endeavouring to install a sense of decorum and manners into me. 'No well brought up young lady allows *any* man to catch a glimpse of an ankle or petticoat. Most immodest.' Obviously Merlake had its own rules.

How strange that such conventional advice should come to mind under present circumstances, with everything so dim and bewildering and far removed from the decorous behaviour of well-bred current society. I almost smiled: If I'd not been so on edge I'd have laughed aloud. Ivan may have sensed my brief change of mood. At the top of the first flight of stairs he released my arm, glanced down at me, under a watery glare of light, and said, "Glad to see you're not shivering any more. Merlake isn't a warm place, but you'll find your bedroom has a fire lighted. I hope you'll have a comfortable night."

"I hope so too," I replied, matching my formal manner to his.

"Don't try to wake early in the morning," he told me, staring straight ahead. "After the journey you'll be expected to rest, and breakfast will be brought to you by one of the servants."

For that I felt grateful.

We walked along the broad landing for quite a distance, then turned a corner on the left and continued for some yards. This corridor was not nearly so wide; there were three doors, two on the right, one at my left hand, where the housekeeper stopped, holding the lantern as high as possible so Jed could turn the handle and enter the room with my valise. Then he and Marte turned and still carrying Mr Sterne's bags, went back to join the wider landing where his premises presumably were.

Mrs Traille waited for me to pass through. Before I did so Ivan said a polite 'goodnight', turned quickly and walked away, leaving smudges of damp footsteps from his wet boots on the floor. My shoes had also left puddles there. It didn't really matter, I told myself. The floor was of stone and could easily be cleaned. The few rugs were thin and I guessed a little threadbare in parts, very unlike the thicker carpeting of the stairs.

"Come along," I heard the housekeeper say irritably, "don't stand there in them dripping things. You'd best hurry and change and get warm by the fire. There'll be soup and a bite of something brought up later. The master will be eating on his own, of course. In the dining room; downstairs."

She spoke smugly, and although in the candlelight and glow from the lamp her broad elderly face appeared expressionless, her small dark eyes set closely together over a bony nose, held a shrewd look of power. Her mouth was small and primped into a button shape over a heavy jaw, her figure plump under the starched black dress she wore. A dark satin apron embroidered with tiny flowers and birds was tied and fell from her waist over the spreading voluminous skirts. Her hair, under the shred of lace cap, was black — too black, perhaps, to be completely natural. Later I discovered I was wrong there. She was of Spanish descent, which explained her strong features and colouring.

After the discomfort of travelling I was relieved to discover that the bedroom, if not exactly welcoming, was pleasant in an old-fashioned way; the furniture was fairly simple for that period, including a wash-stand, dressing table, wardrobe, and a carved, canopied bedspread with drapes. There was a patchwork quilt already turned down, rugs partially covering the wooden floor. A fire burned from the grate. A small but amply upholstered leather-back arm chair stood nearby. Candles flickered from either side of the dressing table. The room could have been used previously for unimportant guests, I thought, or perhaps an upper servant. The only magnificent piece was the bed which towered over the rest of the furniture. I'd have preferred one of a smaller size, and wondered why it had ever been placed in such a countrified interior.

Then I noticed the windows. There was an ordinary square one over which Curtains and blinds had been drawn, and high up — far too high to peer through without some kind of a ladder — two small gothic-looking apertures of stained glass, obviously of a more ancient date. Without taking in such details at a first glance, I was aware of mixed periods having come together during the passage of time. Later I was to discover that the whole building was the same — rising from monastic simplicity in earliest days to an anachronism of monumental proportions as the centuries came and went.

Presently, when I'd unpacked my few possessions from the valise, a maidservant with rather prominent eyes and a scared-rabbit look on her plain face appeared with a can of warm water which she poured into the ewer standing by a pot basin. She made a little bob, stared at me sullenly for a second, then hurried from the room without a word. Her manner suggested resentment mingled with furtive fear, and I wondered if it was because I was a stranger, or because the dominant housekeeper had forced her into attending me. Deciding the small problem wasn't worth bothering about, I dismissed it, removed my bedraggled travelling gown, boots, and was deciding to wash, then change into night-clothes and a wrap when there was a second tap on the door. It was the girl again with a bowl of soup on a tray and something hot in a dish under a cover.

She dumped it down on a side table near the fire.

"The master said I was to bid you goodnight, an' you'll not be expected down agen. 'Tell 'er to see she sleeps well', 'ee said. An' if you wants anythin', ring."

She indicated a brass bell standing on the chest, once more threw me a resentful look, and turned to go.

"Thank you," I remarked politely.

She marched out with her head up; there was the click of a latch, so sharply snapped to, that the key fell out. A key! — that was *something*. In stockinged feet I ran to the door and locked it. Then I crossed to the bed and rested there thoughtfully, leaning back against the pillows, which were very soft, with my hands under my head. The fire's glow gave a pleasant dreamy feeling. Realising I should fall asleep unless I stirred immediately, I forced myself up again, had a quick wash, pulled a wrap round my shoulders and went to the fire. The rosy glow was gradually dying. I took two logs from a bucket and threw them on. As I settled into the chair to eat the meal, there was a spitting of wood, followed by a brightening leap of orange and yellow flame.

Before taking a spoon to sample the soup I held out my hands to the warmth. I was surprised to find how cold my fingers still were. I was also shivering a little, but guessed it was from reaction as much as the chill journey. The food was simple but good, although I could not swallow all the stew, which was seasoned with various herbs and spices. I wished a dog or cat could appear from nowhere and eat the remains. Probably the cook or housekeeper, or whoever it was who'd prepared the meal, would be ruffled at so much being left. But did animals like spice? *Would* cats devour herbs? What ridiculous notions.

I had the queerest sensation suddenly of being caught up into some weird illogical dream. I had a struggle to keep my eyes open. The experiences of the last twenty-four hours became curiously mixed up — a conglomeration of faces, events, and being pushed here and there — of Aunt Clarissa's face swimming ridiculously under her piled-up hair against a back-cloth of sea, driven rain, and tall towers about to topple and crush me. Through the booming of waves Ivan Sterne's voice emerged and died again, and the shrieking of gulls became the grating of Jed's harsh laugh. I studied my face peering through the mirror and glimpsed only a pale disc swimming against a sea of shadows. Had I been drugged? Was that it? If so, by whom?

Ivan? Or the grim-faced housekeeper? If so, why? *Why?* I closed my eyes, rubbed them hard, and looked again at my reflection. It was my own normal face confronting me from the glass. With relief came sanity. Automatically, I finished undressing, pulled my nightgown over my head and climbed into bed.

I'd already lapsed into unconsciousness, when a thunderous bang woke me. My heart jerked, and started hammering. I sat up and for a few moments didn't answer. Then I cried, "What is it? What's the matter?"

"Let me in. What you doin' lockin' that theer door? There's things to collect."

Relief flooded me. The housekeeper.

I got out of bed, padded across the floor, turned the key in the lock, and opened the door. A very ruffled-looking Mrs Traille confronted me.

She stared, said nothing, but marched by, picked up the tray, rattling the cutlery and china as she did so. Before she went out she turned and deliberately took the key, slipping it into a pocket of the black taffeta skirt.

"That's *mine*," I protested.

She flung me a grim smile.

"*Nuthen's* yours at Merlake. And if doors are locked tes from the outside. You understand?"

"No. And in the morning I shall ask Mr Sterne about this."

"You do," she said smugly. "You just *do*, an' I shall be very interested to hear his answer. *Very*."

When she'd gone I returned to bed feeling not only annoyed but once more uncertain and afraid. Then commonsense returned. The unpleasant character was merely jealous, I told myself firmly — possessively determined to retain full domestic power at Merlake.

The power, however, was not solely hers, as I was to learn later.

That night, in spite of utter weariness — perhaps because of it — I slept fitfully. At one point I was roused uncomfortably by a faint thudding from outside by the landing. The wind and pounding of the sea had died. This sound was different — more like the furtive, stealthy footsteps of some giant cat on the prowl.

My heart quickened as they paused by my door. I looked round wildly for a candle, fancying the knob was turned. The next moment all was still again. Whether the door had been opened a chink or not I never knew. Before daring to close my eyes again, I pushed the chair against the woodwork, so that if any intruder attempted entrance I should hear.

As far as I knew, no one did.

But in the morning, when I woke, I found the chair was once more in its usual place by the fire.

Had I then, been suffering from an illusion, or a dream? This seemed the logical explanation. But I knew it was not the truth. Someone *had* been in. Why?

Everything else was in place — my clothes and wrap, and slippers by the bedside.

One fact was obvious. At the first opportunity I must confront Ivan and ask him to explain the curious incident and Mrs Traille's insistence on retaining the key.

As soon as the decision was made, I felt better, until, with amazement, I noticed something very peculiar indeed.

The key was once more in the lock.

On *my* side of the door!

This was no illusion. I knew then that something was wrong at Merlake — something it would probably be best not to probe into, and when I went downstairs later I mentioned nothing, after all, of my peculiar experience. Even if I'd wished to I couldn't have done so. Ivan, Mrs Traille informed me, was out.

"Do you mean he's gone to the mainland?" I asked.

Her expression became bleak, bland.

"There's other business than over theer," she answered, "business where the master rightly belongs — on Merlake. He did say you could take a look at the gardens though, if you liked. They're on the west side leadin' out of the conservatory from the large parlour. But tell 'er 'bout the rule of not goin' further, he said. There's walls all round, an' no one but the master an' Jed goes beyond. Or if you'd rather, you could look at the books. He gave me permission to show you the library."

"No, thank you", I replied rather abruptly. "I'd like a breath of air."

"A breath?" She gave a short laugh. "There's more than a breath round here. Well, then, you tell me when you want to go, an' I'll show you the way."

"Now," I answered, "if it's all right with you."

"H'm! Very well. Best get wrapped up. The storm's left cold about. 'Winter's comin',' I said to myself when I looked out earlier."

"My cape was taken to be dried last night," I reminded her.

"An' is that the only one you do have?" Faint contempt underlay the words. "Still damp in the dryin' room. Wet as a drowned gull it was."

"Yes. All the luggage I brought was packed into my valise."

"Hm. Then you'll have to borrow one of the girls'." By girls I supposed she meant servants.

The article she produced was dull brown, heavy and unbecoming.

I drew it round me, and led by the broad squat figure, was presently following her past the foot of the stairs towards the parlour and conservatory. As I went by a cackle of sound that could have been laughter or an exclamation of command, startled me. I looked up. At the bend of the staircase, an ancient hawk-like countenance crowned by a mass of ribbons, combs and artificial flowers stared down. A stream of light from the narrow stained-glass window, emphasised the bony structure of the predatory nose and formidable jaw above the wrinkled chins. Slits of eyes held the hard curious gleam of some ancient parrot considering attack. I had the impression of jewels glinting, and two bright spots of colour gleaming garishly from the reddened cheeks.

I looked away quickly.

"What was that?"

"Miss Augusta Sterne — Madam, as she likes to be called. The master's great-aunt."

"Oh." I was nonplussed, a little shaken. So that was Great Aunt Augusta.

"Now, remember — Miss Augusta edn' no concern of yours. She's been here always — right through the old master's life. She won't ever leave heer until she's carried out. You mark my words. A part of Merlake Miss Augusta is. Has her own quarters in a separate wing."

"I see."

Mrs Traille shook her head slowly. "No, no you don't. An' what's more, you never will." Her voice softened perceptibly. "In a way, I'm sorry for you, because it seems to me you haven't an inklin' o' what you've landed yourself into."

"I shall have to do the best I can then," I stated automatically.

"Hm." She turned a few paces to the left, pushed the parlour door open and went through. "Here tes. Follow me."

She marched into the room which was dark and over-cluttered with heavy furniture. A small fire crackled from a marble-framed grate. The atmosphere was oppressive, as though windows were seldom opened. A heavy framed portrait of a sardonic-looking old gentleman hung on the wall to the left of the mantelshelf. The expression was imperious and aggressive. I guessed it might be Ivan's grandfather. Everything about the interior held the musty smell of old leather. On a mahogany table papers lay by a file. The very shadows seemed imbued with a dreary identity conveying hostility as we moved over the brownish shabby carpet to an opposite door.

It was slightly ajar. Mrs Traille pushed it open, and beckoned.

I went in after her. Strange plants trailed from pots on shelves and from hanging containers. A few of an exotic variety that must have been imported from abroad at some bygone date were in bloom. But the few blossoms looked tired and uncared for. Ferns had a yellowish tinge. Pipes ran under the lowest shelf, emitting a sultry heat. At the end a beam of early watery sunlight penetrated the glass, filtering over a film of dust on an iron seat with a broken arm. I was surprised by the derelict atmosphere. Mrs Traille must have sensed it.

"Times haven't bin easy heer," she muttered. "Jed and Marte has other thin's to do than gardenin', and Master Ivan has a load o' worries on his mind."

"Worries?"

Her head turned sharply for a second or two in my direction.

"Everyone in his position has worries,"

she told me acidly. "But don't be askin' me what they are. Folks here mind their own business an' you'd best do the same."

"I've certainly no wish to interfere," I remarked coldly, "but as I'm going to work at Merlake it's natural I'll want to know a little of the background — "

"Background?" She gave a grunt of a laugh; but there was no humour in it. "Well — theer's your background." She pushed the door wide, waved an arm to the garden. "Go out and have a look. But remember what I've bin sayin'."

She stood against the wooden erection, which needed paint and attention to the hinges, watching me with a dead-pan expression as I passed through. I had a feeling her eyes were still upon me when I turned a corner of a short path and came to an expanse of lawn enclosed by granite walls. Shrubs crouched beneath. The ground sloped downwards. From a narrow gap at the bottom, the glint of sea was visible. The sound of waves breaking on the rocky shore boomed in heavy persistent rhythm. Although I couldn't recognise the locality of the land facing me — the night of my arrival had been so misted by rain and storm — I guessed, from the gleam of rising sunlight behind a low belt of cloud that the short pier was not far away.

A few glasshouses were huddled at a more sheltered corner of the garden, with a gazebo standing above. A path crossed the base of the house, cutting into another side door. Over all, the towers and turrets of Merlake rose like some fantastic erection from a medieval fairy tale. There was no sound but the fitful moaning of the wind, intermittent wild crying of curlews and gulls, and the everlasting encroaching tide. A hungry tide, I thought, drawing the cumbrous cloak more tightly round me, yet never able to claim the island, which was in itself a fortress defying the elements.

I cut down and peered over the gap in the wall. About the pier I had been correct. It curved to the path we must have climbed to the house through the rain. It was wider than I'd thought, almost a drive, running upwards, but beyond the garden wall. The track was very steep, bordered by boulders shining black and grey on either side, and still wet from the storm and wind-blown sea.

I moved again, taking an opposite bend which gave me a view of precipitous cliffs, jagged and angry-looking, holding a blackish glassy sheen where the giant breakers flung their spume.

Fascinated, in spite of a giddy feeling, I stared and stared, thinking how terrible it would be to plunge to the swirling depths below. Yet there appeared to be a very narrow track zig-zagging this way and that between boulders that finally disappeared round a corner of the island. What lay beyond? It was then that movement ahead startled me. For a second or two afterwards nothing stirred. I blinked; from behind a rock a face took shape — broad, piggy-eyed, with a cap pulled down over both ears. Wiping a strand of hair from my forehead I craned my neck to make sure I wasn't mistaken, that the confusion of mist, wind and blown spray, wasn't creating a mere impression from the rugged granite.

The face watching me was real enough. Jed.

He drew himself up, waved an arm in

a gesture of dismissal, put a telescope to one eye, then when I still hadn't moved, he started clambering over rocks towards me, not along the narrow track, but higher, negotiating every dangerous twist of cliff above the precipitous line of coast. Realising the distance between us that way was considerably shorter, I turned and hurried from view across the garden, missing the side door of the conservatory, eventually arriving at the front entrance.

The great door was closed. I rattled the knocker, and pulled the hanging bell. There was no response for minutes. I was about to go back and hopefully locate the conservatory before Jed arrived when the sound of heavy footsteps approaching halted me. There was the grinding of hinges and a bolt being pulled. The door opened. Mrs Traille looking flushed and indignant confronted me.

"So!" she exclaimed. "It's you."

"I'm sorry," I told her. "I missed the conservatory. It was Jed. He — "

"Come in, come in," she told me impatiently. "What d'you mean, Jed? What's he to do with et? Been wanderin' where you shouldn't, is that it?"

I felt suddenly angry. "*No*. I never left the garden. I simply *looked* over the wall where there's a kind of gap, and he appeared from the other side, *threatening me*."

"*Threatenin'?*" She laughed contemptuously. "Why should he? Warnin' you from danger, I s'pose. That's his business."

"Keeper of the Island, you mean?" I said scathingly.

"Yes."

Her lips closed with a snap. "You've got the right word. He's keeper for Master. An' I advise you to remember, Miss Ellan."

I went up to my room, took off the ugly cape, touched my damp hair and went to the mirror. What a sight I looked — my dark curls ruffled by air and the hood, had fallen back behind my ears to the shoulders. In rushing from Jed I must have caught my left cheek on a bush, or jagged point of rock. It flamed slightly near the temple, where a thin trickle of blood had dried. There was water in the ewer. I poured some into the basin and sponged it, then applied a coating of rice powder over my whole face. The new pallor added lustre to my eyes; they appeared enormous through the shadows. Why I bothered to use lip-salve, I don't know. There was no one to comment either approvingly or to the contrary.

Ivan was out somewhere — fishing perhaps? or cruising round in his odd vessel, the lugger. In any case, he had no interest in me or my appearance. If he noticed me at all it would be to my detriment. I was in his service — a menial position while I stayed at Merlake, which had been indicated quite clearly. And servants — even 'companions' or any domestic help were not expected to use cosmetics or flaunt any particular physical attraction. I made my way aimlessly to the window and looked out.

Over a grey roof and chimney of an apparently smaller wing of the house, I could discern, to my left, a patch of rough grassy moor sloping to the cliffs and grey sea beyond. Through a gap in the clouds a streak of pale sunlight lit up the whole scene briefly, and in the distance a hump of land was clarified like the shape of some monstrous beast against the horizon. How far? Four miles, perhaps — or five. Could it be the mainland? If so, I must be facing south.

But what did it matter? I'd no intention of returning. Even if I wished to it wasn't possible without Ivan Sterne's permission, and the last thing I wanted just then was to humiliate myself by asking such a favour.

So stiffening my spine, and determined to put on a facade of dignity, I pinned a cameo brooch at the scrap of lace bordering the neckline of my dark dress, and presently went downstairs again.

The servant who'd brought me tea earlier was in the hall with a brush and pan in her hands.

"Do you mind showing me the library?" I asked. When she didn't reply but just stood staring dumbly, I added a trifle superciliously, "I have permission. in case you haven't been told. But don't worry. I have eyes in my head. You'd better get on with what you're doing. I'll explore the house on my own."

My last remarks jerked her to life. She waved the brush behind a shoulder and said, "That door. Not the first — the next."

"Thank you," I said icily.

She passed me without another word.

I took a few steps along the hall and entered the room she'd indicated. It was panelled, with two large bow windows on one side — obviously of the Regency period. A small fire glowed from the grate which was at the far end set into an oak recess containing wooden benches on either side. The other two walls had bookshelves filled with ancient-looking volumes, mostly bound in leather. A refectory table under a window held an ink pot and feather pen, with a few papers lying casually by.

A bewhiskered, heavy-jawed character — obviously a seafarer — was depicted in an oak-framed portrait over the mantelshelf. Like himself, the leather seated high-backed chairs appeared forbidding and inhospitable. Everything about the interior was somehow intimidating, suggesting I was a trespasser, and had no right to enter. It was worse even than the parlour.

Nevertheless, I went forward reluctantly

to the fire, held my hands to the meagre blaze and impulsively took a log from a bucket by the hearth and threw it on. A few sparks kindled, throwing a brief rosy glitter over the dark surround of the grate. There was a spatter of sound, then silence. The wind must have suddenly died; or perhaps the room had been cunningly contrived to shut out all suggestion of a world outside. I had an impulse to pull the windows wide — to free the interior of its own musty identity, but when I studied the glass of a bay window between the heavy brown drapes, there was no sign of a catch and I rubbed a hand across a pane. The room must be facing the same direction as the conservatory; the outlook, however, revealed nothing but the grey outline of a tree with a patch of indefinite shadowed land beyond. I turned away and wandered to the nearest bookshelves. Many of the volumes appeared to be historical accounts of a sea-faring nature, intermingled with early editions of Chaucer, Shakespeare, Bacon and others. Above the shelves on the opposite wall facing the windows was a framed map on yellow parchment. I went over and glanced at it with rising interest.

It was obviously an ancient definition of Merlake Island, showing by scale, an area slightly under three square miles. There were landmarks and signs I did not understand. The southern and western portion appeared to be higher and more rocky and precipitous than the opposite coastline where the pier was depicted. The house was highly placed, appearing as a fortress rather than a dwelling. Obviously, it had been considerably added to since the drawing was made. I was about to move away when something startled me. I hadn't consciously heard the doorknob turning; but there, with what frail light there was striking full on his face, stood a youngish man. He was slender, narrow-faced, good-looking in a Byronesque way, with curling black hair waving back from a wide forehead, and side burns. His eyes also were brilliantly black under elegantly arched brows, his attire, though dark, slightly foppish as though calculated to emphasize his narrow waist and hips.

He gave a little bow. "Good morning. You, I suppose, are the new lady-help. I'm enchanted to meet you."

He stepped forward and took my right hand in his. His grasp was cool and impersonal.

"Good morning," I replied mechanically, adding after a brief pause, "Yes, I'm — I'm supposed to be that — the help I mean, although I don't know my duties yet."

He smiled, but without humour. "I don't think you'll be overburdened, Miss — ?"

"Ellan."

"Ah, yes. Now I remember. And I'm Claude Lang — Maurice's tutor."

"Maurice?"

"Mr Sterne's ward." He looked back over his shoulder. "Come here, Maurice."

A boy appeared from the shadows of the hall. He could have been seven or eight years old, and was handsome in a sturdy way, if a trifle truculent-looking. He had curly reddish hair, wore a dark bottle green coat with breeches of the same shade reaching to mid-calf length above silk stockings and buckled shoes. His assessing stare held a hint of insolence.

"I'm pleased to meet you, Maurice," I remarked politely.

"Are you? Why?"

"Well — because — because I'm going to live at Merlake and it's best we should be friends, don't you think?"

He shrugged.

"I don't care. I don't want friends."

Claude Lang took the boy's arm, gave it a little shake and said sharply in a voice meant to show disapproval, although I fancied a quirk of amusement touched the well-sculptured lips, "That's very impolite. Apologise, Maurice."

The boy's full underlip took a belligerent thrust. He was about to refuse, but thought better of it. Glancing from his face to Claude Lang's I saw that the tutor's mouth had quickly hardened into a thin line. The young man, then, could be more of a tyrant than I'd imagined.

"Sorry," Maurice murmured, with his cheeks reddening.

I smiled. "It's quite all right. I understand."

I didn't, of course.

71

I understood nothing of what went on at Merlake, and realised that it was probably better I shouldn't. So far any contacts I'd made hadn't been at all encouraging.

After a few further brief words Maurice and Claude Lang left the room.

I waited until their footsteps had receded down the hall, or it may have been along a narrow corridor facing the library, then I too went out, closing the door quietly behind me. From the kitchens at the back of the house there came the distant clatter of work going on. Not wishing to encounter the housekeeper or any other servant, I hurried, half running, towards the foot of the stairs hoping to avoid human contact or further questioning.

It was at that point that the wide front door ahead of me swung open, and Ivan Sterne's tall figure swung in. Spray sprinkled his dark hair. His high boots, over the fawn breeches were also damp, also his cape and the cuffs of his jacket. I guessed my surmise that he had been doing something at sea was correct.

He smiled, brushing a strand of

hair from his forehead. Somehow he looked younger than I remembered, more approachable in his slight disarray.

I relaxed.

"Ah, Miss Ellan. You look refreshed. I hope you had a good night — what was left of it."

I nodded, and replied in the affirmative. I'd meant to question him about the key incident, but suddenly it seemed unimportant and better delayed for a future moment when the matter could be referred to casually. He took off his cape, slung it over one arm and continued, "I must get this dried. I've been messing about in one of the boats. With Marte."

"Oh? I didn't see you."

He showed momentary surprise.

"You went out then?"

"Yes, for a stroll. Mrs Traille told me I could see round the gardens."

"Of course. Once they were worth looking at. Now I'm afraid they're very neglected. The upkeep of this island costs more nowadays than it should. My grandfather was too concerned with other things towards the end of his life, and

after his death my father wasn't well — "
he paused, continuing in more practical
tones, "However, in the future all may
be remedied. In the meantime, there are
matters here in which you may be of
great help."

"I hope so," I told him.

"Maurice, my ward, is inclined to be
wayward," he went on. "He has only
his tutor and aunt for companionship,
and — "

"I met them," I interrupted. "A good-
looking boy — "

He frowned.

"You did? When was this?"

"Oh — only a few minutes ago. I was
in the library, and they both appeared at
the door. Maurice and Mr — Mr Lang,
wasn't it?"

"Yes."

"Was it wrong of me or something?
Shouldn't we have spoken?"

"Of course you weren't wrong. I was
just surprised. Maurice at this time
is usually in the schoolroom studying.
You'd have met them later in any case.
I've arranged for us to have the midday
meal together — in the breakfast room

adjoining Miss Dupont's apartment. Miss Lalage Dupont. She's Maurice's aunt."

"Oh. I see. Is she — is she — "

"Yes?"

"I saw an old lady looking down over the stairs when I came down," I told him, speaking quickly. "Mrs Traille called her Miss Augusta."

"My great-aunt," Ivan said. "Quite a character, but very different from Lalage." He sighed. "You'll see what I mean over lunch. Aunt Augusta will not be there. She has her own establishment, as Mrs Traille may have told you."

"Yes, she mentioned it."

From staring at me intently, too personally for my comfort, he turned away.

"An informal meal with just Claude Lang, Lalage and Maurice seemed to me the best way of breaking down barriers," he said casually. "And now, if you'll excuse me, I must change and make myself respectable. Do whatever you like this morning, Jade-Anna — " again his use of my full name stirred me strangely, " — only don't go wandering where you're not supposed to. The boundaries

75

of the grounds are well defined, and if you disobey my express wishes there'll be trouble." Little wrinkles of amusement crinkled the corners of his eyes. "I'm not an ogre, but my own particular method of dealing with naughty girls might not appeal to you."

Without another word he had passed me, striding down towards the kitchens and drying room with the cape over his arm.

During the rest of the morning I mostly idled the time away, tidying up my own few possessions unnecessarily, wandering from my bedroom downstairs again, and having another look at the conservatory, which as the light brightened, looked a little less archaic, but neglected with cracks in some of the glass, and dust glittering in tiny filaments over leaves and the few blossoms. I could imagine that in winter when frost lay crisp over the brown moors, extra heating would have to be used; a kind of chill filled me. So many ghosts of the past must once have moved here and sat on the old iron seat in conversation — whispering, laughing? — even lovers, perhaps? When times were more prosperous at Merlake, there might have been parties. If I closed my eyes I could wilfully conjure up a picture of some bygone gallant bending down to place a flower in a lovely girl's hair.

Instinctively I lifted an arm and smoothed a dark curl from a temple. I wore it curled behind my ears that day, and had changed before coming downstairs again into the one attractive day dress I had — deep blueish green that emphasized the colour of my eyes. There was a tiny ruffle of lace at the neck, tied with a narrow brown velvet bow. I had suddenly felt it important to look my best at this first arranged introduction to the family.

Ivan appeared a few minutes later, to accompany me to the breakfast room. He lifted a finger, beckoned me, took my arm lightly, and led me out. As we reached the main hall he released me, went ahead, and opened a door further down on the right hand side. From there a comparatively narrow but well-carpeted flight of stairs wound upwards, taking a turn halfway up before continuing to a landing.

"Miss Dupont has her rooms here," he told me, "also Maurice and his tutor. In the past the breakfast room was included in the housekeeper's special domaine, but Mrs Traille prefers now to live on the ground floor nearer the kitchens."

"Oh, I see," I said, rather stupidly, adding quickly, "it must be rather difficult having to remember so many corridors and stairs and rooms — "

"Don't try," he interrupted, "you won't be required to."

I almost asked him bluntly at that point what I *was* supposed to know about Merlake, and what not, but controlled any impetuous questioning and walked on silently for a few yards before being shown through another door.

The room we entered wasn't large, and a blazing fire gave warmth and a sense of welcome to the interior. The furniture was oak, the hangings and upholstery orange and rust coloured. From a large oval table in the centre, china and cutlery glistened. A decanter of sherry was waiting with glasses sparkling on a carved oak chest. Nearby stood a woman. She was raven-haired and exotic-looking, extravagantly attired in red silk. At first glance she did not appear to be over thirty, but when the fire-light caught her face from a sideways angle small lines and the contour of a double chin above the creamy round neck suggested she must be approaching forty — perhaps more. Claude Lang and Maurice were waiting by the fire. Both turned, staring at me, as we went in. Then the boy looked away again and reached for a bronze figure astride a horse on the mantelshelf.

"Don't touch that," I heard Lang say sharply. "You've been told before."

Maurice scowled, but obeyed. All three stood motionless until Ivan Sterne introduced me — to the woman first. She came forward and took my hand, smiling not with warmth, but with what I sensed was assumed politeness. I noticed that the red silk was slightly strained over the voluptuous breasts and that she was breathing rather quickly. Small beads of perspiration glistened on her upper lip, and a glass half full of brandy stood near her other hand.

Her features were boldly modelled, and in youth could have been beautiful before too much flesh hid the natural bone structure. Spots of rouge on each cheek heightened a theatrical quality about her that now appeared decadent rather than dramatic. An aura of heavy perfume emanated from her ample form. And yet despite her exotic exterior I was aware of a hard cat-like glitter in her eyes which was disconcerting. They were curious eyes — of pale grey, almost colourless and rather prominent, under heavy brows that had been obviously darkened.

"How nice to meet you," she said in throaty, slightly slurred, tones.

"Thank you, Miss Dupont," I replied.

"And this is Maurice, my ward, but apparently you've already met," I heard Ivan saying, beckoning the boy forward. "And, of course. Mr Lang."

Claude bowed; Maurice held out his hand in a grown-up fashion. He was smiling, and immediately — although his colouring was so different from his aunt's — I was aware of a likeness between the two. The well-modelled lips were similar — bold and sensuous. In a few years I guessed the boy could have matured into quite a womaniser.

The meal that night was simple, well served by the maid I'd previously met, and the conversation dealing with ordinary everyday matters. No suggestion of what my exact duties at Merlake were to be was referred to, but I had a shrewd idea that they might include supervision of Maurice during Claude Lang's free time, and when Lalage Dupont, his aunt, either did not wish the responsibility or was incapable of dealing with her nephew. That probably was the case. She was quite clearly over-fond of her brandy or whatever alcoholic drink was available. More than once Ivan eyed her sternly when she reached for a decanter, addressing her sharply with just her name 'Lalage' then changing the conversation into something trite and ordinary. Each time this happened, Miss Dupont's face dulled into sullen red as her full underlip gave a rebellious thrust. But she always complied with his command.

Yes. I had no doubt at all that Ivan Sterne was in every way master of the island, and that I was there, partially, to reinforce his domestic position when he was not on the scene.

If so, I didn't look forward to it. I could feel a curious bond existing between Claude, Lalage, and Maurice — some secret relationship which would be very hard indeed to break, and which I really had no wish to. I'd previously envisaged being employed to share some of the household duties — linen, sewing, even helping supervise the kitchen, if necessary, or going on walks about the island with Maurice in his leisure time, and reading aloud to his aunt when she needed amusing.

Now I had met her, I knew this was a futile idea. Lalage Dupont might tolerate my company on occasions, but she would never wish for it.

I was an outsider, and would remain so. Feeling suddenly very lonely, I decided at the first opportunity to have my position clearly clarified by 'Master' Sterne.

The chance came the next day when at his invitation I accompanied him to an enclosed part of the island towards the back, behind the pier where beyond acres of moor, a few sheep and cows grazed on gentler grassland. It was more sheltered and verdant than I would have expected on Merlake, being bordered on either side by rising rocky ground. A barn and stables crouched in a hollow, and as we approached I saw the figure of Marte cross and disappear with a bucket in his hand.

I was surprised. Farming seemed so uncharacteristic of the island, and I would have thought impracticable.

When I commented on the fact, Ivan said, "There has to be a certain independence here. We rely quite a lot on our own produce for living purposes. We have to. In the past, before my grandfather's time, more acres were utilised. In fact, we had a stamp of our own. The head of the family regarded himself as a kind of monarch — Lord, or King of Sterne, if you like."

"How strange."

"Yes. I suppose it does seem so to you. But being quite a distance from the mainland, Merlake, during centuries of intermittent warfare with the continent found it wise to carve its own identity, becoming at one period a kind of fortress. Things are different now, of course — at the moment. But it still has something to battle against — something I'm determined to overcome."

I glanced at him curiously.

"Such as?"

"Never mind." He spoke sharply. "As you've gathered — I told you, didn't I? — the whole estate in my father's time went to seed. Now I'm going to see it's pulled together again."

"Ah."

He gave a short laugh. "Not very forthcoming, am I? All this must be boring to a young girl."

I lifted my chin.

"No, though all I'm *really* interested in, Mr Sterne — is what exactly I'm supposed to do here, apart from the little secretarial work. You did mention something of the sort earlier."

"There won't be much of that, Miss Ellan. Yesterday, except for Aunt Augusta, you met the — residents — shall we say — of Merlake. At the moment, we're understaffed for such a large place, so I'm sure Mrs Traille will be able to find a few useful tasks to keep you occupied — arranging flowers, light duties, that sort of thing. But — "

"Yes?"

"To be frank I'd like you to see that Maurice is not left too often in the company of Lalage — Miss Dupont — when Lang isn't with him. She's got her weakness, as you must have noticed, and I don't want my ward influenced by bad habits at such an early age. By being yourself companionable to Miss Dupont whenever possible, and also by interesting the boy in some way, they won't have the chance of being so much together — " He glanced at me questioningly.

"I'll do what I can, of course," I said rather abruptly. "But from what I saw of Maurice I can't imagine that I've an earthly chance of influencing him in any way. He seemed rather to dislike me."

"Then use your charms to change that."

"*Me!* How? You overrate me, Mr Sterne."

His eyes darkened as they stared at me, making me feel for a few moments ridiculously embarrassed. Then he said, very firmly, "No. I'm sure I do not. At Mounterrith you very effectively captivated my attention, under circumstances that would normally have left me cold."

Feeling the warm colour flooding my cheeks, I turned my face away.

"I'll do what I can," I told him. "But I'm afraid you'll be disappointed."

There was a pause between us until he remarked casually, "Well, we shall see."

After that the conversation turned to more practical channels, concerning the sturdy short-legged breed of Cornish sheep, plans for extending vegetable cultivation on the island, and his determination that Maurice should be brought up to be a good landowner.

"I have made him my heir," he told me as we went back to the house. "So his education is in every way exceedingly important."

He spoke with optimism. But underlying the statement I fancied was a faint intangible doubt, which I fully shared.

3

DURING the period before Christmas I did my best to become acclimatised to the isolated condition of life at Merlake. It wasn't easy. Mrs Traille, from the beginning of my arrival there, seemed determined to allow me as few duties as possible, which left me with lonely hours in which I had nothing to do but roam about the house and desolate gardens and dutifully endeavour to make some kind of contact with Maurice. His manner to me continued to be supercilious and resentful, and the more I saw of him the less I could bring myself to like him. He could be charming to Ivan when it suited him, but he had no regard or sensitivity to animals. Once I'd seen him kick Leo, the golden spaniel, for no reason at all, and he had a habit of collecting and stabbing any small insect or wild creature he noticed, watching it writhe in torment before adding it to his 'collection'.

"Why do you do that?" I asked him once, after one of his cruel acts. He glanced up at me with astonishment on his face, which I knew was not genuine. He'd meant to shock me.

"*Flies!*" he said. "Unhealthy dirty things."

"Then why do you collect them?"

He smiled; a very cold smile that went oddly with his healthy handsome countenance.

"I shall be master here one day," he said, with chilling certainty. "I shall collect whatever I like. Even — "

"Yes?"

"Never mind. It's not your business."

I felt my temper rising.

"Don't talk to me in that way. I'm supposed to help you — teach you a few things."

He laughed.

"What? A woman like you. Lang's my tutor. He says you've no right to interfere."

"Then I shall have to speak to Mr Lang," I told him firmly. "Your guardian, Mr Sterne, is very anxious for us to be friends"

"*Him?*" Maurice's voice was scornful. "He's just got you here for himself, that's all. Like my aunt — "

I felt faintly sick.

"How *dare* you!"

"Well, it's true. Ask her. Or him, if you like."

"Very well." My voice sounded hard in my own ears. "I *will*. I can promise you that."

There was silence between us for a few moments, then Maurice said more quietly, "You needn't. I was only joking. Can't you take a joke?"

"It depends on the kind it is," I answered. "Yours seem particularly nasty sometimes."

He glanced downwards, sighed, and said rather forlornly, "Perhaps that's because of living here."

"What do you mean?"

"Well — it's not much fun at Merlake, is it?" When he glanced up he appeared younger again, more vulnerable. "Most people don't have to be on an island with — with only Mr Lang and Uncle Ivan and Aunt Lalage. Then that horrible old Aunt Augusta — she's always poking and prying, and cackling when there's no one else about. I hate her. She laughs at me. She has a cane. Once she told Mr Lang to beat me. And he did — " He broke off, flushing. "Afterwards I found the stick and I put it between the door and broke it. I told Uncle — Mr Sterne — about it, and he was cross with both of them. 'Never touch my ward again,' he said, 'without my permission, or you'll regret it.' After that Claude Lang was more careful, and the old witch keeps away. But I wouldn't trust either of them — or Aunt Lalage, although she's different of course."

"What do you mean 'different'?"

He flung me a knowing look.

"She *does* things."

"What things?"

He shrugged. "Oh, you know — with Claude Lang; and Uncle Ivan, I shouldn't wonder, like I said. It's men. She likes men — "

I was horrified. The whole situation had become obnoxious and unhealthy to me.

* * *

Christmas came and went, with a show of the usual seasonal festivities which seemed to me curiously unreal. There were presents for Maurice and one for mc — a bottle of expensive perfume from Ivan delivered in the dining room where we all ate together during the few festive days. There was a note with it which said, 'You will find something upstairs in your room, which I hope will fit. Please wear it tonight. Ivan.'

I was astonished and cast him an enquiring glance. My heart had quickened, and his expression, though veiled, held a penetrating gleam in the eyes. What did he mean? The word 'fit' suggested wearing apparel of some kind. But what? And *why*? Was it that I appeared so drab against the colourful Lalage?

As soon as possible I went upstairs to find out. A box lay on my bed. I opened it. Swathed in tissue paper was a shimmering sea-green silk gown trimmed with lace and tiny flowers. I took it up, shook it, and holding it out in front of me crossed to the minor. But it was lovely — *lovely*. I gasped. How had he got it? And where? Then I remembered that the previous month Ivan had gone to the mainland with Jed and Marte on business dealing with shipping. I'd heard him vaguely referring to a project of taking over some merchant shipping line that was in need of finance to keep it going. Isaac Polglaze his agent had been due to meet him in Penzance, so probably Ivan had purchased the dress there.

Caught up in a whirl of excitement I scrambled out of the dull gown I was wearing, and with trembling hands stepped into the blue-green. I could hardly wait to fiddle with the tiny hooks and eyes of the bodice, and fastenings at the waist. The style was cut very low on the shoulders bordered by rows and rows of fine lace. At the front the shadowed curve above my breasts was clearly visible, and emphasized by the tight fitting below. The bodice was pointed, from which full panniers were gathered, falling apart over a second skirt showing a wide frilled lace hem. Bunches of tiny gold flowers bordered each pannier. How beautiful it was. And I? A spray of flowers with a shred of net veiling lay also in the box. I reached for it, held it casually against my hair for a moment before fixing it on the russet curls, and then I knew.

Yes, *I* was beautiful too. At that moment, I really was. Brilliant jade eyes cast butterfly shadows from thick lashes on the cheek bones I'd always thought too high. My cream skin was glowing satin smooth in the candlelight. Never in my wildest dreams had I imagined Jade-Anna Ellan could appear so.

I reached for the tiny mother-of-pearl fan that Evadne had so casually and half-contemptuously given me as a present, then I returned to the mirror again, posturing this way and that, turning my head at various angles to reveal the full graceful curve of throat and well defined chin, curtseying, bowing and smiling all the time, until quite suddenly there was a tap, a creaking and movement from the door.

I turned abruptly.

The macabre jewelled figure of Miss Augusta stood there attired in voluminous cream silk and lace sprinkled with tiny jewels of every colour. Her hair was piled high with osprey feathers and flowers, under which her ancient hawk-like face and yellow wrinkled skin appeared dry and drab as old parchment. Only the eyes seemed alive. They were bright and inquisitive, darting this way and that like a snake's about to seize some prey.

I attempted defensively to cover myself by reaching for my shawl and flinging it round my shoulders.

She laughed.

"Don't bother about me, gel. When I was your age I had several like you in attendance. All beauties, but I could beat the lot. Hard to imagine, isn't it? Miss Augusta Sterne — Mistress and Queen of Merlake — " The smile died from her withered lips, as her ancient chin jutted out aggressively. She rapped her stick on the floor. It was ivory, with a silver knob. "Well, speak, can't you? Are you dumb, gel? Don't you believe I was ever beautiful, eh? Can't you imagine it?" Her tone, though harsh, was imperious, and unnerving.

"Of course," I managed to say, "I'm sure you were."

"Don't lie. They all lie to me. 'Old Witch' they call me behind my back.

'That old witch.' Well, maybe it's true. But I still reign here, and don't you forget it, gel. Another thing — " she poked her head forward at me aggressively, "don't go thinking to catch that swaggering heir of mine — Ivan — with your fallals and fancy airs. He collects what he wants of 'em and that's that. He could have the richest woman in the land if he wanted, but he don't. There ain't no chance for you there, nor ever will be. So keep your place, gel. In the end I'm the one who matters. D'ye hear? If I'd known about it, that slut — the Dupont woman — would never have got in either. Shove her in the sea I would, like all the rest — "

Her words and manner horrified me. Involuntarily, I stepped backwards. She stared; then, quite unpredictably, her mood changed. All rancour seemed to desert her, she appeared merely what she was — a very old woman whose thoughts and mind had been wandering.

"Don't worry about me," she muttered. "Don't mean any harm, gel. One day you must come upstairs and I'll show you things, my treasures. Like that, would you?"

"Very much," I lied brightly.

"But say nothing." She put a finger to her lips. "Just our secret. Yours and mine. Eh?"

I nodded.

Satisfied, she turned and left, closing the door behind her.

My joy and excitement over the new gown had temporarily faded. I took it off and laid it on the bed. Then I tidied myself, redressed, and went downstairs again. Later, in the afternoon, I told Ivan I could not possibly accept his gift.

"You mean the dress?"

"Yes," I said more calmly than I felt. "I'm sorry. It was very kind of you; but — "

"Doesn't it suit you?"

"It's lovely. And it must have been very expensive — " I broke off hesitantly, then continued determinedly, "I haven't earned it. I must be independent."

"And not a kept woman." His voice was ironic.

"I never suggested such a thing, Mr Sterne." My hot temper was rising. I turned with my head up, and tried to march past him towards the foot of the stairs. A piece of holly decorating a nearby standing state of Venus, caught my hair. I lifted a hand to disentangle it, but he was there first, freeing the caught tendrils from the spikey leaves. I could feel the warm colour staining my cheeks. "Thank you," I said.

"Not at all. It's a pleasure." His grey eyes were on mine unswervingly. "All the same," he continued, "wear the gown tonight. It's a command, Miss Ellan."

I was about to give a hot reply when a hand touched my neck briefly. My whole body reacted as though struck by lightning. He smiled, a slow secret smile that told me he was quite aware of the impact. With a quick flash of memory I remembered Miss Augusta's warning that he could have any woman he wanted — the richest in the land — if it suited his purpose. But then Evadne had rejected him. Was I then just a puppet — something to allay his wounded pride? No. I was not. And I would prove it to him if he attempted any further overtures.

"It's understood?" I heard him saying.
"Very well. Just for tonight. After

97

all — " recalling Evadne's green satin, " — I'm used to wearing borrowed plumes."

"Exactly."

He stepped aside, allowing me to pass and go to my room. I didn't look round, but knew he was watching. I could feel his eyes probing my back until I'd turned the bend of the stairs.

When at last I sat on the bed my heart was racing ridiculously.

I waited until it had eased, then went to the window and looked out. Everything outside appeared grey and lonely. Grey turrets above dark moors sloping down towards the grey sea and curling tip of the pier.

I shivered involuntarily, feeling suddenly very cut off and alone, at the mercy of the elements, inhabitants and shadowed history of Merlake. Perhaps after all it would have been better to remain at Mounterrith under mean and fussy Aunt Clarissa's supervision. Eventually, I supposed I'd have ended up as a governess or help in some perfectly ordinary household, or with a prosaic husband not of my choice, but one forced on me by my circumstances. I wandered idly to the dressing table and took out the first communication I'd received from my aunt. It held the typical lecture.

I hope you're settling down and behaving in a manner suitable to your position. Be careful to observe your duties with propriety. You are extremely lucky to be taken into such an esteemed house-hold . . .

Esteemed! What a ridiculous word, when all the fusspot matrons of Aunt Clarissa's circle cared about was the Sterne wealth, the Sterne shipping company and the power of an ancient name. Feeling a little contemptuous, I read on:

Evadne sends you her love. As Sir Bruce Ferris's daughter-in-law she is now well and truly launched into the upper ranks of society, and there are plans I believe to have her presented to the Queen. Imagine it. Your Uncle and I are both delighted. Now — another word of advice —

Having had more than I wanted already, I tore the letter across, threw the bits of paper into the wastepaper basket, and took a good look at myself through the mirror. I didn't appear at all beautiful then — just rather young and vulnerable, a little stubborn, too, because Evadne seemed to have everything; riches, adulation and love from the man I'd cared for so much.

Would anyone ever love me, I wondered? Love me not only with desire and passion, but gently, protectively?

I sighed. Perhaps I wasn't that kind of person. Perhaps the Spanish part of me was in reality stronger than that of my father — the Ellan blood that coursed equally through my veins. There was no point in speculation anyway. I was Jade-Anna; myself. A girl with few attributes to commend her except a determination to make the best of the future, whatever that might be. At the moment matters certainly wouldn't be helped by defying Ivan Sterne.

So that evening I wore the dress. I went into the dining room with my head high.

Madam — Miss Augusta — was already seated at the far end of the dining table, facing Ivan's place at the other. On one side Claude Lang and Maurice waited. Lalage was standing by the fire, with a glass in her hand. She was wearing black chiffon trimmed with immense artificial red roses. The dress at the front was cut so low that an inch more would have completely exposed the full white breasts. Her black hair was piled high with ribbons and flowers, her lips obviously painted. Yet in spite of all efforts of being sensational, she appeared slightly untidy. A lock of hair, damp with perspiration, strayed to one temple. A smear of white powder blurred a side of her corsage.

She stared at me, and at the same moment old Miss Sterne, looking more than ever like some glorified ancient macaw started to speak. Then Ivan came in. He threw me a quick glance. That was all. But I noticed when his gaze travelled towards Miss Dupont, her colour deepened under her make-up. The glass tinkled as she put it down with a trembling hand. The look between them was highly charged with something I could not understand. Rebellion? Passion? Contempt? — Or had Miss Augusta been speaking the truth when she'd implied or rather asserted, that Ivan 'collected' women? It was odd how such a flood of suspicions raced, in that flash of time, through my mind. If only this could have been an ordinary Christmas occasion, I thought, as I took my place at the table next to Lalage — a dinner similar to those at Mounterrith, when in spite of Evadne's flirtatious chatter and Aunt Clarissa's inane gossip there would have been a normal atmosphere and jokes from my Uncle. Still, I'd chosen my course, and surprisingly, instead of being embarrassed by the new dress, it did give me courage.

A complimentary word from Ivan could have helped reinforce it, but after the meal when I passed him, following his great-aunt and Miss Dupont to the drawing room, he merely said, 'Quite nice' with a slight inclination of his head, then turned to Maurice and Claude Lang.

I could have slapped his face. But what a good thing I didn't. And why on earth was I becoming so sensitive to his moods?

Later, when the household had retired to bed, including myself, I crept downstairs again, slipped the bolt of the front door as soundlessly as possible, and went out on to the terrace. The air was keen, but holding a tangy sweetness blown on the winter wind from the sea. I stood there with my woollen wrap held close against my chin over the white flannelette nightgown given to me by Aunt Clarissa on my last birthday. She had always chosen 'useful' presents for me, whereas Evadne had received frivolous pretty things. Just then I was grateful for the warmth. My hair, too, fell thick over my shoulders almost to my waist. The sky was dark-velvet deepest midnight dark, studded with pin points of stars glimmering like a million candles. My heart and senses responded to the beauty in a deep stirring of longing.

I remembered my father. How, as a small child, he had held me on his shoulder at a window and pointed out the constellations. 'Men like me paint pictures,' he'd said, 'but the wonder of everything's up there. Think of it, Jade, love — so many whirling small worlds of light. Light is very difficult to understand. Light and dark — morning and evening — who made it? God, perhaps?'

I tried to think fleetingly of what he himself was trying to tell me, but I was too young; the mystery too great, and I'd stirred restlessly, looking back over his shoulder for my favourite toy — a small fluffy monkey in a red cap.

Then suddenly he'd laughed, lifted me higher into the air, showing a flash of white teeth for a moment then put me down on my bed.

The incident had seemed unimportant to me at the time, but the memory had lingered, returning occasionally through the years of growing up; now it was with me again, enclosing me with the poignancy of bygone things. I was so lost in my own emotional reactions, that I was unaware of anyone else's presence, until the quiet tread of a footstep behind me woke me from the dream. I turned my head. Through the darkness no features were clearly visible. It could have been, at first, anyone's tall figure standing there — even some ghost born of the strange occasion.

But the strong hands encircling both my cheeks a second later and the pressure of lips on mine were no phantom's. Neither were they forceful and demanding, but gentle and comforting. My heart jerked with surprise. He released me, and then, in spite of the darkness and cold air blowing a drift of hair across my eyes, I recognised him.

Ivan.

"A Christmas kiss," he said, "and to thank you for wearing the dress."

My fluttering heart steadied a little. So that's what it meant — gratitude. Gratitude for acknowledging a gift. No more than that.

"Thank you, sir," I answered lightly, trying to match his mood.

"You looked very beautiful, Jade-Anna," he told me after a short pause.

"It's a beautiful dress," I replied mechanically.

"It wasn't only the dress." His manner

had changed, become almost curt. A hand touched my head lightly, with fingers that lingered briefly, almost as a caress on the thick waves of my hair.

"Why did you come out here so late?" he asked a moment later. "To tempt me?"

I stared at him. "Of course not. You'd all gone to bed. I wanted to think."

"What about?"

"I really don't know. Anything — nothing. I was sort of half-dreaming."

"A pleasant state," he agreed casually. "I've felt the same myself under certain times and conditions, especially when I was out east — a non-reality existence. Helpful in periods of stress, but frequently dangerous. Opium has the same effect."

"Opium?"

"You *have* heard of it, I suppose?"

"Oh — just vaguely." I answered. "Before I left Mounterrith my Uncle used to hum and hah, and even damn a bit sometimes about the war — the war with the Chinese. He thought all the fuss was ridiculous."

"Did he?" I could sense Ivan's figure stiffen. "That, Miss Ellan, was because he knew very little about it. And now — " once more he became the stern matter-of-fact remote Master of Merlake, commanding rather than asking " — you had better return to your room immediately, before you catch cold. Mrs Traille certainly wouldn't appreciate having to nurse a sick employee."

Employee!

Indignation made my face burn. How dare he speak to me so indifferently — almost with contempt? — especially when he'd had the nerve, the temerity to creep up unawares, and kiss me? Or had he forgotten that already?

Probably so, if what old Miss Augusta Sterne had indicated was true.

Without another word I whirled quickly passed him, fled down the hall, and half stumbled at the foot of the stairs; I managed to adjust myself with all the dignity I could muster, and with my hand on the rail for support, made my way to my room.

Once there I took the key, which was safely on my own side of the door, and locked it.

I had no idea whether Ivan would

follow me or not. Part of me half hoped he would, and be thwarted by my mistrust and defiance — the other side of me, the desperate hungry emotional side, was remembering the pressure of his lips on mine, and wishing they could have held more fire and desire.

But of course Ivan Sterne did not feel in such a way about me. 'A Christmas kiss' he'd said, which meant I must regard it as just that.

I decided I would be careful in future it never happened again. I was no light woman or servant girl to be taken advantage of when any opportunity arose.

If the master of Merlake wanted casual indulgences of such a kind he must look elsewhere.

It never occurred to me that a time might come when I would be defenceless against him.

4

IN January the weather turned unusually cold, shrouding Merlake with intermittent gales of lashing seas and wild snow-laden winds. Except for the moaning and beating and creaking of old wood from the elements, the house seemed unusually quiet. Ivan was preoccupied with business affairs, shutting himself away for long periods in his study. As the days passed Mrs Traille became more defensive of her own domestic position, allowing me only minor duties such as arranging flowers and foliage from the conservatory, and when the girl was busy indicating that I might flick a duster over the library if I had nothing better to do, but to leave the books alone.

My efforts at entertaining Lalage in any way were futile; she didn't want my company, and it didn't appear to me that she was anxious for Maurice's either, or he for hers. When Claude was not in the schoolroom the boy secreted himself in a small adjoining room referred to as his 'den', where he had a water tank filled with small strange reptilian creatures, and holed boxes containing insects and flies. He fancied himself obviously as a naturalist. But the scientific, destructive element in his nature horrified me when I imagined what strange processes might be indulged in behind the closed door.

I *did* discover something about Lalage, however, that didn't surprise me in the least. She had night visitors. Or maybe just one; I don't know. As I lay awake one evening unable to sleep because of the lash of rain against windows and walls, I heard, above all other sounds, a sudden slam of a door followed by a shrill cry, and murmur of protestation in a male voice.

I sat up abruptly in bed, got out, hurried to my own door, unlocked it quietly, opened it just a little and stared through the darkness. At the end of the corridor where a partition divided Miss Dupont's apartments from the rest of the house, the frail light of a candle flickered. There was a fleeting glimpse of white arms raised — a momentary shadowed vision of a pale face as the blurred form detached itself from a woman's and with head bent moved stealthily along the landing. All light was obscured suddenly. I closed my door, locked it without the key grating, and stood for some moments with my back to the wood, listening. From the distance I thought I heard the soft padding of footsteps approaching. Whether it was my own imagination or not I couldn't tell, because a high shrieking of wind rose with violent intensity, subduing all else to the moaning, whining echo of the elements.

When I was sure no one was on my track, I went back to bed and lay for a time trying to recall exactly what I'd seen, and whether there'd been any indication at all of the man's identity. The woman I knew was Lalage. But the man? Claude Lang? Or could it have been Ivan? Both were tall. Both slim. Through the darkness it had been impossible to tell. Was it credible — and I tried to tell myself it was — that even Jed had been making a nocturnal visit?

I wouldn't put it past him. But almost as soon as the idea occurred I had to dismiss it. Jed was so much larger and lumpier. His form would have eclipsed any pale glimmer of light. No. It couldn't possibly have been Jed.

At last, after an hour or so I fell into a troubled sleep.

I didn't wake until it was past nine, when the girl knocked and entered with breakfast.

"Mrs Traille said as how I should wake you," she told me a trifle truculently. "She wants everythin' on time today. There's comp'ny comin'."

"Company?" I rubbed my eyes. "Who?"

"Mr Polglaze. Mr Isaac Polglaze."

"Oh. I don't know him. Who is he?"

"The master's agent. Comin' by boat from the mainland he is." She spoke smugly. "There'll be somethen special for the meal today. O' course, it'll be the master and Mr Polglaze eatin' together. *You'll* be with Mr Claude an' Maurice, or perhaps with Mrs Traille." She paused, then added, "Mr Polglaze is gentry. A really fine-dressed gentleman." She giggled stupidly. "Las' time he come he give me a slap on the behind, and pushed a rose in me hair. No one see'd it but me." A sigh passed her lips. "I like Mr Polglaze. He's rich 'n got a fine place over theer — at Penzance."

"Oh. Have you seen it?"

"No. Course not. None of us ever crosses the water except the master and Jed and Marte. Once I thought I'd like to. Now I knows I wouldn', 'cause of the wrecks an' thin's an' them pirates you get on the sea."

"Pirates?" I laughed. "We don't have pirates anymore, not round here."

"Don't we now?" she sniffed. "You doan' know nuthen 'bout this place, Ellan — "

"*Miss* Ellan," I corrected her.

She gave me a surly look, tossed her head and went to the door. Once there she made a mock curtsey and said, "Or should I say y'r majesty? Mebbe yu'd like that."

"Don't be insolent," I told her angrily. "If you ever speak to me like that again I shall tell Mrs Traille — or the master. Yes, I shall complain to Mr Sterne.

"He wouldn' listen. He — "

113

"Oh, yes, I think he would," Something in my manner must have disturbed her. She once more appeared the cringing rabbity looking creature she'd appeared on my arrival. Although in making such a comparison I was certainly being unfair to the rabbit.

"He wouldn't then. Mrs Traille said you was nuthen. Nuthen but a stuck-up skivvy, she said. Well — sumthen like that — " Her words faded. I was aware of my mouth hardening.

"Then I shall have to speak about Mrs Traille, too," I said coldly.

"No." The girl's head sagged forward. "Don't. Not her."

"Why not? If she says such things behind my back it's only right I should enquire why, and inform her who told me."

All trace of belligerence faded from the plain countenance.

"Please don't, Miss. P'raps I shouldn't've said."

"You certainly shouldn't. And I hardly think Mrs Traille would talk in such a manner, considering Ivan — Master Sterne — brought me here personally.

Obviously, you don't like serving me, and if it offends you I'll come down to the kitchen and make breakfast for myself. That won't worry me in the least."

"Better not — oh much better not — " Momentary fear flooded the watery eyes. "Mrs Traille doan' like her plans upset. She'd tell that theer Jed, an' — an' — " Her words faded as she glanced back over her shoulder.

"Why are you afraid of Jed?" I asked. "Has he ever hurt you?"

She nodded. "Once. When I was fust workin' proper here, he took a strap to me because I wouldn' — I wouldn' — "

"Well?"

"I'm not tellin'." From the sulky determination in her voice I knew she wouldn't.

"What about the master — Mr Sterne? Did he know?"

She shook her head.

"No. I didn't say, and shan't, ever. He's got things on his mind, see? He doan' want botherin' what goes on in the kitchens. An' it's not all fun, I c'n tell you. Not with that mad old creature upstairs — Miss Augusta, an' high-an'-mighty Lalage, too. Not that *she's* got anythin' to boast about. Drinks she does, an' man-mad into the bargain. I tell you — " her manner became confiding and secretive, almost friendly, " — if I had the chance I'd be off tomorrow — "

"To the mainland?"

"Mebbe. I dunno. Anywhere."

"What keeps you here?"

"I was paid for. *Bought*. That's what."

I stared at her, shocked.

"*Bought?*"

She nodded.

"I was on a ship see? An' it was wrecked — off the back of the island. I was only a little 'un, — 'bout four, I s'pose. 'Bout twenty year ago, Jed says. My pa was drownded. All of 'em — except me an' a furriner who was sent back to one o' they far off places. Coloured he was, an' the ole man gave him a guinea to say nuthen and tek off, or he'd hang. So you could say I cost a guinea, couldn't you? I bin here ever since. Long before Mr Ivan came o' course."

"You mean you've not been anywhere else all your *life*?" It seemed incredible, but would explain her primitive mentality.

"That's right. Anyways — where'd I go? An' what for?" She sighed heavily, and continued, "Not but what I wouldn't like to see a few o' them shops, that theer Miss Dupont talks about. I doan' believe her quite, mind you. She's a born liar. Once I heared the master tellin' her so, so there!" The oration ended on a note of triumph.

"You shouldn't listen at doors," I told her, in my most prim voice.

"Why? Wouldn't you, if you got the chance?"

I found myself blushing. "It would depend. Anyway, what the master discusses in private with anyone else is entirely his own business. You shouldn't really have told me. Do you understand?"

A look of cunning crossed her face. "If that's so — 'bout folk talkin' private like — you won' be tellin' Mrs Traille what I said 'bout her then, will you?"

I shook my head. "No. Not this time — so long as you remember your place where I'm concerned and keep a polite

117

tongue when addressing me."

How portentous I sounded! More like Aunt Clarissa than myself. But that short statement did the trick.

"I'll remember," she said, "*Miss.*"

When she'd gone I tried to dismiss the garbled tale I'd heard as only half real, the other part merely the fanciful meandering of a simple mind. But I couldn't help recalling Ivan's allusions to opium, the strange behaviour on the island of Jed with his telescope, and extreme watchfulness of the coast, which, combined with Mr Sterne's recent business of investing or perhaps acquiring the shipping line he'd referred to — suggested a fascinating and mysterious story.

I didn't see Ivan before the midday meal; but Mrs Traille informed me, obviously put out by the news, that the master had said I was expected to eat with the two men.

"It isn't usual," she said, "when Mr Isaac comes, they've always private business to talk about. Still — " she sniffed " — seemingly you'll be taking on a bit of book work in the future.

Business. So the master'll want you to be acquainted with his associates." She spoke with her ample chin raised, looking rather like an inflated pouter pigeon.

I almost giggled.

"I expect so," I answered politely.

"You'll be wantin' to dress proper, then," she said pointedly.

I studied the skirt of my day-gown critically.

"Yes, I suppose so. But I haven't many clothes."

"The evenin' one would be far too fancy," she said. "Mebbe the one you're wearin' would do, given a bit o' smartenin' up with a silk shawl or somethin'."

"Unfortunately I haven't a silk shawl."

"I c'n lend you one," she offered, taking me aback by such an unexpected show of generosity. "You wait a bit, I'll fetch it."

I lingered about until she returned with the shawl hanging over one arm. It was beautiful — pale, regal purples and blues, merging into translucent green, patterned with rose-pink flowers of various shades.

The fringe was thick, shimmering like water under a summer sky, when the light caught it.

I touched it gently. "But how lovely," I murmured. "Are you sure — ?"

"Put it on," she interrupted in her normal sharp way. "Then go take a look at yourself."

I draped the silk round my shoulders and went to the nearest mirror. Then I gasped.

"Well?"

The subtle tones of the material emphasized the green of my eyes, adding lustre even to the dark copper lights of my hair and cream complexion.

"I don't know what to say," I admitted. "It's so beautiful — I've never seen one like this before."

"Of course not. It came from abroad — China or India, or some such place. I dunno. I've forgotten. But if you like you c'n wear it. Maybe I'll *give* it you in the end — you being the sort of colourful creature who can wear such things. The old master passed it on to me when he was turning a lot of stuff out. That was before he went — " she threw me a significant sidelong look " — before his sickness like."

Trying not to appear too curious I asked with feigned nonchalance, "Was Mr — Mr Ivan's father ill for long?"

"Long enough," she answered ambiguously. I thought this meant the end of the conversation, but she suddenly resumed: "It was one o' them theer tropical things I do believe. Affected his — his upstairs, if you know what I mean. His brain."

"Oh. I didn't know. I thought he studied a good deal, and read."

"So he did. Oh, he didn' have fits of madness or that sort o' thing. Just shut 'isself away. Brooding. Moody. Not that he didn' have cause."

"I suppose it must have been difficult for him with Miss Augusta always here, and his sons away. Then Miss Dupont — how long has she been at Merlake?"

Mrs Traille's face set into its usual fierce mould. "You're askin' things you shouldn', Miss Ellan. Tisn' your business. What happened in the past es only Mr Ivan's affair. So my advice is, go about your duties. Get sumthen pretty from the conservatory, an' see the dinin' room an' library look welcomin' — that's where they do go when Master Polglaze comes — the library. Then tidy yourself up as befittin' your place." She eyed me very directly, continuing critically, "That dark hair o' yours is forever falling out of place. Can' you do sumthen to keep it in place? Use more combs or a bit of chiffon or sumthen' — When you went out the other day a real gipsy you looked, all wild an' windblown prancin' towards the pier — "

"I like the wind in my hair," I told her. "And I didn't know you were watching."

"I just happened to be. An' others could've seen you. Madam — Miss Augusta — Marte, or Jed."

"I can well imagine that Jed's always watching."

"It's his job. An' Marte's too, when he's not tendin' the farm work or goats. So just you remember, Ellan." She forgot the 'Miss' this time. "Attend to your own duties here, and forget the rest."

She jerked her head up, turned, marched away, and left me to my own thoughts.

After a minute I realised I hadn't really time to let my mind wander. With the flowers to attend to, and an inspection of the library to make, not to mention dealing with my own appearance, and seeing that I looked sufficiently elegant yet dignified to eat with Ivan and his guest, I had quite enough to attend to.

My first meeting with Isaac Polglaze at the meal later proved easier than I'd anticipated. I'd expected someone either loudly dressed and overbearing, or a little coarse, according to my conversation with the maid earlier. He appeared to be neither — he was dressed in a dark waisted coat above lemon knee-length breeches and stockings, over which he'd worn boots for the sea journey, then changed into buckled shoes. His gold waistcoat was topped by a cream neckcloth. It was difficult to imagine him frivolous or sticking a rose into a servant girl's locks, as she'd said. His face was ruddy and broad, framed by side whiskers and greying, carefully groomed hair; he was polite, but not extravagantly so, small in height, but a trifle portly. A very ordinary man, I thought, until I noticed the eyes. They were small, shrewd, of no particular colour, but quickly moving, as though missing nothing. My introduction to him by Ivan was brief and perfunctory.

"Miss Ellan may accompany me to Penzance one day in the future," Ivan explained, after the first formalities had been exchanged. "There will probably be an occasion when I need a feminine hostess — and for secretarial duties as well." Feeling his eyes on me, my skin burned.

"Very good, very good," Isaac Polglaze remarked. Then turning to me he asked, "Are you a good sailor, Miss Ellan?"

"Not very," I admitted, recalling my journey from the mainland to Merlake. "But I wasn't actually ill."

"Hm."

"It was a stormy night," Ivan said, "and Miss Ellan was weary. She showed considerable stoicism."

"It's often the way," Isaac Polglaze remarked non-committally; "Women of an attractive feminine exterior can sometimes possess unexpected character beneath."

124

I supposed this was meant as a compliment, although the man instantly looked away, showing little interest in me. After this the meal continued in comparative silence except for the clatter of cutlery on plates, the tinkle of glass, and ordinary trite snippets of conversation concerning the weather, and occasional references to Cornish mining ventures between the two men. There were brief allusions I did not understand to the take-over of the new shipping line, and most of the time I felt that my presence at the table was quite superfluous.

I retired early, leaving Ivan and his guest talking over cigars and further drink, in the library.

For a time I wandered aimlessly about the room, tidying the dressing-table where a few toilet accessories, ribbons and combs were in careless disorder. Once or twice I went to the window, staring out over grey roofs and garden to the moorland slope and sea below. I realised that my bedroom must be overlooking Miss Augusta's apartments which were on the first floor. I could just define the tip of a squat tower jutting out and the edge of her small private scrap of walled-in land which was sufficiently sheltered to have well-cared for rose beds and climbing fruit trees. Trying to picture her domain fascinated me. She must obviously have a personal maid who slept immediately next to her perhaps, or at a lower level, giving easy access to the kitchens. And Lalage? Miss Dupont's quarters, from what I could remember, leading from their narrow staircase, and adjoining the schoolroom and breakfast room would have a view very similar to mine. Gradually evening faded to night.

I was still trying to conjecture and reason out the geography of the building, when a muted flurry of sound and scratching like the tapping of fingers on a wall followed by the heavier tread of footsteps caught my attention. I turned quickly, with my ears alert. Outside the door the furtive noise ceased. There was a sudden silence, then a soft tap, followed by a louder one, but no attempt to enter. I hesitated, then, as I was still fully dressed, and telling myself it could easily be a servant with a message from Ivan wanting me

126

downstairs again, I went to the door and opened it.

Lalage stood there with a candle flaring dangerously in one shaky hand. She was wearing a flimsy nightshift that could easily have caught alight. Through the thin material her voluptuous form appeared broad and sagging — the heavy breasts drooping above the large stomach. She could have been a base caricature of a Rubens' figure. The wan candlelight flickered grotesquely about her face, accentuating jowls and pouches under her eyes, and adding years to her age. There was no longer any semblance of beauty there. The thick hair even appeared coarse and uncared for — a black tousled frame for the concentrated, almost malevolent, glare she threw at me.

Intuitively I stepped back. She said nothing at first. I was about to ask what she wanted when she gave a short throaty laugh, and said in slurred tones:

"Don't interfere with me and mine. Keep off — d'you hear? Don't you dare speak a word against that boy or what goes on between me and him, and others. You just take care of yourself, and mind

127

your own business or — " she thrust her face forward, " — you'll regret it."

Her hand was shaking. From her manner and the strong smell of spirit, I knew she was drunk. I did my best to reason with her and keep my voice calm.

"Please go back to bed," I said. "I've no intention of interfering with anyone. Certainly not you. Please, Lalage."

She drew herself up. Her large mouth was belligerent — a sneering red gash above the heavy chin.

"Oh, indeed!" she repeated in mincing, mocking tones that had lost any trace of refinement, "Ai've no hintention of interfering'. Well, you just remember it. And my name's Dupont to you. Would you like to know the rest? The truth?"

With my hand on the knob I answered firmly, "No. I don't want to hear stories — about you, or your nephew, or anything else that concerns you — "

"That's why you've come though, isn't it? To spy? That's what you are, a dirty stinking spy. Someone to whisper in darling Ivan's ear."

I sighed and forced the door against

her intruding form.

"I've no idea what you're talking about. Now — please go, will you?"

"No I won't — I *won't*. Touch me, and I'll burn your hair off — " The idea seemed to amuse her. She started laughing in an obscene, jeering way. "That'd be funny, wouldn't it? You a baldy! The high-and-mighty Miss — Miss — holier-than-thou, is it?" Her large figure heaved as a series of meaningless chuckles rose from her throat. The candle dropped to the ground. She stared stupidly for a moment as I bent to pick it up. It had already singed a corner of her thin wrap. When I faced her again she was still staring, her full mouth shocked and open. All belligerence had left her. She looked what she obviously was — an unhappy, intoxicated creature on the verge of madness, suddenly brought to her senses through an awareness of danger.

"Go to your room now," I said, "before anyone finds you. I'll follow you with the candle."

She didn't resist when I took her firmly

by her plump arm and accompanied her down narrow corridors to her own premises. She knew the way by instinct, but later when I returned to my own bedroom after seeing her safely ensconsed in her room, without candles or light I could not have exactly recalled the route. The unpleasant intrusion had left me shocked, and quite determined that in future after locking my door I would not open it to anyone unless I knew who was outside.

Hours passed before I could get to sleep that night. I lay staring restlessly through the darkness trying to quieten my uneasy thoughts. One point at least was clarified — the reason for Ivan's anxiety concerning Lalage's influence on Maurice. She was not only an alcoholic, but an unstable one.

Two days later, however, when I left through the conservatory for a stroll in the garden, I saw them walking together hand in hand towards the far edge of the lawn.

Remembering Ivan's instructions to intercept contact between them whenever possible, I wandered on, stopping idly at intervals to touch a spray of blossom or the petals of a flower. Once a blue butterfly settled on my hand, opened its velvety wings for a moment, then delicately fluttered away into the quiet sky. Nearing the gazebo I came face to face with the couple, hardly recognising the well-corseted woman confronting me.

She was an erect, statuesque figure in grey silk, wearing a black lace shawl over her ample shoulders. Her manner was confident, almost condescending. Except for a faint mottling of her complexion there was no indication of self-indulgence. Her hair was parted in the centre and looped over her ears under organdie frills edged with lace. She bowed her head and said in controlled tones, "Good morning, Miss — Ellan, isn't it?" And then, turning to her nephew, "Remember your manners, Maurice."

The boy smiled automatically and offered me his hand. "Good morning," he echoed dutifully.

"It's a lovely day, isn't it?" I remarked, trying to show no surprise.

"We'll have rain later, I expect," Lalage

131

told me. "Or a gale, perhaps. Quietness like this doesn't last long at Merlake." She smiled. Her eyes held mine unswervingly. It was as though she sensed the inward war between us concerning Maurice, and was determined to outshine me. I didn't return the smile; it was false and completely without friendliness. Maurice also had a certain secret triumph in his eyes.

"We won't keep you any longer," I heard Lalage saying, "and we must get back to the house. Maurice's lessons are due and Claude will be waiting for him." She swept past me arrogantly. I turned my head, watching them move side by side towards the conservatory. As I paused, the figure of Claude Lang appeared at the end of the path leading to the side-entrance. He obviously saw me. His pale face and static figure appeared, to my heightened imagination, to emit a menacing quality like that of some threatening phantom conjured up especially to haunt me. For that brief pause I was aware of a strange bond between them — something holding the impact of a thunderous dark cloud threatening to break. Yet why? What reason was there for such hatred? I didn't wish them any harm. All I wanted was to assist Ivan without causing trouble. Quite clearly this was going to be extremely difficult — even impossible.

After the trio had disappeared I lingered about for some time before returning to the house. When I got back, there was no one about. I went up to my room curiously disturbed. The little interlude in the garden had upset me more than I'd realised at the time, and it was for this reason, partly, that later — in the afternoon — I threw discretion to the winds and decided to explore any part of the island that was possible.

Lalage had been right about the change in the weather.

There was no rain, but following the extreme calm a wind had risen, driving massed dark clouds in galleon shapes across the sky.

Impulsively, I slung my cape over my arm in case a storm broke, and went out, unseen, cutting down the garden path to the gap in the wall which overlooked the moorland drop towards the great cliffs below. The salt sting of rime was driven through the air leaving its fresh tang on my lips, whipping through the heather, against boulders and my blown hair. I paused, looking towards the precipitous forbidden line of coast, half expecting to see Jed's large form appear gazing in my direction, or into his telescope pointed seawards. There was no sign of him. Nothing but a froth of white where the great waves broke against the rocks and a few gulls rising screaming above. I darted forward recklessly, clambering between great clusters of granite in the hope of locating the narrow track I'd glimpsed in my first glance that way. It seemed to have petered out, becoming only a thread of short turf zig-zagging uncertainly between boulders — wavering down then upwards again, starred at points with the frail pink of thrift and sparse undergrowth. I paused as the land took an abrupt turn round a jutting line of cliff, wondering whether to go back. But curiosity defied common sense, and I went on. The boom of the sea grew louder crashing below with thunderous force. Suddenly the wind's fury intensified. Clutching at a spike of granite with one hand, I tried to steady myself, and wipe my eyes free of driven spray with the other.

Then I glanced down.

Terror seized me.

I was standing on a small plateau of rock not more than four feet in width, overlooking a sheer drop of dark glassy cliff cutting to a swirling mass of water below. At each ebb of giant waves the tips of crags showed briefly like hungry great teeth before the tide rushed forward to cover them again. I tore my eyes away and stiffened my spine against the cold granite, still clutching the rocky spike for support. It was as though I myself was paralysed — turned to stone. I couldn't move either way. One false step — a slight slip — and I'd be taken by the elements and hurled down — down, into the yawning wild abyss of raging sea.

I closed my eyes for a moment, and held my breath as a strand of wet hair was whipped against my face. Above the moan of wind and waves I heard different sounds — the shrill crying of gulls — or was it the greedy shrieking of others who'd been taken before me and now lay crushed as broken skeletons in their cold sea tombs? In lightning speed the series of macabre visions flashed through my mind. The sweep of rain mingled with spray, now half blinded me. I made an effort to edge back the way I'd come, still with my spine stiff against the icy rock. But it was useless. If once I loosened my hold on the crag of jutting cliff, I knew I'd be helpless. Giddiness could claim me, and send me swirling to death.

"A miracle," I prayed inwardly, "there must be a miracle." I think I was crying as I prayed. I didn't really believe in miracles, and my prayer was only a desperate appeal to live — for life, whatever kind of existence it was — either with dull domineering Aunt Clarissa at Mounterrith or in my locked bedroom at Merlake.

My tears began to tremble into hysterical laughter. It was so stupid to think of Aunt Clarissa just then, when any moment might be my last. But it shouldn't be — it *mustn't*. The wild instinctive desire to endure was suddenly reborn in me with such force

I managed to free myself momentarily from rigidity.

Keeping my eyes firmly away from the cold ugly cliff face, I loosened my hold on the crag, and clutching at an overhanging growth of short turf above, took a step sideways towards the spot where the coastline bent back abruptly cutting to gentler terrain. How I managed to reach safer ground, I don't really know now. But I did, and as the precipice faded behind the thrust of bulging cliff, I was able to find a firm foothold, and a place to rest in behind a barrier of larger boulders. I waited with my head bent forward in my hands. My whole body was trembling. And then, to my astonishment, I heard a man's voice.

"What the hell — "

Jerked to attention, I looked up comparatively recovered, but still shivering.

Ivan was standing there — a dark forbidding figure against the cold sky. His expression was strained and drawn and angry. He reached down, stared into my face for a moment, then pulled me up, gripping me quite cruelly by both arms.

137

"What are you doing here?" he demanded. "You were told never to come this way. Then why the devil did you do it — why? *Why?*" There was a sort of agony in his voice — an agony I couldn't understand, because after all it was only me, Jade-Anna, a penniless stranger who'd been forced on him by circumstances and a little effort on my own part.

"I don't know," I answered. "I shouldn't have I suppose, but I wanted to see the view — I — "

"The view!" he shouted. "You could have killed yourself. Know that?" He started shaking me. My jaws chattered. Then, before I knew what was happening, he'd picked me up, and his lips were on mine. The kiss was hot and hungry and demanding, wild with desire and bitterness — the bitterness of the elements that claimed us irrevocably in that wanton place. He laid me down. There was darkness, and light, and a leap of pain that became joy unutterable. Terror was forgotten as flesh was unified with flesh, at one with the surging spirit of ages gone and yet to be. Thought or words were superfluous. What happened was inevitable — as merciless and hungry as the cruel tide below.

When all was over silence held us, broken only by the soughing and breaking of wind and waves. Then Ivan drew me to my feet, pulled my wet cape round me, swept the hair from my eyes, and said, just as though we'd been resting following a normal stroll together: "We'd better get back now. I was looking for you. I wanted to show you some books. If Marte hadn't spotted you taking off this way I might never have found you."

"I see," I answered stiffly, quite shocked by his attitude, his casual acceptance of the unpredictable passionate scene of only moments ago.

"No need to apologise this time. But if I ever catch you disobeying me again you'll get a walloping you'll never forget. So just remember, will you?"

"Providing you stop threatening me like a child," I answered, shrilly.

"Good."

Grasping me by an arm he pulled me back the way I'd come, in places taking a route slightly more inland.

Near the house we met Jed coming from the opposite direction. Ivan stared at him grimly. "You missed out this time, Jed," Ivan cried. "In your absence this — this young — Miss Ellan — nearly got herself killed."

"I can't have eyes everywhere," Jed replied, in rather a surly way for a servant, I thought. But then perhaps he didn't count as a 'servant' — what was it Mrs Traille had called him? — 'Keeper of the Island'. Yes. And if I remembered rightly, so had Miss Augusta, in one of our brief exchanges of words together.

"Then see Marte does a bit more," Ivan told him coldly. "You know there's no relying on Thorlock these days."

Jed's heavy jaw hardened. He walked away, saying, "I'll do what's possible. If you want more help you'd better go about getting it." He was clearly very put out, and so was Ivan. If I'd not been there I knew he'd have gone after the burly figure and that some confrontation could have ensued. As it was he controlled himself, gave another jerk to my arm, and a few minutes later we were entering the house through the conservatory.

"Go to your room," he told me, before we reached the hall, "and stay there until I give permission for you to come down. At the moment I've had enough of you."

Biting my lip I ran past him, though the parlour, and upstairs. How *dare* he? I thought wildly. After doing what he'd done — scolding and shouting and then taking me like any cheap whore? Oh, I hated him. It was unforgivable. I sat on the bed, breathing heavily. I'd show him though, I determined, with tears of humiliation half choking my throat. Somehow I'd pay him out — make Mr Ivan Sterne regret the day he'd ever brought Jade-Anna Ellan to Merlake. Following the wild decision my nerves and outrage quietened a little. I recalled against my will, my own response to the passionate encounter. I'd wanted him as much as he'd wanted me. I hadn't fought or denied him. Why? Because I'd been scared out of my senses — a fact he'd realised and taken advantage of.

No. That wasn't strictly true. It wasn't

only circumstances that had drawn us together, not weaknesses or my own fear, but something darker and deeper and far more tormenting — something I'd felt on that first meeting at Mounterrith when our eyes had met in the crowded room following Evadne's marriage to Christopher.

I didn't understand the tumult of my own emotions. At the time it was hard to fathom their importance or get the episode into true proportions. Possibly I'd behaved like a 'loose woman'? — Aunt Clarissa would certainly say so. If so — what matter? — Nothing seemed normal or straightforward at Merlake. Thinking things over more coolly later, I recalled another peculiar detail — Ivan's reference, while talking to Jed, of someone called Thorlock. Who was Thorlock? And how did he fit into life at Merlake?

I wandered to the dressing table, seated myself at the mirror and stared at my own reflection — loose damp hair curling crisply about a face still perplexed yet burning from those passionate moments on the cliff. My jade eyes seemed to have darkened almost to black, lightened with darting feverish sparks that gave haunting intensity to the pallor of my face. Against one cheek were two tiny red marks where male lips had bruised the flesh. Automatically I put up a hand and touched them.

My heart quickened.

It couldn't be, I thought resentfully, oh, surely it *couldn't* be that I'd desired him? Was in love?

A second afterwards I dispelled the idea ruthlessly.

Love had gentleness in it, and trust; and there was nothing any more about Ivan Sterne that I trusted or even liked. He'd taken me from a boring, dreary, safe life at Mounterrith to something frightening and dangerous, and utterly despicable.

The collector of women!

What could be more humiliating?

Nothing, I told myself. My situation at Merlake was ignominious, and the only course just then seemed that I must leave the island on the first opportunity.

I didn't go downstairs again that evening, but turned the key in the lock of my door, and refused to answer any knock.

The following week passed comparatively uneventfully.

Mealtimes were silent, superficially polite affairs. On the few occasions when Ivan and I met by chance in the hall or passed on the stairs, I said nothing, and he appeared morose and preoccupied.

On the Monday morning following the wild episode on the cliff, however, he found me alone in the library, and informed me curtly that he had to make a trip to the mainland on Friday, and that I was to accompany him.

I was too astounded at first to speak. Then, after a short pause, I asked coldly, "Why?"

"It was in our contract, I believe, Miss Ellan. In any case, you should do something about your clothes."

"What's wrong with my clothes?"

He looked hard at me for a moment, as though assessing every line and curve of my figure.

"They don't flatter you."

"I didn't come here as a — a —" I

floundered helplessly, and turned away continuing abruptly, "I'm an employee. Supposed to work."

"And you'll do so. That's why it's important for you to live up to your position. I've business acquaintances for you to meet at Penzance. You'll be required to play hostess to guests at my table, and take notes when required."

"I've had no proper training as a secretary," I reminded him.

He glanced away, put a hand to his stock as though to tidy it. "Don't worry. A bright child would be able to handle what's required on such an occasion. And whatever else you may or may not be, Jade-Anna, I'm quite sure you're no dullard."

Having no remark ready for such a statement, I held my tongue, and without giving me another glance he walked smartly past me and left the room.

5

DURING the next few days life at Merlake seemed quieter than usual, although with myself it was mostly façade. I saw Ivan very little except at mealtimes, and then he seemed preoccupied, concerned, I supposed, with the forthcoming visit to the mainland. Apart from inward apprehension, I felt puzzled and humiliated. His remoteness seemed so unnatural after what had happened between us. Perhaps he would unbend later, I told myself, when we reached Penzance. Perhaps even he was waiting until we got there before he informed me that after all I was not suitable for the post. Certainly I'd done nothing so far to prevent Lalage meeting her nephew. I'd seen them only once again since that brief glimpse of them in the garden, and there was nothing I could do, because Claude Lang was also present.

Once Madam — Miss Augusta — left

146

her own premises and startled me in the hall by calling from the bend of the staircase above.

"Leaving, are you?" she cried, poking her gaunt face over the rail.

I shook my head. "No. Not yet."

Her macabre smile vanished. The jaws snapped tight. She turned away, drawing the lace shawl high under her neck and muttering something like, "You will — you will. There's no place for a gel like you here."

I hurried away, wondering what had given her the idea of my departure with Ivan. But probably she was only guessing, I thought — trying to goad me into an interlude of argument or gossip.

Later that day something happened — information from Ivan that completely swept all other matters from my mind.

He came into the parlour where I was arranging flowers and said, "Our trip is tomorrow, Jade-Anna. I've been remiss in not explaining before. Sit down — "

Something — a note of quiet determination in his voice — made me obey. He went to a cabinet, brought out a decanter, and poured a glass of madeira for me and one for himself.

"If you'd been a more amenable character I'd already have told you," he continued, half seated on the edge of the table. "But to be frank I didn't want a scene."

"Why should there be a scene?" I demanded quickly.

"Exactly." He studied me intently, as the old feeling of confusion mixed up with wild attraction brought a hot wave of embarrassed excitement flooding my whole body. Then he resumed, "Following our little — escapade — on the cliff, I've decided there's only one course open to us."

"What do you mean? You want me to leave Merlake, for good?" I should have known, I thought dully. It was the obvious solution for him.

I was startled by his answer.

"No. That wouldn't be the decent thing to do."

"But — "

"Listen, and for heaven's sake keep your sharp tongue quiet for a moment while I'm talking." He took a pinch of snuff — something I'd never seen him do before. Was snuff a cure for nerves, I wondered stupidly, remembering that my uncle had generally resorted to it whenever there was an argument between him and Aunt Clarissa. I had always considered it an unpleasant habit and turned my face away.

"Look at me," I heard Ivan say a moment later.

I did so defiantly.

"And don't glare. It isn't — " he paused, putting the snuff box away, " — exactly tactful under the circumstances."

"What circumstances?"

"Questions again!" He smiled unexpectedly. "Well, why not? You have the right. The circumstances, Miss Ellan — " a tinge of mockery touched his lips and was quite apparent in his voice " — are that a marriage has been arranged."

"A *marriage*?" I jumped up. "What do you mean?"

He reached for my hand, enclosing it so firmly I could not draw away.

"Are you frightened?"

"Yes. No — not frightened," I stammered. "Just shocked. Perhaps I shouldn't be, perhaps I've not understood. Do you mean we'll be attending it — or — or — " I broke off helplessly.

"My dear girl — " he released my hand and slipped an arm round my waist. "Don't prevaricate. You should know very well what I'm talking about. *Us*, my love."

"Us? — but you're not 'my love'. I never said — "

"It wasn't for you to say," he interrupted, "and obviously we both acted over-hastily the other evening. However, in my own particular fashion I'm a man of honour; also it's possible I need a wife. You certainly need a husband."

I could feel one tooth cutting my underlip. My head was whirling. After all recent conjecturing this was the last thing I'd anticipated; in fact the idea had never occurred to me at all. A passionate affair was one thing — marriage quite another — especially when he was most probably still secretly yearning for Evadne, my beautiful cousin who had stolen Christopher from me. Stung by his cool assumption that I could be used so lightly over so serious a business,

150

I retorted hotly, "No, I'm sorry. I don't love you, and I wouldn't demean myself by marrying a man I — "

"You what? Desire with your body but not your romantic heart?" He touched my chin again with a finger and tilted my face up to his. Then his lips came down on mine. His kiss was different from any he'd given before — gentle yet sensuous, causing a great longing in me, which dimmed commonsense into a cloud of forgetfulness. When it ended he told me with a wry smile, "You've still quite a great deal to learn, Jade-Anna, but I'm sure you'll be able to — in time."

Bewilderment once more engulfed me. The consequence was that in spite of all protests and emotional conflict, Ivan won, and later, when I was able to face matters objectively, I was no longer in the slightest rebellious, but titillated with excitement, and a sense of wild anticipation for the future and becoming Mrs Ivan Sterne, Mistress of Merlake.

I temporarily forgot the existence of Miss Augusta, or the unpleasant presence of Lalage Dupont. My new position at Merlake would surely prevent any interference on their part. I was, of course, being unduly optimistic, as the future was to prove in a cruel manner I could not remotely have anticipated.

The following afternoon we set off early, about three o'clock, for the mainland. I was wearing the best clothes I could muster from my sparse wardrobe, and carried with me only my small valise. The weather was calm and fine. The sea unruffled, showing only a ripple of silvered waves on the water. Jed and Marte rowed steadily. No sail had been hoisted, and I was spared the queasiness from any rolling tide.

It was a strange crossing. Ivan was unduly silent. Several times I made an effort to start a conversation, but words were swallowed up — died — into a limbo of unreality. I wouldn't have been surprised if I'd woken suddenly as from a dream, to find myself in my old bedroom at Mounterrith. However, when at length we reached Penzance Harbour, truth registered. Ivan helped me ashore, and my heart jerked alive, hammering wildly. The grip of his hand on mine was forceful, and was not withdrawn until I was able to walk steadily over the shingle and rough stones.

"Are you all right?" he asked.

I nodded. "Perfectly, thank you."

He took my arm then, and guided me between fishing boats, ropes, and away from large vessels anchored by the quay. Sea-gulls screamed, sailors shouted intermittently as cargo was unloaded. Sometimes caps were touched respectfully as Ivan and I passed.

Behind us Marte dealt with what luggage we had, leaving Jed to attend to the boat. When we reached the pier we mounted some steps and found a cab waiting, with a driver ready to spring down and open the door. From there we were driven into the town, up a road past an inn, and a warehouse, and from there took an abrupt turn to the right along a cobbled byway. The buildings — mostly commercial — grew taller, but at intervals narrow entries showed glimpses of the sea below. Strange distorted shadows played across the ground. A man with a patch over one eye, and a wooden leg, looking like a character out of fiction, was slumped against a wall with a bottle to his lips. A seaman obviously. Instinctively I drew my cape more tightly round my neck.

"What's the matter?" Ivan asked.

"Nothing. It's got colder, though."

"We shall soon be there. My house-keeper's niece will have a meal waiting."

I didn't question him about the niece or her aunt, deciding their presence was immaterial since in future I was evidently destined to shoulder what social duties were necessary. But I did enquire before the cab stopped, if I should be expected to deal with domestic chores in Penzance.

"Certainly not," he said. "How could you? Your life will be at Merlake, and in any case, I wouldn't wish my wife to undertake menial work." The word 'wife' mildly shocked me, but I tried not to show it as he continued more casually, "Beth will find a caretaker for me. She's a capable young woman. Her husband runs The Golden Cow, so she's well in with the local population."

There seemed nothing more to say. I sat back, and a few moments later the cab drew up by a flight of granite steps leading up to a high rather higgledy-piggledy looking building silhouetted against watery sunlight. The cabby descended, took our luggage from us, and carried it ahead, leaving Ivan to assist me. I didn't need assistance, I told him. He released my arm then, leaving me free to lift my skirts with both hands above the ankles.

The steps were steep and took a bend at the top where a heavy door had already been opened slightly. The house, I noticed, had one or two brass plates placed irregularly at other smaller doors and above, obviously indicating business premises or professional offices. Beside the main entrance the name 'Sterne' followed by 'Shipping Company' was emblazoned boldly on a large plaque.

After depositing the luggage on the top step, the cabby waited until Ivan had paid him, then touching his cap respectfully returned to his vehicle, leaving Ivan and me alone.

Ivan pushed the door wider, and held it for me to enter. I obeyed silently. The interior had a faintly musty smell. The heavy mahogany hall furniture was well polished though, and shone from a side window. From the back of the house a woman emerged wearing a blue dress, white apron, and something white and lacy pushed to the back of her head. She was comely, stoutish and friendly looking, with an ample bosom and pink cheeks.

"There'll be something to eat in the parlour, sir," she said, when the first introductions were over, "and the bedroom's ready for the young lady. That's right, sir, isn't it?" She paused doubtfully.

"Quite right, Beth," Ivan answered. "I shall sleep in the back office."

"Just as usual. Very good. I thought so, sir, and I've a fire going in both places."

It all sounded so commonplace and matter-of-fact, I had a sudden urge to laugh, but was able to restrain myself. How ridiculous and really funny her words seemed, considering the wild episode on the cliff which had led to the situation I was now in. Of course Beth might not be so conventional or prim as she appeared. I rather fancied there was a twinkle in her pale blue eyes, when she conducted me to the bedroom a moment later. Like the hall, the room was furnished sombrely in mahogany, but a bowl of fresh roses had been placed on the dressing table. The blind at the square window was up, and the lace curtains parted revealing an immediate view of rooftops and chimney pots. The bed was a four poster, large, with a lace spread over the thick crimson quilt.

"I hope you'll be comfortable," Beth said, a little breathlessly, depositing my valise on the rug near the wardrobe. "I hear — " she paused, eyeing me speculatively, before continuing " — I understand you'll be marrying Mr Ivan tomorrow?"

I could feel myself blushing.

"Yes. He's told you then?"

"Of course, miss. He had to, didn't he? With Auntie leaving, and all these new arrangements having to be made. I hope you'll be happy. You won't be here much though, will you? Mr Ivan doesn't come all that often — generally only for business meetings, and they're what you could call mostly male affairs." She laughed. "I expect this time's a special one — just for the wedding like."

"I'm here also for secretarial duties," I told her, realising instantly how prim the words must sound.

She shook her head good-naturedly. "I shouldn't worry about *that* too much, Miss Ellan. Mr Ivan — or Sterne, I should say, has always been one for using his own head and taking his own notes. You'll be an asset though, for showing off to his friends. My John — that's my husband, always says there's nothing like a pretty skirt to help pull off a tricky business deal. And you're certainly that."

"What?"

"Well — take a look at yourself in the glass. Pretty isn't the right word, perhaps, but — handsome, colourful and picturesque."

When I didn't answer she touched my arm lightly. "Embarrassed you, have I? Spoken out of turn? Forgive me, miss. I shouldn't have. But really! To find Mr Ivan getting married at last is such a surprise — it's quite shaken me up. In a nice way of course. Keep what I've said to yourself, will you?"

"Of course."

"I won't be there tomorrow, though."

"Where?"

"At the registry place, outside, waiting to see you come out. That's where it is, isn't it?"

I shook my head. "I'm not sure. Ivan — Mr Sterne — hasn't told me much. I mean — " I broke off, realising how naive I must sound.

"*What?* Not sure? You don't know about your own *wedding?*"

I forced a smile.

"He wants to surprise me, you see. He's — he's like that."

"Is he now!" she sounded doubtful, then shrugged. "Well, people have funny ideas sometimes, especially men. Anyway, I suppose he'll want me here — to prepare things like tonight — a meal. So it doesn't really make much difference. I wouldn't be able to go — church *or* office."

"I don't see why you shouldn't," I told her impulsively. "In fact, I shall *insist* on it, and ask him myself."

Over the meal which was simple, but well served, I broached the matter. The parlour was surprisingly large, combining as well as leather covered armchairs, a sofa and carved mahogany sideboard with a table sufficiently large to seat a dozen or so people. An oleograph of The Battle of Trafalgar hung on one wall, two maps, and an ancient framed document containing details and drawings of geographical interest, and various shipping routes. I wondered if it was here that Ivan entertained any of the important guests he'd previously referred to, and found this rather difficult to believe unless the company were all men. It was certainly a 'male' room, not calculated as a background for feminine fripperies or furbelows.

It was between the fish course and the mutton pie, which I did not really want, that I casually referred to the forthcoming ceremony.

"I suppose the — the wedding — will be at the Registrar's?" I enquired over-casually, fiddling with my napkin unnecessarily.

"No," Ivan replied. "What made you think that?"

"Well — you said something about a

special licence, and being a very private affair."

"Licences, in certain cases, are needed in church," he pointed out. "You should know that, Jade-Anna. Privacy? Yes. There'll be no congregation. I thought you'd prefer it that way."

"I wasn't given much time to think. It was all so quick."

"Which is why I obtained the special document necessary." He paused, eyed me closely for a moment then asked, "Are you against taking religious vows? If so, tell me and no doubt we can alter the arrangements. It really makes little difference to me. I thought all girls preferred church marriages."

"Yes. I just thought — well, this isn't an *ordinary* wedding, is it?"

He smiled.

"*Nothing's* ordinary where you're concerned." I was annoyed with myself for feeling the tell-tale blush staining my cheeks again. Seconds ticked by before he said, once more quite casually, "The church is a small one, well tucked away. You needn't be afraid of publicity. St Day's obviously would have attracted attention, and if you'd had time to be fitted with a worthy wedding dress, veil, and an entourage of bridesmaids — I couldn't have objected to a fine show. But there *wasn't* time. So my choice is best, and I hope the presence of a clergyman will make you feel a proper bride — more married to me than by some legal Johnny without an ounce of sentiment in him."

I was surprised that Ivan had considered 'sentiment' at all. When he'd asked me about my parentage and date of birth a few days before, he'd sounded so business-like and almost offhand I'd resented the sudden curiosity, and I'd decided he might be trying to use facts in some devious way to get rid of me.

Instead — how mistaken I'd been.

I was about to enquire why the marriage had had to be arranged so speedily, when Beth entered with the pie. I managed to eat some of it, but had to refuse the rest. I was suddenly tired, and longing to be on my own.

Ivan must have sensed my mood, for he remarked politely after the meal, "I can see you're weary. Well, it is understandable. Have a nightcap — a glass of wine will help you relax. Then we'll say goodnight, and you can go to bed. I shall sleep as I usually do — on the couch in my offices."

"Oh."

"We must appear respectable," he pointed out, "and seem to be so — by Beth, who has a cubbyhole next to you, which her aunt sometimes used."

I had the impulse to enquire what the bedroom allotted to me had been for. But, of course, such a question would have been futile and out of place. Women mostly, I told myself, with a surge of quick bitterness, remembering calculated remarks by Lalage and others. I was just one of his 'collection' and yet he was marrying me.

Bewildered and apprehensive, I somehow forced myself into a state of acquiescence, and kept comparatively silent until the time I could politely withdraw to the solitude of the bedroom.

Ivan had been right about the wine. It helped me sleep, and when I woke it was morning. Pale sunlight streaked thinly between cracks in the blind and lace curtains. When I got up and went to the window, the vista was a misted panorama of glimmering damp housetops and a distant glimpse of St Michael's Mount rising above a thin belt of cloud. Hearing footsteps along the corridor I hurried back to the bed. There was a knock, and Beth entered with breakfast on a tray.

I took it bemusedly, and when she'd gone I realised with a shock that this was my wedding day.

The church was neither very old nor picturesque. It was small and squat, situated in a huddle of buildings near the waterfront, on the fringe of the town. Jed and a black-bearded man I had never seen before were the only witnesses. One or two curious natives had gathered at the doors, but didn't attend the ceremony; probably they'd been kept from doing so. Beth was present after all, and smiled at me encouragingly as I passed. She was wearing a pink silk dress with something flowery on her hair, and I remember thinking ironically that she must appear far more bridal-looking than myself in my best day dress which was subdued in comparison. I had been a little chagrined to have been given no time to buy something new.

"You can go shopping later," Ivan had told me before we left Merlake. "My own plans have changed slightly. You probably won't be needed to be present at my business meeting this time. Well? — " when I didn't reply, " — that's all right, isn't it? I did mention you needed new clothes."

"Yes, so you did," I'd agreed tartly, "and I'd have thought *before* a wedding would have been better than afterwards."

I'd walked away before he'd had time to answer; or if he had, I'd not heard.

My sudden recollection of that brief conversation soon passed, It didn't matter. The whole of the short ceremony seemed unreal, almost as though I was taking part in a charade or play.

When I left the church on Ivan's arm, Jed, who was staying in Penzance for the few days we were there, went off to a nearby hostelry with the bewhiskered stranger, leaving Beth seated by the cabby, in front.

Inside Ivan and I sat together, saying

little, curiously subdued for a newly married couple. Bewilderment filled me. I wasn't *really* subdued, just shocked and exhilarated at the same time; wondering again at how all this had come about, and what the outcome would be. It seemed so strange that the wealthy Ivan Sterne should have entered matrimony under circumstances amounting almost to secrecy, taking a penniless girl for his wife. No doubt, in his own eyes, he had acted honourably. But I would rather it had been for more personal reasons. At one moment I almost hated him, because the situation seemed very similar to that of a wealthy man having seduced an 'inferior' in a lax act of passion, and then soothed his conscience by doing the 'right thing'.

Well, I told myself determinedly, I wouldn't be soothed. I would show him from the very first that my dignity was equal to his. This time I would have to be wooed and won, and then perhaps he would see me in a different light.

As it happened I need have made no plans at all, because we did not sleep together that night. During the afternoon, following the meal, Ivan unexpectedly received a message, calling him to Truro.

"I shall have to go," he told me with what seemed genuine regret. "I'm very sorry indeed. I do apologise — but a John Porter has arrived without notice from the North. He's an engineer I'm embroiled with concerning important business over a mine — he has to return to Derby by night, so you'll have to excuse me — " He was staring at me expectantly.

"When will you be back?" I asked bluntly.

"It will be late. I'll get word through to my shipping colleague, delaying his visit until tomorrow. In the meantime, an early sleep won't do you any harm. In fact — " he smiled slightly, " — I expect you'll be glad of a little peace and quiet. Then, before returning to Merlake, you'll feel refreshed for your shopping expedition."

"I see."

"You don't mind, do you?"

Of course I minded. But I didn't say so.

"No," I answered. "Business comes first, naturally."

His lips twitched. An arm slipped round my waist, suddenly bringing warmth and life again to my stiffened body.

"Jade-Anna — " His tones were almost endearing.

"Yes?"

"I didn't *plan* this."

"No. I understand."

"You don't, you know. Never mind — " He released me. "We have plenty of time ahead. Be patient till we get back."

"To Merlake, you mean."

"Yes, to Merlake."

Always Merlake, I thought. The name had become obsessive somehow. Yet at the same time I couldn't help a thrill of anticipation flooding me when I recalled its wanton influence — the thunder of wind and waves crashing, and Ivan's lips hot on mine as we'd lain together, with senses and pulses pounding, at one with the wild elements.

Ivan had been right when he said I needed rest, but I was too keyed up to take any, and shortly after he'd left I set off, accompanied by Beth, for a tour of what costumiers and dress shops there were in Penzance.

168

There were few, and the only store displaying sufficiently picturesque or stylish gowns to please me, extremely expensive. However, I went in there, because my husband — how odd it seemed to realise I was now actually Mrs Ivan Sterne — had provided me with the necessary money to be wildly extravagant if I chose.

I *did* choose.

Madam Le Fauvre, shrewd, black-eyed, and extremely complimentary whose French accent and appearance, I guessed, had been carefully learned and adapted for business purposes, made me feel very important as she had the most exotic silks and satins brought out for my inspection. She gesticulated, bowed and primped, sighed, and threw up her hands in exaggerated excitement while I tried first one outfit, then another, uttering such compliments as — "Ah! but Madame looks ravissante — so chic — the true Parisienne."

Beth, I knew, was quite bewildered, even a little shocked when I said casually, "Yes, I think I'll have that — the crimson silk, and the blue velvet.

Then I shall need something more formal, black perhaps?"

"Ah!" The sound of gratification made me think of a sleek seal sighing with pleasure on a sun-washed rock, and I almost giggled aloud. "The black? Yes, Madame. How right you are. The one with the tucks of lace, *non*? So smart, yet so veree feminine. And a cloak? Does Madame require a cloak? Or a waisted coat — fur-edged, per'aps? — the very latest style — ?"

"Both, I think," I told her recklessly.

In the end I had so many boxes and smaller parcels packed that Beth suggested wryly, "We shall have to order an extra cab for all this."

"If Madame Sterne wishes we can arrange for delivery at any address," came the haughty answer.

"Oh, no, I'm sure we shall manage perfectly well," I assured her with a grim look at Beth. Luckily I was right. The cabby appeared a little surprised to see such a conglomeration of parcels being taken to his vehicle but after a few minutes all, including Beth and myself, were packed inside, and for the first time

I realised how recklessly I'd spent Ivan's money.

Never mind, I thought, lifting my chin an inch higher. He'd told me to have just whatever I wanted, and after all I'd not had a wedding dress, so I was fully justified.

I changed into rose pink for the evening meal, but Ivan did not return in time to see it. I ate alone, served by Beth, feeling chagrined, disappointed, and angry.

The anger drove me to bed early.

I lay awake for a long time listening for his footsteps along the corridor and at the door. When at last they came, they paused outside, but only for a moment. There was no turn of the knob, no tap, or sign that he wished to enter. I said nothing, but just lay there, feeling suddenly humiliated and determined that later, in some way, I would pay him out for his rejection. I didn't at the moment know how, and it never occurred to me he could have a legitimate business reason. But the time would come, I determined, when Mr Ivan Sterne would realise I was no mere plaything, to be used just when he chose, and put aside whenever it suited him.

The next morning, early, we set out on the sea journey once more for Merlake.

6

OUR marriage night at Merlake was curiously restrained and lacking the ardour I'd anticipated following our primitive coming together on the first occasion. Ivan was considerate and gentle, but his very politeness flattened me. It was as though, subtly, he was attempting to erase the past, and obliterate the memory of the wild night when he'd taken me with such desire. An apology! Was that it? Had his conscience alone driven him to make me his wife? The thought was humiliating.

After the first greeting by servants when we'd arrived, I'd fancied sly, amused looks passed between them. Later, when Miss Augusta had appeared from her quarters to join in the toasting, her fierce old face had an almost malignant smile on it; she had dressed more extravagantly and garishly than usual, with jewels, feathers, lace and chiffon, giving her the appearance of some aged old queen out of a fairytale.

"I wish you well, gel," she'd rasped in her crow-like voice. "And luck. You'll need it — both of you." She had started fanning herself, while her small bright eyes rested for a moment on Ivan.

"Thank you, dear aunt," Ivan had said coldly, planting a brief kiss on the withered beringed hand suddenly thrust out to him.

She gave a short laugh and turned away. Lalage, who had been standing by the sideboard, lifted her glass in a toast. She was wearing bright green, which accentuated her opulent looks and plump yet still handsome figure. With her chin raised, and away from the direct light, years were diminished, and I had imagined her briefly as she must once have been — compellingly beautiful in a dramatic way. Why, I'd wondered, had she been content to bury herself at Merlake? And once more — what was the true relationship between herself and Ivan? Once or twice I'd noticed his eyes slide towards her, as though drawn there against his will. The looks had been mutual. Secretive; on his part a little condemning. My old suspicions revived. Had he ever been in love with her? Did some unacknowledged bond exist that neither could entirely break? If so why had he married *me*? Why, *why*?

So many times during the night and days that followed, the question returned to taunt and depress me. I began to feel I walked a mental tightrope, at one moment caught up on a bright wave of anticipation, the next cast down into despair. I tried reasoningly to assure myself such changing moods were due simply to the fact I was so shut off from normal more ordinary company. After all, living on an island with a husband who for the most part appeared abstracted and concerned with other things, was not conducive to natural contentment.

I became very restless, inwardly frustrated, though I tried not to show it. Frequently Ivan did not sleep with me in the new apartment set aside for us shortly before the wedding. He always had an excuse; he had papers to attend to; there were matters he had to discuss with Jed. I needed my rest, so he'd spend the night hours in his old room. What papers, I wondered on such occasions, and what possible business could there be concerning the obnoxious, burly keeper of the island?

In bitter moments I pictured such assertions of his as mere excuses for having hours alone with Lalage, whom I was beginning to detest. I seldom saw her, and when I did she appeared slyly contemptuous or ebulliently aggressive. Mostly, like Miss Augusta, she ate her meals in her own premises where I'd gathered she either preferred or was supposed to remain. But when she felt like it she appeared at most unexpected moments that could be embarrassing. It was like living in the middle of some fictitious melodrama. Of the mainland, and the real world beyond Merlake, I heard little, and what I did held no real significance for me.

Occasionally, I found a newspaper left open in the library or perhaps on the hall table. From quick glances I saw Palmerston's name mentioned, concerned with the effects of Britain's war with the Chinese — also that of Mr Gladstone, who opposed him. Opium smoking apparently had caused considerable warfare in Parliament, and I recalled occasions when Ivan himself had let drop remarks dealing with the subject. But what could such things have to do with Jed? — or even Ivan himself. Was the Chinese business in any way related to my husband's recently acquired new shipping line? Once, when Miss Augusta joined us for dinner, conversation inadvertently turned to political affairs. Later I realised that the old tyrant herself must have mischievously switched Ivan's mind in certain directions.

From appearing mildly bored, as he generally did in her presence, he referred in sharp condemnatory terms to, 'Those despicable despots, the kings of Greece and Naples', then, with a challenging glance at his great-aunt, relaxed into silence again.

Madam's bright button-like eyes lit up with malicious amusement.

"Ha!" she croaked. "Let 'em alone, nephew. You don't have to worry about foreign monarchs. Enough worries here, haven't we? — and one queen. Only *one*.

Remember? *Me*." She drew herself up thrusting her predatory jaw forward over her bejewelled scraggy neck. Diamonds glinted from her ears and corsage. Feathers bobbed from her hair which must have been a wig.

Ivan gave her one ironic stare and continued with his meal.

The wide, almost toothless grin, vanished from her wrinkled mouth.

"So you won't bow; no acknowledgements — no respect for your elders, eh? Fifty years ago you'd've got the switch for that, young man. Ha! the country's lost its fire, its values. No spirit any more." She stared at her plate, then commanded irately, "Pass me the pepper. Where's the pepper? You know I need it, especially with this stuff." She prodded a fork at the food on her plate. "What is it, eh? Fish? Can't abide it without the proper sauces and condiments. No one cooks properly here any more. Can you cook, gel?" She glared at me fiercely.

"I — I — no, I never have," I admitted.

"Thought as much." Her tones were derisive. I thought the tirade had ended there, but I was wrong. Suddenly she looked up again, still directing her attention to me. "Then why did Ivan marry you? Eh? Just to warm your bed?" The unpleasant sly grin crossed her face again. "The more fool him, then. *And* you, gel. There are plenty here to do that. That's so, isn't it, nephew?"

As I bowed my head in angry humiliation, Ivan came to sudden life. "Aunt Augusta, I will not have such talk at my table. Unless you can behave politely to my wife and myself you'd better leave and go to your own apartments. Do you understand? I won't have such nonsense spoken."

Her eyes flashed fire, then she crumpled.

"Sorry, m'boy. This tongue of mine *will* start wagging on occasions. Tek no notice. Blame the fish. Nasty stuff, isn't it, gel?"

When I didn't reply she added, "You don't have to believe all I say, you know. After as many birthdays as I've had — and in *my* position it's my right to make a joke at times, even if this prig of a nephew takes offence. Don't you agree, gel?"

I neither agreed nor disagreed, but decided she really was a little mad. All the same her jibes about my marriage remained like tiny swords in my brain, recurring and pricking at unexpected moments.

I saw very little of Claude Lang during those early summer days, and learned nothing about his past or plans for the future, when Maurice would be too old for his tuition. When I questioned Ivan about this I was told that the time was not yet ripe for definite plans, but that the boy later would probably be sent to Oxford to obtain a degree.

"On what subject?" I asked curiously. "Science? Archaeology?"

"Why do you suggest that?"

I shrugged.

"He and — and Mr Lang go walking together quite a lot — studying rocks and wild life. I've seen them wandering about by the pier, and Maurice is quite obsessed by his collection."

"Of what? Butterflies? Insects?"

"Yes."

"Oh. So you've seen them.

"Once, when your ward was unusually

180

forthcoming. He took out glass cases from a drawer in his chest and showed me."

"I see. And were you impressed?" His calm tones gave nothing away.

"No," I answered. "I thought it horrible. Why should beautiful living things like butterflies be pinned down in such a horrid way?"

"Boys do it. Certain studies unfortunately demand brief cruelty."

"So you approve?"

He sighed. "Jade-Anna, I didn't say so. I'd far rather Maurice was involved in something else — the land, for instance. I've tried to get him interested in the farming project here, and if he had been I'd planned to send him eventually to the mainland for training at a horticultural or agricultural college. But Maurice, in some respects, is like my father. An individualist. Studious — outgoing in one way, in another reserved. It's difficult to know him properly."

"Oh, I agree."

He touched my hand briefly. "Try and like him."

"I will, I have. But I don't see him

much. Another thing, Ivan — " I was desperately searching for a way to change the trend of conversation.

"Yes?"

"Am I ever going to be allowed to do anything here that matters? That is of some use?"

Warmth suddenly replaced the impersonal cool glint of his eyes. "My dear love, what a question. You're needed. You're my wife. Isn't that enough?" He tilted my face up towards him, and I could feel myself responding as I always did to his touch, to the deepening ardour of his glance as his other arm enclosed my waist, travelling to the base of my spine where his hand lingered sensuously.

Then, as I waited expectantly for an increase of passion and desire, he suddenly and determinedly drew himself away.

"Don't tempt me, my love. I've pressing business to attend to." He strode sharply to the window, glanced out, turned then and went to the door.

"Business! *Business!*" I echoed scathingly. "Always that." I lifted my head, and my expression must have been fierce when I added, "Well, don't expect me forever to stay here twiddling my thumbs saying 'Yes, Ivan, thank you, Ivan, or no, Ivan, I understand'. Because I *don't* understand, and never will, why you married me except that you wanted to feel good, and honourable, and that you'd done your duty to your employee, Miss Ellan, whom you'd seduced under most unpleasant circumstances — " I broke off breathlessly. He took his hand from the door knob and in two strides had me by the shoulders.

"Don't ever talk to me like that again," he said, and his eyes were fire in his lean face. "You know very well you were as anxious as I was for that wild revealing incident. Perhaps even you had something of the kind in mind when you first came to Merlake. Did you?"

I struggled and tried to free myself, but it was no use, and I knew in my deepest heart that what he'd said might well be true.

"Let me go," I cried, "you insufferable — "

"Go on, do tell me — "

I managed to free one hand and bring

it stingingly against his face. Unwittingly a nail scratched it and it bled.

I stared, shocked and dismayed as he took out a kerchief and wiped the blood away.

"I'm sorry — I — I — "

"Next time you'll be far sorrier than you are," he told me in a cold voice, though dull angry colour suffused his whole countenance. "Next time, you little madam, I'll put you over my knee and give you the damn-good spanking you deserve. Remember that; you'd better, because I mean it, and it would be most infra-dig for you to have to eat your meals standing, wouldn't it?"

I stared at him, infuriated and humiliated beyond words.

When he went out he was still dabbing at his cheek with the stained piece of lawn.

For a few moments following his departure, I hated him, or thought I did. Then, gradually, violence died, leaving me encompassed by a strange feeling of desolation and loneliness.

Except for a brief stroll towards the farm I did not go out that day. The sky was grey, and by afternoon a thin rain was falling. The next morning, however, it had cleared, leaving a blue sky behind trails of white cloud blown on a fresh wind. My spirits soared. There was a feeling of adventure in the air. Jed, as usual, was occupied with his telescope at the southern end of the island. Ivan had already informed me that he would be shut away in his study until lunch time. What servants we had were occupied in the kitchen or upstairs. There were no signs of Claude Lang, Maurice, Lalage, or Miss Augusta, and on impulse I slipped on a loose cape over a russet-coloured gown, one I'd purchased in Penzance, and unseen left for further exploration of Merlake territory.

7

ONE day in late June, feeling curiously restless, I decided once again to ignore the boundaries of the island laid down by Ivan and Jed — perhaps after all, Jed was half responsible — and to explore territory above the farm. No one specifically had ordered me not to go there, and if the land and cliffs appeared too dangerous I could always turn back.

The weather was sultry and heavy, holding no breath of wind. No wild flowers stirred; there was no cry, even from gulls or sudden whirr of wings rising to the cloudless sky. A veil of thin mist, prediction of heat to come, shrouded rocks and under-growth, taking turrets into silvered obscurity. A high track cut upwards towards an abrupt bend from the wider path above the pier, where Ivan and I had clambered through the storm on my arrival at Merlake. I paused several times, listening for any indication of activity from barn or out-buildings below. There was nothing.

I cut round the corner, treading carefully upon short turf under boulders which were slightly overhanging. The extreme quiet was uncanny. The scent of sea, heather, bracken and bluebells in sheltered places was heady with summer sweetness. Glancing down I could just perceive the misted bell-like shapes crouched among springing green. Unexpectedly a branch of foaming white thorn caught me, pricking my hand. Sudden splashes of gorse flashed gold, then died into wreaths of spreading grey.

Once round the corner the narrow path widened slightly. The land for a time became gentler, although it appeared to slope into nothingness. So I kept well under the rocky summit with one hand intermittently grasping at the rough cliff — listening; ears alert for any faint sign that my departure from the house had been seen by Marte or Jed, or by Miss Augusta, under whose towered premises I'd had to pass. There was nothing except the calm lapping of waves breaking somewhere far below.

I proceeded cautiously, hoping Ivan hadn't decided suddenly to leave his study where he'd told me he'd be as usual, for the rest of the morning. If so I might be missed.

"All right," I'd assured him, "I have quite a lot to do — letters to write, and a few things to wash."

"Washing? You? Can't your maid do it?"

"I haven't a maid of my own," I'd reminded him, "not yet, and these are delicate articles — lace and fine lawn. After that, I shall deal with the flowers."

He'd seemed satisfied; probably relieved, I'd thought, since his mines and shipping company — especially the latter — had seemed, so far, much more to him than myself.

Quite suddenly a fierce jutting crag of granite loomed ahead in a precipitous spike over the sea.

I rubbed my eyes and stared. The path had become a mere pale thread cutting abruptly downwards, winding in a ghostly line until it disappeared altogether. I paused, waiting. Presently, as the mist lifted a little, the rim of land and water was visible. Instinct told me to go back, but I was then too curious to obey, sensing that far below perhaps was something that might provide an important clue to the mystery overshadowing Merlake.

Why I imagined it possible I don't know. There was at that point no sign of human life — no indication that anything awaited me except another dangerous panorama that would eventually lead to the western side of the island — the wild coast where my passionate encounter with Ivan had occurred.

I continued the descent until the ground again took a gentler angle, winding over short turf sprinkled with pink thrift. A ray of sunlight suddenly pierced the lifting mist. A few yards further on I found myself looking down directly upon a rugged thrust of rocks and pale sand. Waves broke leisurely against the granite which was easily negotiable. I lifted my skirts an inch higher, although they were already dripping from air and spray, and went on, picking the way carefully between slippery stones and clumps of weed.

And then I saw it — the mysterious dark mouth of a cave opening from a cramped cove. Sea-plants and cobwebbed filaments of plant-life overhung the entrance. A board, and the remains of an old saucepan, lay to one side. Quite obviously the shadowed recess was tenanted, or had been, at some time. Who by? A tramp perhaps, or some fugitive from the sea? Moving closer, my eyes became more accustomed to the fitful dim light. There was a line slung from a spike to rock ceiling. Something whiteish fluttered from it; and behind, a coil of smoke curdled the grey air. I hesitated for a few minutes, hidden and clinging to a stunted bush, listening for any sound or movement — any indication that the secret place was occupied. Very faintly, merging into the rhythmic sound of waves breaking on the shore — there was a tinkle resembling that of metal — tin probably — from within.

A gentle soughing of wind was now rising from the west stirring branches of weed with a tapping motion against stones and earth. Tensed up, but more than ever curious, I continued along a narrowing ledge, and clutching what support I had, swung round the projecting arm of cliff.

When I reached firm ground I glanced down. If the distance to the beach had been greater I'd have been terrified. The drop was sheer, and the few yards I had to cross before negotiating the cave's entrance, extremely narrow.

I looked ahead again abruptly, and springing lightly, arrived in a few seconds by the inlet. A screen of tangled scrub and bulging granite made it possible for me to wait unseen from any prying eyes. When no one appeared, I emerged and moved cautiously a few feet inside. The mist momentarily seemed to have thickened, but was obviously intensified by smoke. Something was burning, and dimly, through the blurred air, a reddish glow gleamed down the aperture. Throwing discretion to the wind I moved on. Cobwebs brushed my face, but the ground was smoother underfoot. Almost on tiptoe I ventured further, one hand and arm pressed against the damp granite wall for support.

As the spreading light increased it became obvious someone lived there.

An old wooden chair stood at one side, a piece of ancient tapestry hung from a spike, and there was a wooden bench with a tin bowl on it a little further on. A second later the passage, or cave, took an abrupt turn to the right. I looked round and was quite astonished. The misty interior widened suddenly, and there before me was an oddly shaped room formed by nature, but utilised by human hands into living quarters holding a crudely made table, a bench, and numerous nick-nacks and domestic implements strewn about.

There was something else.

As the fire at the far end spluttered, a flaring log lit up the far wall, where a woman's portrait hung in a broken frame.

I must have gasped, or perhaps I held my breath — I'm not sure which. But my heart quickened. The face, though cracked by one cheek, was so very beautiful — fair, almost greenish pale from damp and the passing of years, with a tilted mouth curved in a half smile, and eyes lit from a soft blueish darkness to brilliant turquoise in the fitful glow. It was obviously an old painting, although no clue was apparent defining any particular period. Indication of jewels shone briefly against white neck and shoulders; all else, below the shadowed breasts, was blurred. Whether she wore a gown or not I couldn't even tell. The painting, except for necklace and earrings, could have been of a nude woman — some legendary fey creature born of sea and cloud and rain-filtered sunlight or moon. My shock was so great, I forgot caution and stepped foward quickly, catching a stone with one foot. It was dislodged and fell with a rattling sound. Almost instantly there was movement from the recess of darkness beyond the fire.

I stood as though petrified, waiting.

Slowly, with a shuffling motion a dark bent form emerged from a twisting of the passage. A man's form. He was old — very old, with one bony hand clenched on a stick, ancient eyes like two twin burning coals in his withered face. Bedraggled white locks fell about his shoulders. His beard, too, was tangled and grey, straggling in cobwebbed wisps to his knees. His coat was long and ragged, his expression fierce.

I stood petrified as he shuffled forward. Then he lifted the stick, and shouted in thin rasping tones.

"Off with thee — get off. No one's allowed here. *No* one — understand?"

The cracked voice rose into a scream. "Thorlock! — that's me — and this is my place"

As if from a distance I heard my own voice crying, "I'm sorry. I didn't know. I — "

Words faded on my lips as he lunged towards me with surprising agility, head thrust at a macabre angle from his bony shoulders. I made a wild effort to escape, turning and grazing my forearm against the rock, half stumbling over something on the slippery ground underfoot. It was a bag, and as it moved in a crumpled heap, bits and pieces of china, jewellery, and other small articles, were spilled over the floor. I had no time to distinguish anything clearly. But for a second, through a spurt of yellow life from the fire, glass glittered in a myriad of different shapes. There was something round that looked like a magnifying glass or end of a telescope. Everything suddenly became a jumble of confused screaming and whirling shapes — of contorted shadows that leaped and played through the mist, and of a pale green hand wielding a spiked weapon at me.

Clutching my skirts to my knees I somehow clambered up a slope immediately above, not daring to attempt the way I'd come. The old creature was after me, I knew that. But I was quicker than he was in the ascent, and realised fearfully that I had to go on, even if I eventually died by falling down some unexpected precipitous ravine.

The mist had thickened again. At last, exhausted, I fell to my knees and bowed my head to get some breath back. When I'd recovered I waited for any sound, any sign of the old man — Thorlock's — approach.

There was none.

At last, quite suddenly, the air lightened. There was no clarity ahead, mist still silvered short turf and clustered scabious. But the land rose in a gentler line. The boulders were rounded, and somewhere in the distance a thin ray of watery sunlight caught the tip of what appeared to be a tower.

How long it took and how far I went to reach the house I couldn't say. All that registered was to keep going. I'd no intention of trying ever again to locate that wild and terrifying place.

I managed to get into the house by a side door near the back, and made my way unseen down a maze of narrow side passages that led to a flight of back stairs. At least I *thought* I was unseen. But at a corner of a corridor cutting into a main landing, Maurice's form appeared suddenly, ambling towards me. He had a knowing smile on his lips.

"Hullo," he said, "aren't we wet? Look at the floor."

I glanced down dismayed at the damp trail of footsteps and wet skirt along the carpet.

"I've been for a walk," I said coldly. "Perhaps you'd better get a servant to wipe it up."

He shrugged. "I shouldn't worry. It'll soon dry. No one comes this way much." He paused, adding slyly, "*I* shan't say anything. I like secrets too."

With a conspiratorial wink, he turned then, and skipped ahead of me into the shadows.

Mist still lapped against the windows, drifting through chinks in the old building.

Disconcerted, with my heart beating heavily, I hurried to the bedroom. There was no sign of Ivan, for which I was thankful, but one look at the clock told me it was only half an hour to lunchtime.

I hurriedly took off my damp clothes and changed.

Later, as Ivan and I ate alone for once, he said, "You look quite flushed, Jade-Anna, what did you do all morning?"

"Oh, just the small things I told you about," I lied, "and then went for a stroll — in the garden."

"Not very pleasant out," he remarked, "but it will be sunny and quite warm after the mist."

He obviously believed me, and I wished I felt as calm as I sounded. Strangely, it was not only old Thorlock who'd frightened me, but the adult cunning look in young Maurice's eyes.

For the next few weeks routine at Merlake continued without any out-standing incident. The weather, in July, became oppressive and thunderous. No rain fell. The sea was glassily calm under skies unflecked by cloud. The short turf of the island began to brown and wither. Heather and gorse bloomed, but scabious and wild flowers wilted and died. Even roses in the walled gardens shed their petals. Miss Augusta's temper worsened; she would appear away from her own apartments at unexpected places in the house, demanding why there were no fresh blooms in her rooms? Why was her bedroom so stuffy? And what were the servants thinking about not to see that the water in her carafe was not changed more frequently?

"Yellow, it is," she grumbled. "Trying to poison me, are ye?"

The maids and men generally scurried — or faded away — when her ancient face poked round corners, topped by her macabre wig which was generally askew. All except Jed. If Jed was around he merely threw her a surly look and went on with what he was doing. Once she rapped his strong knuckles with a fan. He appeared not to notice, which infuriated her. "Bow to me," she screamed, "on your knees — *serf!*"

Hearing her parrot cry Ivan came from the library and led her away.

All seemed comparatively peaceable with Maurice and his tutor. Lalage spent most of her days lying on a chaise-longue, with — Maurice asserted — a bottle of tonic beside her, and I could guess what the tonic was; I knew also that she still had a nightly visitor to her room. Reason told me it must be Claude Lang. But the thought also occurred that it might be Ivan. Jealousy gnawed me then. Although I couldn't complain that he neglected me — our nights together were mostly warm and sexually rewarding — a part of him remained withdrawn from me, and I wondered about the cause.

Lalage!

Was he secretly lusting for her? If so, why hadn't he openly avowed it and married her instead of me? Her gaze was frequently turned upon him. Had there been some obstacle to their union? Her health? Or the longing for drink, other men? But then, what about Evadne? It was Evadne he'd really cared for, and perhaps still did.

This fact troubled and hurt me more than any other. I knew I had no right to grudge him his memories; I did, all the same. Very often I wished for a second trip to the mainland so my mind could be diverted from emotional delving and digging into my husband's secret life. Once, in a recurring fit of curiosity I questioned him about Thorlock.

He frowned slightly, but didn't appear unduly perturbed.

"What makes you ask?"

"Oh!" I shrugged. "You mentioned him once. Is he a — farm hand or something?"

Ivan's voice was quite frank when he replied, "He's an old man, a retainer, who used to work for the family before I came. A hermit. Has a place of his own on the western coast. Cranky now, with a hatred of people."

I thought a moment, then said daringly, "Will you take me to meet him? I rather like cranks."

"No, I will not. His territory's dangerous. And I don't want you wandering about there." He paused before adding, "You do understand, don't you, Jade-Anna?"

"Oh, perfectly," I replied lightly, restraining any further questioning on my part. I'd have liked to know about the portrait, its identify and age, but realised any prompting on my part would have completely given me away. So I kept silent and the subject was dropped. But at nights, when I lay wakeful sometimes, waiting for Ivan to come to bed, I went over the incident time after time, wondering. Bewilderment intensified through the dark hours, and was only stilled when my husband appeared, to take me to him in love, soothing apprehension away.

Because I never — or seldom — openly defied him these days, we were happy. He was mostly a gentle lover, and there were occasions when I could hardly believe he was the same man who'd taken me so violently on the cliff. The touch of his mouth on mine was warm and desirous, but controlled — the hands on my body, though sensuously able to rouse me in passion, were soothing and tender. This, I told myself, was real love. But where was the first fire — the abandonment he'd once shown? Was it just that he was merely trying to prove his own self-control? Or was it that the flame had died?

Frequently I became restless and provoked by inner impatience. He was being oh so polite and considerate, and my spirit rebelled. I had part of him — yes. But I wanted all — *all*. During those hot summer days, the emotion of our marriage, like grass, earth, and undergrowth of Merlake — the very air — seemed to wilt under a veil of inactivity. Even the farm animals seemed tired. Marte lunged about his work with heavy shoulders, head thrust forward from his big neck, only quickening his pace at a sudden gruff warning from Jed.

Jed alone remained stoically determined not to flag, keeping his watch round the island's coast, with his telescope always at his eye or under his arm. On the few occasions I met Miss Augusta, her form appeared a little more bent, her shrewd eyes slightly dulled in her ancient face, her breathing more of a quick rasp, and her temper quite unreasonable.

Lalage kept mostly to her own apartments, and on the few occasions when she was invited to dine with us, arrived at the table perspiring heavily, her plump naked shoulders glistening with perspiration over the muslin gowns which she wore distastefully low over her plump breasts. She flushed easily, and the rubicund glow of her cheeks under the masses of rather wiry black hair further aged and coarsened her. She used too much scent for good taste, and once Ivan said irritably, "Your choice of perfume has become as overpowering as that of your liquor, Lalage. I'd be grateful if you'd try to be more discreet."

Lalage lumbered to her feet furiously, half toppling her chair.

"If I offend you, I'll take off to my own place. Don't worry, your company's not all that important, Mr High-n-mighty Ivan Stern — " she was breathing heavily. He waved a frilled cuff.

"Sit down. Don't be a fool."

The crimson complexion dulled to a deeper shade.

"*Fool? Me?*"

"Yes. In some things. You always were, and you always will be." His quickening temper died suddenly. "Oh, Lalage, for God's sake don't make a scene. Any moment the fish will arrive. Try and behave in front of the servants — *please*."

The last word — the plea — did the trick. Following another sullen glance Miss Dupont lifted her ample chin, and settled herself unsteadily on to her chair again.

The next time she joined us in the dining room her manner was carefully composed, her gown subdued, and her hair tidily dressed, revealing something of the beauty she must once have been when she was younger.

But the heat continued.

Then, suddenly, in late August, the weather changed. High winds rose from the west bringing a spatter of rain that was gradually whipped to fury round the island. Massed clouds in heavy billowing shapes obscured the ocean's rim and great waves dashed thrusting rocks and cliffs with mountainous breaking spray.

Despite summer's heat, the old house shivered from the impact of the elements. Fires were lit again in the grates — but there was no rest or peace. Lalage amazed Ivan by leaving her premises frequently and wandering the corridors, staring through windows at the frenzied scene of tossed sea and cloud. By afternoon on a fatal day I was never to forget, the thunder came. Soon all walls and glass of the house were darkened and streaming. Ivan went out to help Marte, he said, with the animals, although from my own lookout, I watched his figure cut the other way, head thrust forward, purposefully defying the weather's onslaught. Jed, I guessed, was somewhere out on the island — ever menacing, ever watchful. For what? — for *what*? — I wondered again as I had so many times before. As time passed the blinding flashes of lightning and thunder became more frequent. From far out at sea I thought I heard a ship's siren. And then — shattering all other sounds, shaking for a moment it seemed the very foundations of Merlake — something else. The great blast of a cannon surely?

205

Without taking a second thought I rushed upstairs for my cape, and on the way bumped into the housekeeper. She carried a lantern to light the darkened corridors. For a second or two she prevented my progress.

"Where are you off to? Have sense, girl. This edn' the time for hysterics."

I pushed her away.

"Leave me alone. I'm going out. I want to know what's happening — " I rushed by her, went into the bedroom, slammed the door, and pulled on boots and my heaviest cape. Then I left, and found her waiting in the hall. She appeared obdurate and somehow menacing, trying to block the way, both hands planted on her ample black-clad hips.

"Don't dare go out in that," she cried. "The master — "

"I'm going to find him — " I shouted. She put out an arm, I dashed it away, and as I ran down the hall heard a fleeting cackle of laughter from above, and knew that Madam had left her room and was enjoying the scene immensely.

I didn't look up, but continued racing towards the kitchens, cutting off halfway, and going out through a side door some distance from the conservatory.

As I took the path leading through the gardens towards the headland a tremendous gust of wind blew my cape over my face. Distentangling myself after a few seconds, I went on, battling against the wind, half stumbling then recovering, finding by instinct, or perhaps a miracle, the gap in the wall bordering the forbidden territory.

I waited, recovering my breath and wiping the wet tumbled hair from my eyes, before clambering upwards through the rocky barrier. Then there was a further blast of heavy firing. The whole land and sea-scape were momentarily lit to yellowish orange flame, and with horror I saw the blackened stark shape of a ship at sea beyond the jutting cliffs. The splintering, roaring and curdling smoke inbued the scene with all the terror of some tortuous black hell.

I was petrified.

Why? *Why?* — was the vessel armed? Or had some ancient cannon been used from a secret position on Merlake to attack? Through the sting of rime lashing my face, and salty wind whipping tears from my eyes, I saw dots of figures flung into the air and taken back again into the sea with pieces of wreckage and splintered wood. The ship reared on a great wave for a moment before diving into the swirling waters. I think I screamed, or it may have been the wild crying of gulls in my ears, merging with the shrieking of human beings caught by the carnage.

Obviously I could do nothing. The narrow track round the headland would have meant certain death in the gale. The drop to the shore from the point where I stood was sheer, and in any case I would have been helpless against the holocaust. When my cape was once more drawn back over my face, I almost slipped, and in a surge of fear clutched wildly at a spike of granite, hanging on to it until I was able to turn, and somehow make my way back to the house.

I went in through the kitchens this time. Mrs Traille appeared from her own sitting room and eyed me condemningly when I went through to the hall.

"Look at you!" she exclaimed, "wet

and dripping as a dead fish. And look at the floor; soaked and dirtied again as though there hadn't been a cloth to it all day. What do you think you've been doin'? Eh? An' what d'you think the master'll say when he knows?"

"Oh, bother the master!" I shouted. "And get one of the men to wipe it up."

I was rushing by, but she caught my arm, and pulled me round to face her. Her dark eyes were blazing.

"Men? *Men?* They've enough to do this night without botherin' 'bout clearin' your high-an'-mighty footsteps — "

She broke off, breathing heavily.

"How *dare* you speak to me like that?"

"Oh, I dare all right, madam. An' if you were a younger child you'd find the sting of my hand at your back. But maybe — " Her lips tightened. "Maybe the master'll see about that. He will if he's any sense."

I shook myself free.

"It will be *you* who'll suffer, I'm afraid," I told her, with my temper blazing, but my voice cold. "Say what you wish to my husband, that's *your* affair. But as his wife I shall demand your dismissal."

"Demand? *Demand?* You little fool." Her lips twisted in a sneer. "I'm *needed* here — can't you understand? All who work at Merlake's *needed.* So if I was you — " she paused, then added more quietly " — I'd get upstairs, calm your temper, and change into dry clothes. Maybe I'll inform Mr Ivan when he gets in — maybe I won't. It's all depending."

"So he *is* still out there!"

"What d'you think?"

I didn't know what to say. I'd guessed, of course, or I'd probably never have ventured out in the first place. "If you'd explain — " I began on a more conciliatory note.

She shut her lips firmly.

"*I'm* doing no explaining, and I advise you to get to your room before *you* have to start — Marte or any of them may be back directly."

I didn't wait to hear any more, or to reply, but hurried away, leaving her staring after me as I ran along the hall.

At the bend in the staircase I looked down briefly.

She was still standing, a lump of a figure, quite motionless, watching me, with one hand on a hip.

When I reached my room I was trembling. I undressed, and changed into dry clothing before re-arranging my hair and toilette. Then I took the wet things along to the wash closet.

For two hours I waited about for Ivan's return, but it was already evening before he appeared. He was a sight. Pale-faced and haggard-looking, with blood streaming from a cut on his forehead. His clothes were half torn from his back. There was such anguish in his expression, I winced.

I tried to question him, but realised quickly there was no point. He swept by me without a word, and that night slept alone in his study.

In the morning the rain had stopped, leaving leaden skies over the island. Bit by bit I learned there had been a wreck — of which I didn't need to be told — 'a bit of an affray', and that all hands and passengers had been lost.

All, that is — except one.

A girl.

In the afternoon I met her. Her name was Siri.

Nothing was said of the cannon fire, and at that point I did not enquire. Ivan appeared morose and disinclined to talk with me.

Well, I could understand that, with so many dead lying in the sea beyond the great cliffs.

If it hadn't been for the look of hurt in his eyes I'd have hated him, because I felt in some way he'd been responsible. As it was, I felt dazed and unable to make up my mind in any way concerning the terrible incident.

8

MRS TRAILLE was obviously irritated at having to take charge of the castaway and see that she was trained for some kind of domestic duties in the house. I wasn't surprised. Siri's knowledge of the English language was so limited it was almost nil. She was too shocked during her first few days at Merlake to do anything but lie in bed recovering from her bruises and injuries which mercifully were slight, then later wander round the kitchens, with a curious air of detachment about her that was more frightening than any outward show of grief or hysterics. She had a small room in the servants' quarters, and following the first week simple tasks were allotted to her, and attempts made to draw her out, but she remained sulkily impervious to pleas and signs. All she would divulge, pointing to her breast, was, "Me Siri."

She was slow in her duties, though

I sensed not really unintelligent. Her movements were languorous, 'lazy' was the word used by Mrs Traille. But on the few occasions I saw her, a sudden glint of her tilted fawn's eyes suggested she could be quick enough if she wished. There was a sly secretive quality about her — unmistakably oriental — that troubled me.

One day I asked Ivan what eventually was to become of her.

"Who?"

"The girl. The one from the wreck."

"She'll stay here, of course," Ivan told me. "What else is there for her?"

"She must have relatives somewhere. Or — well, she might want to go to the mainland to work."

"The girl is my responsibility. She'll remain at Merlake."

"But why — ?" I broke off helplessly.

"My love, don't ask questions. Her presence will be reported to the proper authorities. Sometime in the future she may be returned to her own people — if we discover who they are, which I doubt. In the meantime there are other more important matters concerning the sorry business to get settled with the authorities."

"Such as how a cannon could be fired from Merlake?" I asked recklessly.

He frowned.

"What on earth are you talking about? The vessel was — well, call it a pirate ship, or smuggler — whatever you choose. It was in forbidden waters, *Merlake* waters, and the cannon you refer to so naively must have been a figment of your own wild imagination. Big guns have the-same impact, and that ship was heavily armed. Now — " he surveyed me sternly.

"Yes?"

"For my sake will you please stop wondering and probing? I've more than sufficient practical details to deal with. Some bodies have been recovered and will be given a decent burial. But most have been swept out to sea. Some are still being washed up by the tide. I want you to keep away from the coast for a time — until the proper authorities have dealt with salvage and humanitarian issues."

When I didn't say anything he

continued, "Do you understand, Jade-Anna?"

"No," I answered truthfully. "At least — yes, in a way. You don't want me to know anything about the wreck."

"Exactly."

Knowing I should get nothing more from him at that point, I let the matter rest, although my mind was still a riot of unanswered puzzling questions. Whatever Ivan suggested to the contrary, I knew that somewhere round the forbidden corner of the island dangerous weapons were secreted, and that Merlake was defended as a fortress.

Shortly after this conversation, Preventive officials arrived from the mainland. There was a good deal of activity round the coast and lengthy discussions at the house between Ivan and the officers.

How many bodies were eventually taken away, I never knew.

To have defied Ivan's command not to wander about by the shore would have been futile. Even when the affair was settled, Jed was more than ever on the alert, and demanded more time from Marte, who had to shoulder certain hours of 'sentry' duty, besides running the farm.

When the excitement and horror had faded from my mind a little, I thought again of the ancient Thorlock in his cave home, recollecting vividly the beautiful face of the portrait in the broken frame. I was tempted to question Mrs Traille subtly, but thought better of it. She would no doubt have informed Ivan, and he'd have guessed I'd been round there. On the other hand, except for her awareness of the old man's existence, she might know nothing else about him. It was highly improbable that she'd made the treacherous journey to his hide-out, and certainly Ivan would not have taken her.

As autumn approached I grew more and more restless.

"When are you going to take me to the mainland?" I asked Ivan abruptly one morning after breakfast. "You told me I was to have some sort of hostess's duties in Penzance. And I'd like to see some shops again."

"Are you so bored?"

"Yes," I answered promptly. "There's

not much diversion here. Nothing normal seems to happen. There's no one to talk to except Lalage when she feels like it — she doesn't like me anyway — and of course your unpleasant old aunt, and Maurice. It's very limiting."

"I realise that," Ivan conceded. "But then our marriage was an unusual one, wasn't it? And when you induced me to bring you to Merlake — "

"*I* induced you?"

He gave a lopsided half-smile. "Well, didn't you?"

Remembering the circumstances of our meeting at Mounterrith, I flushed.

"Marrying me was *your* idea," I pointed out. "And when I agreed — "

"It was certainly to your advantage," he told me coldly.

"In a way perhaps, but if I'd known — " I broke off, not knowing quite how to express my list of grievances.

"Yes?"

"I hadn't thought about boundaries, and wrecks, and — and not being allowed to walk here, or there, and being watched every minute I go out for a stroll by that awful Jed or Marte. And I didn't expect to have that strange girl peeping at me from her sly eyes whenever I go near the kitchen — ”

“But she's had a very bad shock, she can't speak our language — you probably frighten her. You can be very intimidating when you rein a temper, Jade-Anna, and I must say you've had plenty of those lately.”

“*Thank you.*”

“You see?” he remarked tartly. “You're already in a rage.”

With my hands clenched and chin raised fiercely, I made a bold stride towards him. “And why shouldn't I be?” I demanded rashly. “Especially when you're so concerned about her. And don't tell me you're not. You never miss a chance of speaking with her, or smiling, or flattering. It's quite clear you admire her.”

“Oh?”

“Yes.”

He gripped my shoulder. I turned my face away, but with the other hand under my chin he forced my eyes back to meet his.

“What a little fool you are, my love,”

219

he said softly. "In one way so bright and clever — in another so naive." His lips touched my cheek, resting there until desire gradually spread, and glowed in me. Then he released me, and drew a kerchief across his brow. "One day," he said, "I'll prove what folly it is for you to be jealous. In the meantime, be pleasant to Siri. And that's an order."

"But why?"

"I don't have to give reasons. Just do what you're told for once. *Please*. I mean it."

Sullenly I watched him walk out, every nerve in my body tensed to rebellion.

After that I became more than ever suspicious of the unwanted girl, although I tried not to show it. In her own peculiar foreign way, she was entrancing to look at; not specifically beautiful, but graceful and feline, with a golden skin, tilted amber eyes in a small heart-shaped face, and luxurious black silky hair which she usually wore tied back behind her pearly ears into a ribbon. The simple clothes provided by Mrs Traille could not entirely hide the sinuous lines of her figure, and she would languorously, almost soundlessly, go about the numerous tasks allotted to her. I was on the point several times of telling her to hurry up and not loiter about her work. But this was not my province and with difficulty I kept the words back. In any case, she had by then become surprisingly adept at following Mrs Traille's instructions in a minimum of time.

Once, as I watched her disappear into the dairy, Lalage appeared from the garden.

There was a knowing smile on her lips.

"Better keep an eye on that one," she told me. "If you ask me she and Ivan have quite an understanding between them. Cosy, you could say."

She was trying to goad me, of course, so I did my best to pay no attention. But the barbs hurt.

By October I had abandoned any efforts to like Maurice or understand him. In some ways he was naive — almost dull — for his age, in others curiously adult and knowing. Although he was not supposed to see Lalage more than necessary there was obviously a secret bond between them — and one which Claude Lang didn't appear to resent. The unpleasant thought occurred to me more than once that the tutor might be using his charge as a go-between — a contact with the sensuous, indulgent Miss Dupont. Several times I had seen Lang in the vicinity of her apartments, and guessed he had either been visiting her, or was on the point of doing so. I wondered if my husband knew. But he must, surely, I told myself, and if this was the case then Ivan couldn't have any personal interest in her, unless — once again old suspicions rose in me. Claude's presence could be very convenient for any dallying on Ivan's part.

I recalled former allusions by the odious old Madam — Miss Augusta — concerning her great-nephew's addiction to women. The collector! Could this really be true? And was I merely another conquest? A boost to his wounded pride, following his rejection by Evadne?

A torment of dark emotions flooded me. Confused and unhappy I steeled myself against him, avoiding physical contact whenever possible, under the

222

façade of having a headache, or being tired, or pretending to be asleep when Ivan came to bed.

He made no attempt at that period to enforce intimacy, for which, on the whole, I was grateful just then. But there were moments when I chafed, inwardly jealous and angry, convinced bitterly that his acceptance of my mood was not due to consideration on his part, but because he could find satisfaction elsewhere.

Sometimes, as we sat at table, or met casually in the hall, parlour, or conservatory, I could feel his eyes on me speculatively, and fancied he was about to question me over some matter. But my polite smile and quiet manner apparently chilled him, and the words were never said.

I was careful always to retire early, and occasionally would be seated at the dressing table in my nightdress and negligée, brushing my long hair before the mirror. Once I glimpsed his reflection darkly silhouetted behind me. He stood static for a few moments, then a hand was raised slowly; he took a step nearer, treading very softly; the candlelight lit his eyes briefly, in which, it seemed, just for an instant, longing stirred. I didn't look round, and the next moment he turned and left the room again.

Warmth, and the dawning of excitement in me, died into disappointment and chill.

I shivered.

Outside the golden dusk had already faded into violet night. Through the slit of open window, the bittersweet smell of heather and sea drifted insidiously with that of fallen leaves, blackberries and damp dying vegetation.

I parted the curtains and glanced out.

What I saw astonished me.

A shape was moving round a point below Miss Augusta's turret, crawling and walking with head thrust forward like an animal on the prowl, up the side of the house where it was quickly lost in the shadows.

Not Jed, or Marte, or Claude Lang, and certainly not old Thorlock. For a second the form had been clarified by a momentary beam of torchlight.

I was puzzled and intrigued, wondering whether I should sound the alarm, or go downstairs and find Ivan.

Then I decided to do nothing.

All was mystery at Merlake.

Let Mr Ivan Sterne solve this one on his own.

Later I felt a little mean, but in the morning I put the matter aside telling myself it had been a trick of the imagination, no more.

I was, of course, quite wrong, as later events proved.

★ ★ ★

October passed into November a period mostly spent by Ivan on the mainland. His business commitments, he told me, were heavier than he'd expected.

"Once I have everything finalised with the company," he'd said, alluding to the new Sterne Line, "I shall be comparatively free for a little socialising, and will take you with me on a tour for Christmas shopping."

"In Penzance?" Perhaps my voice was ironic. He looked slightly amused as he answered, "Well, I may have one or two of my friends there for you to meet, but there's nothing to stop us going further afield. Plymouth maybe, and certainly Falmouth. A week or ten days of delayed honeymoon. Would that please you?"

I couldn't help smiling. "Will it include business also, Ivan?"

He had the grace to admit, "Naturally I'll spend an hour or two at the new offices, but I can assure you, my love, it shouldn't interfere with your pleasure. Trust me."

"You haven't talked of new offices before," I pointed out. "Where are they?"

"Falmouth, naturally."

"Will Jed go with us, and Marte?"

He laughed outright.

"My dear child — "

"I'm not a child," I interrupted petulantly.

"My much honoured wife then," he amended quickly. "You'll have the most up-to-date sea-passage possible, manned by an expert crew that certainly won't include either Jed or his son."

"Oh. And what kind of boat will it be?"

"Very modern. One recently built for the Sterne Line. An iron steamer, with paddle wheels." I noticed that his voice had quietened perceptibly. His eyes had a fleeting speculative far-away gleam in them as though he was envisaging a future holding a whole new trend and achievement in shipping. "You've probably never heard of Isambard Brunel?" he queried a moment later, and not waiting for me to reply, continued: "Brunel — one of our greatest engineers — is about to launch a screw propelled iron-built vessel — a steamer, for Transatlantic service. This design will make tremendous impact, and eventually — except for pleasure purposes, will most probably mean the decline and eventual demise of great sailing ships. I mean my own line to be in the front rank of commercial shipping when this occurs — " He broke off, lost in his own dream.

"Oh. I see," I was faintly bored. The future he was speaking of seemed so far away from Christmas shopping and delayed honeymoons. He suddenly jerked himself to the present. "You're not interested," he remarked. "Well, why should you be? Anyway — " a small anxious frown appeared between his eyes, "I only meant to explain why I had to go away now. It will only be for a fortnight or so. And during that time you'll be able to make lists and plan the way women do for what you're going to buy when we set off together."

"Of course." But I was wondering what use there was in planning, when plans so far, where I was concerned, had failed to mature. However, I knew that no doubts of mine would alter his business arrangements, so I tried to accept his decision philosophically, and one late October day saw him leave for the mainland, heading for Penzance.

I felt not only desolate when he'd left, but on edge. If there was one single nice person on the island to talk to, I thought frequently, it would not be so bad. But everyone living at the house seemed in some way abnormal and resentful of my presence. It was very like wandering through an old fashioned fairytale, except that in this instance the meeting with ancient Thorlock, Maurice's cruelty, the malicious attitude of Lalage Dupont, and above all the macabre memory of the terrible wreck were frighteningly real.

Two days after Ivan's departure I woke up in the morning to find my bedroom door had once more been locked from the other side. I inserted my own key, but it wouldn't work. Feeling angry, and a little frightened, I rattled it wildly, and kept on until Mrs Traille arrived. She used a master key, I supposed, because when she opened the door, I saw her adjusting it on the ring hanging from her waist.

"What does this mean?" I asked breathlessly. "Locking me in. It happened before — at the beginning, when I first came to Merlake — " I broke off with the angry colour burning my cheeks.

The housekeeper sighed. "No need to be hysterical — Miss Ellan — Mrs Sterne — it was for your own safety."

"What do you mean?"

"She's had a turn — Miss Dupont. And when she's like that it's best to be on the safe side."

"A turn?" I remembered suddenly the unpleasant incident when Lalage had threatened to burn my hair off.

"You mean she's drunk," I said

229

contemptuously.

"That, and other things. She's a sick woman. Oh, tedn' often she has to be shut up; very rarely, you could say. Still, the master would go for me if you were harmed in any way."

"And how long do her — turns — last?"

"It's all dependin'," Mrs Traille answered, "on what's causing it. She don't like the master bein' away for one thing, then there's this fear of hers."

"What fear?"

"Now you're askin' too many questions. Let *him* explain when he gets back."

"But he never does. Not anything."

"Hm! Well! that's his own affair," Mrs Traille told me firmly. "Now just you forget about this business, have a wash, and I'll send breakfast up to you."

She lifted her head, stalked out, like a plump pigeon parading itself, leaving me staring irresolutely at the closed door. Her footsteps hadn't completely receded down the landing when I thought I heard banging from the direction of Lalage's apartments, followed by a shrill scream. I couldn't be sure, of course. There was a wind rising, and uneasiness filtered through the house — breathing through every crack and floorboard, rustling under rugs and round corners, tapping at windows and blowing dry leaves against the glass. The sky outside was grey, with a yellowish tinge. Loneliness encompassed the landscape and sea beyond. Ghosts of the past seemed to shiver down the maze of corridors, whispering of unknown bygone events holding no warmth or promise of love or human company.

Breakfast appeared presently. I ate what I could, then dressed and went downstairs, deciding that even conversation with Maurice would be better than none at all.

But he was already closeted in the schoolroom with Claude Lang. So I was forced to idle the hours away attending to flowers from the conservatory, walking round the gardens, doing work on my tapestry, and busying myself with any small tasks that came my way.

A week passed before Lalage appeared unexpectedly in the parlour. From her immediate appearance no one could have guessed that there had been anything amiss with her. Apart from dark smudges under her eyes she looked more composed and far more dignified that I'd have thought possible. She had kept the paint and powder on her face to a minimum, and in her quiet grey dress had a comparatively ladylike air. Her manner to me at first was condescendingly gracious.

"I thought we might eat together," she said. "Just for once. I'm sure Ivan wouldn't mind."

"No," I agreed. "Why should he?"

"Exactly," she seated herself languidly on a sofa, and smiled. "Why should he?" She paused, then added, "Especially as he possesses such a capacity for amusing himself." She spoke a trifle stiltedly as though studying the pronunciation and inflection of each word.

"What do you mean?" I asked. The glint of triumph in her eyes told me I had fallen into a trap.

"Oh — he has friends."

"In business, naturally."

"And not only business. Beth, for instance — that so-called housekeeper woman — " her glance had become wary, sly.

My hand tightened on a shred of lacy handkerchief. I could feel my spine stiffening, but my voice was under control, calm, when I answered, "I think you're referring to his caretaker's *daughter.*"

She shrugged. "Oh, call her what you like. They've been friends — fairly intimate ones, too — for quite a long time. Her husband doesn't mind. Why should he? Ivan was never the one to spare his pocket where his pleasures were concerned."

Her audacity, the meaning of her words, affronted me.

"I don't know what you're trying to imply — exactly — " I said coldly. "But I can guess. And let me tell you, I don't believe a word of it."

"No?"

"No."

She got up, walked to the chest, took out the brandy decanter, and a glass, and poured herself a drink. "Well," she said, gulping the liquor down quickly, "it's all the same to me. What difference does it make? If you want to go around with your eyes shut that's your affair. On the other hand, if you're brave enough to face the truth I've got proof enough — "

My body went cold.

"A letter — " she continued before I could speak, " — from her to him. Must've dropped it, or maybe there was a hole in his pocket — " She laughed shrilly. "Careless of him. Still, I don't suppose it'll worry you. Not been so close together lately, have you? Don't blame you. Oh, no indeed. Men — they're all the same. If you like — " she waited a second or two before adding, "I'll show you the thing. The note, I mean. Not compromising exactly, but aggressive, oh very. Something about him being needed and missed and too long away — oh, she wanted him all right."

I wished I'd not listened to her at all. I wished I'd walked out of the room before her wretched insinuations could have been uttered. I tried to convince myself she was lying, but didn't succeed. Her smile was too smug. Her glance too cold and penetrating.

She moved towards me and touched me on the shoulder.

"Don't fret about him," she said,

with mock sympathy. "He's not worth it really, dear. I've known Ivan Sterne for many years now — a *charming* man — most charming, when he chooses. We were close you see, at one time — "

At that point humiliation and anger burst from me in a torrent of condemnation.

"Don't dare speak like that of my husband. What you suggest is outrageous. I don't want to hear another word. You're concocting a string of lies just to upset me — because you're jealous. You've never liked me. In the past I've tried to be friendly when I had a chance, it's been the same with Maurice — but you've poisoned him against me. You're sick — *sick*."

Her face turned to a sickly grey.

"Don't you call me sick, you — you trollop, with your mincing ways and grand seductive acts. Anyone c'n see through you who's any sense. Out to get everything for yourself you have — from the very start — even my — my son!"

She almost spat the word out.

Shock and surprise momentarily dispelled my anger.

"Your *son*?"

"Yes. You didn't know that, did you? Well, now you do." She broke off, with her breasts heaving. "And when that precious so called husband of yours returns, you can tell him I told you, if you like. I don't care. But it'll make a difference to you, I can tell you that. So just go ahead, it's no odds to me."

She placed her glass with a rattle on the chest, lifted her head high above her plump chins, and swept out.

Before the door closed I thought I heard the cackle of Miss Augusta's senile laughter from somewhere outside.

Minutes passed before I sat down. Then I found I was shaking. I hardly knew what to believe, but the conviction gradually grew in me that what Lalage had told me was at least partially true. However, I had no intention at that point of being driven by her into challenging Ivan about her statement.

I had never been so miserable in my life before.

9

ON the day before Ivan's return to Merlake, Jed, who occasionally combined a fishing trip with other duties that included collecting mail from the mainland, delivered a letter for me from Aunt Clarissa. Unless she had important news concerning Evadne or the family, or wished to indulge in a lecture to me full of advice and her 'sincere hopes' that I was adequately fulfilling my obligations to my husband and 'acting in a manner expected of the mistress of Merlake' — she seldom corresponded.

This time the news came first. She wrote, in her precise neat hand:

You will be delighted to know, I'm sure, that my dear daughter, your cousin Evadne, is expecting a child. I would not of course refer to such a delicate matter, unless I knew how very gratified you would be to hear. Christopher, of course, is in heaven, dear boy. He already has a brilliant career planned for his son. I very *tactfully* tried to point out to him that there was a possibility — only a possibility, of course — that his first-born might be a girl. I expected dismay — one has to be *so* careful over such affairs. But no, no, *no*. 'If my darling Evadne makes me the precious gift of a baby girl in her own sweet image,' he cried, 'what greater delight could any man wish for?' So gallant of him, but between you and me, I know he'd really prefer a son first. You see, Anna, Christopher has a great sense of duty. He already envisages a place in The House of Lords for his heir when the time comes. Don't forget that when old Lord Ferris dies, Sir Bruce will inherit, and eventually Christopher. And there is so *much* for great families to do these days. Lord Palmerston cannot remain in office for ever, and the odious Mr Gladstone is a very great danger with his radical ideas. Thank Heaven our dear Queen *detests* him. Gladstone, I mean. Non-conformists and *pacifists*. Hypocrisy, if you ask me. I was reading the other day that the wretched man actually sympathises with *prostitutes* . . .

Eventually the letter took a more personal turn

Evadne herself is deeply happy, and is proving a most dutiful wife. I hope the same applies to you, Anna. I must admit, and you must well know yourself, that you were somewhat rebellious and difficult to deal with as a young girl. But doubtless Mr Sterne has managed to steer your behaviour in the way suitable to your new position. How lucky you have been, my dear. Remember to thank God every day of your life for the great benefits bestowed on you. I suppose there is a private chapel on Merlake — ?

There was, of course; and once, in the past, a resident chaplain had had his own adjoining premises. Later the incumbency had been removed to the mainland, when it had been arranged for monthly visits from the clergy. Early in Ivan's grandfather's life, however, even these had ceased. Any veneer of religion had faded, in the face of the dark deeds said to have been perpetuated in and around Merlake. The church now was little more than a ruin, huddled in a hollow of land at the back of Miss Augusta's premises. Weeds and ivy trailed its ancient walls — gales had torn the roof, and taken granite stones away. Following my escape from Thorlock's cave I must have passed very near to it.

When I'd questioned Mrs Traille, after looking at an old map, she'd said, reverting to her native burr, "*Church?* House of God?" She'd laughed openly. "More like the devil's claimed it now. A place for wild critters an' plundered tombs, that's all. The sea's encroachin' that side anyway. One day the whole ruin'll go tumblin' into the water. Even now there's things found sometimes — stickin' out of the cliff, like rotted coffins, an' a skull or two. Not that I've seen 'em. None can go that way but Jed. *He's* said though, an' I believe him."

"And old Thorlock?"

Mrs Traille had flung me a quick hard glance. "There's nuthen to know about him, an' the less you ask, the better."

I'd known at that point that I should learn nothing of importance from her, and had let the matter drop.

Now Aunt Clarissa's letter revived the picture. One day, I thought, when my so-called honeymoon was over, I'd try and prevail on Ivan to show me the *whole* of the island, including the ruined church.

But as things turned out the trip to the mainland and Falmouth was again postponed.

Ivan arrived at Merlake during the afternoon. I was in the conservatory. He looked fit and handsome, and had an anticipatory gleam in his eye, which I hoped was for me. Obviously it wasn't. He kissed me in a perfunctory manner on the cheek, but his thoughts quite clearly were elsewhere, although he said, "You look as lovely as ever. I hope you've been good too."

"What chance have I to be anything else here?" I remarked lightly, but with a sharp note in my voice.

"No, that's true."

His facile agreement angered me. Had I become so ordinary — such a casual day to day *commodity* in his eyes, I wondered, that he didn't even consider any other man might be interested? — Claude Lang for instance? I'd noticed early during my life on the island that with any shadow of encouragement from me, Maurice's tutor would willingly have taken advantage of a little romantic dallying, perhaps more than that. At times, I'd noted a sidelong ardent glance in the narrow dark eyes when they'd rested on me. His lips had taken a faint sardonic twist of amusement, as though suggesting, "Someday you may be grateful for my company. You can't fool me. Beneath your chill exterior you are quite a passionate young woman."

Oh yes. Lang was astute. I'd resented his perspicacity from the very beginning — his aptitude for assessing feminine potential, and had therefore made a point of displaying cold indifference whenever we'd chanced to meet.

Now, just for a second, Ivan's attitude made me wish I hadn't. A little coquetry, and pretence on my part towards another man, might have stirred Ivan to a more passionate reunion. Of course, I told myself bitterly — there'd been Beth. Lalage's hints might be true, which would explain the excitement in his eyes, the swagger, and air of confidence; "Like a cat that's just had a saucer of cream," I thought, although the last description applicable to Ivan was feline. He was all human, all male. And how I loved — *and* hated him. Just for a second I wanted to hurt him, to see him wince as I threw the news of Evadne's coming child in his face. But I was instantly ashamed and held my tongue.

He went upstairs to change. I didn't follow him, neither did he ask me to. When he came down to the parlour before dinner he was looking extremely smart in a cut-away tailed black velvet jacket over a gold embroidered waistcoat, cream silk neck-scarf and tie, and lightly fitting dark breeches strapped down over pointed-toed shoes.

As we drank aperitifs before going to the dining room he said, "You look very charming."

I knew I did. I was wearing a deep

rose gown with embroidered panniers. I didn't generally dress *quite* so elegantly when we ate alone together, but because the shade set off my cream glowing skin and dark hair, I'd deliberately chosen it to attract Ivan's attention.

"Well now," he said, in a manner meant to be casual but somehow suggesting he was making a special effort, "you must want to hear the news."

I smiled artificially. "You don't generally confide business matters to me."

"Oh. But this isn't entirely business, and it concerns you quite a bit."

I raised my eyebrows questioningly. "Oh?"

"I'm afraid our — our trip, our honeymoon, will have to be deferred for a bit," he said bluntly, hurrying on to add, "Oh, not indefinitely. But something has cropped up with the company that necessitates me being here for a time."

"I see." My voice must have been hard, cold, even a little bitter.

"Do you?" He sounded doubtful. "Then I must be grateful. Most women I'm sure would feel — disappointed, even slightly resentful."

"I'm not most women. I'm growing used to accepting the primary importance of Merlake's interests."

"Oh, Jade-Anna!" His lips unexpectedly brushed my shoulder and lingered there for a heady second. But I did not relax. He released me, walked away, shrugged and said, "You've a tart tongue. You must have proved quite a challenge to your domineering Aunt Clarissa in the past."

"I had a letter from her yesterday," I remarked.

"Oh? Had she any news?"

"Evadne's with child." His reference to Aunt Clarissa made the statement natural and matter-of-fact.

"So dear Christopher is ensuring the continuity of the noble Ferris line with all speed. Good for him."

Was he chiding me? Subtly taunting me for not yet becoming pregnant? Or was jealousy still gnawing him — jealousy over Evadne, as I'd anticipated?

I said nothing in answer to his mildly sarcastic comment, and when, minutes later, we went through to dinner, I still felt chagrin, with a growing determination somehow to pay him out.

I went to bed alone that night, leaving him in the study, discussing something — one of his important business matters doubtless — with Jed, although what the two men could have to talk about at such an hour I couldn't guess. I was restless, and lay awake with my mind searching this way and that for some satisfactory explanation of his neglectful attitude. But, of course, there was none, and possibly I had no right to expect any. I had forced my presence on him in the first place, at Evadne's wedding. And now he was showing me exactly where I stood. I was still awake, but feigned sleep, two hours later when he slipped into the sheets beside me. He reclined for a minute, head up, resting on one elbow, looking at me.

"Jade-Anna — " I heard him whisper, as his lips touched a cheek, "my love — " During the short pause the warmth of his breathing, the contact, almost broke down my defence. But not quite. Still keeping my eyes tightly shut, I pulled myself away giving a sleepy sound of refusal, of not wishing to be disturbed.

I heard him sigh and turn away.

I wished later I hadn't; but next morning indignation and resentment had mounted in me again. I was not his chattel or plaything, and I would not be shared with any other woman in his life.

And so, goading and hurting myself, I let our relationship drift further into a miasma of misunderstanding.

The following week, as I was taking a walk round the grounds, I came across Claude Lang, quite unexpectedly, standing alone by the gap in the wall, staring out to sea. The air was chilly, the sky grey above the distant water, his figure in its black cape appeared static as an effigy, giving no indication he was aware of my approach. I paused a few yards from him, below a hummock of ground. Then, just like a figure enacting a part in a drama, he turned. His face was very pale in the cold light. For a few seconds we stood regarding each other, silently, held by a sense of queer inevitability, of doom-like purpose — being pulled like puppets, to fulfil our preconceived roles.

As I moved to meet him, he took a step

towards me, and doffed his hat elegantly. I remember thinking how odd it seemed for him to be dressed so formally for a mere stroll in the grounds. How wide and high his forehead was, I thought, the thin mouth pointed, yet in a strange way sensually compelling, like that of some beautiful wicked Pan.

"So our — weather, however inclement — tempted you out, Mrs Sterne," he said, with a malicious undercurrent in his soft voice. "How very fortunate for me. Or was it — could it be — that you were in need of company?"

"Not at all, Mr Lang," I answered in what I hoped was a lofty tone. "I always like to take a breath or two every day."

"A breath or two of what, madam?"

"Of fresh air, of course," I answered, feeling my cheeks burn.

"Ah. Then let me assist you over this decidedly lumpy terrain."

He held out a hand, and just as though I was mesmerised, I took it.

The contact both chilled and excited me. Chilled me because I didn't like him, excited me because I knew Ivan would be annoyed, which made the situation potentially dangerous.

In three strides, I was pulled up the few yards of slope and was standing by him at the gap. "What an extremely pleasant interlude," he remarked, freeing my hand. "All the more so because of its unpredictability — its danger."

"Danger?" The word was meant to sound scornful.

"Oh come now. For a newly wedded young wife to choose an assignation with a man not her husband is surely something of a challenge to the conventions?"

I tossed my head. "You flatter yourself. Assignation? How ridiculous. I didn't know you'd be lurking about, Mr Lang; you're generally with Maurice at this hour. I wanted solitude. And anyway — why on earth should I wish to meet *you*?"

"Oh! Why indeed! a mere tutor. A prisoner, like yourself, on this uncivilized sea-girt terrain."

"A *prisoner*?" I laughed shrilly.

"What else? And what more natural than for a beautiful neglected young woman to wish for a little excitement?"

Under lowered lids his eyes slid over

my form briefly, from head to foot, and as they held my gaze again I noticed a strange brilliance flood them, high-lighting their very small pupils to pin-points of flame against their darkness. A moment later it had gone; he looked bemused, as though impelled from some exotic far-off sphere once more to earth. He rested one hand on the granite wall. The long pale fingers trembled but almost immediately the knuckles clenched over the stone, and he was in full command of himself. For some unknown reason I felt ridiculously nervous, and tried ineffectually to steer the conversation into mundane channels. Yet all the time I knew he saw through the ruse and was secretly amused.

At last I said, "I must go, Mr Lang."

I turned abruptly, but he sprang lightly in front of me, and made a mock bow, and before I realised what he was about, had taken my hand and pressed it to his lips. I tried to free myself quickly, saying, "Don't *do* that! How dare you!"

"*Dare*, Miss Ellan? — forgive me, Mrs Sterne? Oh, dear, dear! how very dramatic — "

There was no tremor in his grip now. His fingers were tight as steel on my wrist.

"Unless you let me go this instant I shall tell my husband and demand your dismissal — " I was breathing quickly. His smile was hard, cold, evil.

"If you do, it's you who'll suffer. I can assure you I shall not be dismissed, neither will your account of our little encounter be believed. You're quite an unknown quantity here, aren't you? Certainly to Master Ivan Sterne. So no tale-telling, madam."

I gave his arm a vicious jerk, inadvertently pulling him forward. For a second his hard mouth was on mine. Then abruptly, he let me go, and with a contemptuous gesture rubbed his lips with a square of silk from his pocket. I stared at him, astonished.

"Those luscious lips have a bitter flavour," he remarked sardonically. "A little sweetness would prove advantageous on your behalf while you remain here. I can be a good friend, but a very bad enemy. Mistress of Merlake in name you may be, but believe me, it's others who wield the power here."

I didn't wait to hear more. Lifting my skirts above the tips of my boots I turned and hurried back as swiftly as possible the way I'd come, not knowing that Jed, from a hidey-hole beyond the gap, had witnessed the finale of the unpleasant scene.

All the evening I felt ill-at-ease. Thin rain was falling from leaden skies that as night closed in turned to sombre starless dark. Lalage insisted on joining Ivan and myself for dinner, and for once I was relieved by her company and intermittent chatter. Ivan was unnaturally quiet. His eyes were frequently on my face, unswervingly watchful, yet with a questioning behind their stillness that unnerved me. Lalage, at moments, appeared secretly amused. Once she enquired bluntly, with a hint of malice, "Have you two quarrelled or something? If so, don't mind about me. Fight and spit as much as you like. The one thing I can't stand is boredom."

Ivan threw her a warning glance. "You weren't asked to the table, Lalage, and if you can't be polite your absence is preferable to your company."

Lalage lifted her head defiantly. Long gold earrings jingled beneath her over-dressed hair. Her cheeks were mottled rosy pink. Obviously she had been drinking.

"There's no need to take that tone with me Ivan — *Sir* — Mr High-and-mighty-master of Merlake. If you can't give your poor dependant a little companionship now and again why don't you arrange a little establishment for me on the mainland? You would be freed then from any unpleasant obligations, which would be to both our advantage. Of course — " Her voice turned smug, "Maurice would have to choose between us. Fair, don't you think — "

"Stop it," Ivan said, sharply. "You're talking nonsense." He reached for Miss Dupont's glass which she was about to refill with wine, and pushed it to the far side of the table. "No more alcohol," he said. "Try and appear a lady, even if you're not."

She made one swift gesture to retrieve the glass, and at the same moment one of the rings fell from an ear. She glanced down quickly, and during that moment I noticed something. In a gleam of light catching the back of her head, fine hairs on her neck revealed roots of a deep flaming red. The glimpse I had, was only momentary, but I was quite astonished. The thick springy locks were not naturally black at all. They were dyed. Wondering confusedly about the reason why, I didn't hear what she said in reply. Ivan retained her glass, and after her muttered comment the meal continued in comparative silence.

Afterwards Ivan, as usual, retired to his study for a smoke and I presumed a measure of his vintage brandy, or port perhaps, having made sure first the drinks cabinet in the dining room was locked with the decanters safely inside.

Lalage laughed unpleasantly.

"You don't exactly draw the best side of him out," she remarked scathingly. "How *do* you manage to make things so goddamned boring, Anna? Or should I say Mrs Sterne?"

I shrugged. "It doesn't really matter

what you call me. I'm tired of arguing."

"Hm! Well — " she paused before adding with a subtle touch of triumph, "you'll get plenty later, I'm sure."

"What do you mean?" I asked sharply, forgetting my resolve not to bandy words with her.

"My dear innocent!" mockingly " — not that you *are* — innocent I mean — if I know anything about dear Ivan — and believe me, I do, quite a lot, he has a bone to pick with you. And on the whole I'm not surprised." Her expression changed, becoming revengeful, almost vicious. "You'll deserve what you get. Every bit of it."

She turned her back on me, and tossing her head with her skirts held up by each plump hand, walked out of the room, tottering slightly in her ridiculous effort to appear dignified.

For some time following her departure, I remained in the dining room, wondering if Ivan would come back. When he didn't I went to the drawing room and started working on my tapestry. I wasn't really interested. In spite of a determination not to be affected by Lalage's words their derisive implication chilled me. Had Ivan not appeared so unnaturally cold and stern that evening I would have tossed the comments aside as mere jealousy. But his uncompromising attitude had held a subtle threat — not necessarily towards Miss Dupont, but myself. I couldn't help wondering, guiltily, if he had somehow got to know of the unpleasant little confrontation with Claude. However, it had been none of my making, I told myself stubbornly. If he'd had witnessed the whole scene — which he surely couldn't have — he'd have known surely that Lang had been the perpetrator. And had my husband paid a little more attention to *me* it would never have happened at all. The latter fact made me angry again, and anger reinforced my wilful mood against him.

I went upstairs early, and when Ivan entered the bedroom an hour later, was already in bed. Hearing the door open and close quietly, I feigned sleep as usual, keeping my eyes closed, and breathing steadily, although I was aware of him coming softly to the bed and staring down on me before he went to the dressing room, derobed, and after his habitual wash, returned and slid into the sheets beside me. He touched a thigh. I managed not to tremble or stir.

Jade-Anna," he said, quietly but peremptorily. I didn't answer.

The hand slid up to a breast. I made a little sigh and attempted to draw away. If he had been in a kind mood how different it could have been; but there was nothing kind in Ivan just then. I sensed it and was determined to delay contact until we could come together in better understanding with no recriminations between us.

For a few seconds I held my breath. Then he said again, Jade-Anna, I'm speaking to you. Do you hear?"

I tightened my lips mutely.

He pulled me forcefully to face him. "Look at me. Open your eyes and stop behaving like a child."

As I stared dumbly, keeping my body rigid, his jaws clenched. I could see a muscle jerking in one cheek. The warmth of him — his closeness and desire for me, both excited and angered me. I attempted to pull away thinking irrationally, 'Let him be hurt, I don't care. He's ignored me so much lately — he deserves it. I won't be played with or put second to any other woman or stuffy business affairs. Let him beg and plead with me. Let *him* know for a change what it's like to be humiliated and ignored — ' I started to struggle. His mouth was a hot flame on mine, willing, urging me to capitulate, but I wouldn't. I could feel my knees pummelling his stomach, my breath came in gasps as his thighs swung their weight upon me.

"So it's like that," he muttered thickly. "You dare to dangle your favours elsewhere, while playing the chaste young madam in the marriage bed. Well — I'm tired of games. Do you understand? This time I'm going to — "

"Leave me *alone*," I cried. "I won't be bullied. You're cruel and ruthless. You've no delicacy or compassion — you — "

A hand came over my mouth. I could feel his flesh hardening against mine as he said in a soft, bitter whisper, "*Compassion?* For *you*? Is that what you felt for Lang when you flung yourself at him this afternoon? Do you think I didn't *know* — ?"

Of *course*, I thought with a shock. Someone had seen the ridiculous little scene and exaggerated the episode completely out of true proportion — someone bent on mischief-making. I tried to laugh, but he slapped my face sharply. The sting of it made me lose all restraint. I caught his hand with my teeth, and as he drew back, I managed to struggle from the bed, and ran for the door. But I was not quick enough. A second later, perhaps two, he'd pulled me back, flung me face down on the sheets, pushed the flimsy nightdress up and brought the flat of his hand smartly on my flesh, spanking me as an irate adult might have treated a naughty child.

I bit my lip, and didn't cry.

But when it was over I turned and with flaming cheeks and the utmost contempt I could muster, said defiantly, "I'll never forgive you for this — *never*.

He laughed in my face then. "I don't want your forgiveness, or need it. What I want of you, I'll take."

And he did, ravishing my body, stirring such a tumult of wild ungovernable emotions in me, that the world temporarily seemed to darken and fade away.

At last he rolled away from me, and presently, when I didn't speak, got up and stood looking down on me.

"You asked for it, you know," he said in expressionless tones. "I warned you once. You're a stupid girl, Jade-Anna. But perhaps — "

With my eyes still closed, I said, "Go away. Don't touch me. And don't talk. I don't want to hear."

"Certainly. I've no wish at all to force my company on a wildcat — even my wife. And in future, madam — " he waited before concluding, "neither will you have the opportunity of flaunting yourself before any other man's eyes."

I looked up then.

"What do you mean?"

"You'll remain here, safely under lock and key, until I can bear to look on you again," he said. "God knows when that will be."

The next moment there was the sound of a key turning in the lock.

He had gone.

Outside a cold wind beat the walls of Merlake, but not so cold as the icy chill — the sudden loneliness flooding my own heart.

10

FOR three days and nights I was confined to the bedroom, seeing no one but Mrs Traille, who brought in food and attended to my toilette. Fires were kept going regularly, and every possible comfort for a prisoner provided, including reading matter. If the weather outside had been more cheerful I might have resented my incarceration more violently. But dreary thin rain fell constantly, enshrouding the island into dismal uniformity — a blurred lump of rock rising in a spectral shape from a vaporous sea. The housekeeper was quick to lock the door before bringing the tray to the bedside table. She needn't have worried. I had no intention of humiliating myself further by struggling with her or making an ineffectual attempt to escape. To the contrary I preserved what pride was left to me, by polite indifference, and a pretence that I was not at all interested in the outside world. What she knew of the truth I couldn't tell, but accepted that she must be aware of the rift between Ivan and me — or why should I be locked up at all.

She referred to my 'malaise' — a word she must have looked up in the dictionary, which mildly, ironically, amused me.

"I'm daily feeling better," I told her once. "Colds at this time of the year are hard to shake off, are they not?"

My artificial, bright but cold smile, must have taken her aback. She looked fussed, with a higher than usual colour in her broad face.

"The master said if there was anything you wanted — "

"Tell your master I want for nothing except to be left alone," I interrupted icily. "Is he well?"

"He's very busy. Working. In his study."

"Ah well — " I feigned languorous indifference, "then I'm the lucky one, to be waited on so attentively in such warmth and comparative luxury."

Her glance at me was dogged and sullen as she turned, stalked heavily across the floor, and departed, locking the door from the outside.

As always, her presence had left me feeling stubborn and rebellious. I went to the window and saw, with relief, that the sky appeared to be lifting slightly, which could mean that it might soon stop raining. Perhaps soon, I thought, Ivan might condescend to let me out. Would he offer me an arm then, and conduct me downstairs to a meal? Would he discuss the weather politely? My welfare? Or his boring shipping line? Or would his glance be stern and cold and forbidding, his hand firm and hard on my arm? Would Lalage be there to witness any farcical reunion? Or would we eat silently, in solitude?

The latter probably, I decided. He'd spare no opportunity of showing his displeasure. How I detested him — his authority and knack of bringing out the worst in me. And why should I stand any more of it? The enforced idleness of the last few days suddenly erupted into a wild desire for action. I was not his chattel. Why should I be any man's? I was not only a woman, but an individual with certain rights of my own.

But what *were* they? What chance had any wife placed as I was, to demand respect and a proper place in her own home? Why, the house wasn't even mine. I shared it with three other domineering creatures — Mrs Traille, Lalage, and the odious Miss Augusta in her turreted domain, all of whom now were most probably revelling in my plight.

As I stood there, defiance deepened into mounting hot anger. The warm blood pounded in my veins, quickening my heart to sudden wild racing.

It was then that my attention was diverted by a shadowed furtive movement in the location of the pier below. Through the greyness, which was now changing from rain to mist, I thought a lamp glowed briefly, swaying for an instant like a hovering will o' the wisp. Then it was gone.

But I knew activity of some kind was in progress. I had the impulse then of some caged thing to break free, and be there too. A second later I realised the futility of the idea. How would I get out? And if I succeeded where would I go? Find Thorlock again? Somehow bribe that terrible old man to keep me hidden until I could find some means of transport to take me to the mainland. He obviously liked treasures. Ivan had given me jewellery as a wedding gift. Perhaps I could tempt him with such a glittering reward?

In my excitement the idea seemed feasible. But the problem remained of how to escape from the house.

I glanced down, noting through the damp mist-washed light, a portion of flat roof joining the pointed tower of Miss Augusta's wing. It was twenty or thirty feet below, but entangled with thick sturdy-trunked ivy. To climb down *would* be possible, provided I could get the bedroom window sufficiently open. After that there would be a further drop to the high land cutting round the north side of Merlake just above the track taken when Ivan and I arrived on that first rain soaked night. Was there a tree there? Or some pipe or other that would help me to reach terra firma?

A childish feeling of adventure seized me.

In thinking he could subdue me by

a spanking and keeping me locked up, Mr Ivan Sterne had certainly made a problem for himself.

But I decided to delay my action until later — probably the early morning.

Unless of course Ivan had a change of heart, released me from confinement, and made a proper apology.

But he didn't.

Several times later I heard movement along the landing, and with bated breath waited for footsteps to pause, followed by the turning of a key, and the opening of a door. Once the murmur of muffled whispered conversation rose, fell, then died into silence. At wakeful periods during the night I was aware of uneasiness, conscious that unless my senses were playing me false, something was going on in the house. Nothing definite, just muted sounds that warned me to be on my guard. I slept only fitfully. At four-thirty I woke with a start, and decided to get up. Pulling the blinds apart I stared through the window at the desolate scene outside. It was quite dark, but the darkness was huddled into its own damp shroud of lapping fog. When the first rays of morning streaked the sky there would still be no clarity. Any watcher from the rocks below would be unable to detect movement unless specifically forewarned. And *nobody* would have the remotest idea that any female could be so reckless as to attempt the kind of escape I was planning, so no one would be on the alert for it.

Even as the wild thoughts raced through my mind, I realised how mad-headed and outrageous they were. A quarrel with Mrs Traille — a quick rush and push past as some unexpected moment when she delivered a tray would have been possible surely, and so much easier. But there was Ivan! He would probably have ordered me back to the bedroom again, or else carried me there. My indignity would then have been intensified in the eyes of the household. At the moment, Mrs Traille had informed me, I was supposed to be suffering from a cold.

A *cold*! How ridiculous. And really how bizarre were the whole circumstances of my life at Merlake. If I wrote events down as they had happened no one would believe them, but take the view privately — or in whispered drawing room conversations between sensation-seeking dowagers — that Sir Humphrey Ellan's unfortunate niece, poor thing — had obviously gone a little mad, although she had shown a childlike talent for concocting fairy tales? I could just imagine the trend of their stuffy gossip, 'A good thing Clarissa managed to get her off her hands so conveniently at such an opportune time. A wild, neurotic creature she's proved to be. Of course, the Sterne family aren't quite *normal*, or Ivan would never have married her. It would be interesting to know — ' and so on, and so on.

I smiled to myself.

Yes. Interesting — very. And now I was going to prove myself as the true mad-cap Aunt Clarissa had always accused me of being. Once I'd made the decision I didn't waste time. First I collected all the jewellery I possessed and secreted it in a pouch. Then I dressed myself in layers of warm underclothes, pushing what I could into a pair of woollen drawers. Ivan, I knew, was not in the dressing room, and there I found a pair of boots — much too large for me, of course, but comfortable when I'd got the pantalettes and other garments stuffed inside. I put a belt round one of my own short coatees, and over everything wore a thick cape. I drew back my thick hair with a ribbon, and when my own reflection confronted me through the pier mirror, was startled to see a boyish-looking individual more like a theatrical highwayman than Jade-Anna Ellan or Mrs Ivan Sterne.

The pouch was a problem as there was no pocket in the cape. I solved it by secreting it in my reticule and tying the whole thing to my belt. Then I returned to the window and managed to open it a foot or two. A drift of icy foggy air blew in. I stretched out an arm, feeling for some trunk of greenery, or a branch sufficiently stalwart to take my weight.

The ivy was thick, and entangled with leafless bindweed and some other creeping herbage. I raised myself over the sill and peered down. Below a billowing screen of milky mist, the ground or rooftops gaped darker than the dark sky behind the cloud. The first daylight was still far away. The only visible vista was one of changing shadows and moving indeterminate shapes conjured on the drift of cold rising wind.

Gripping the wet trunk of ancient greenery I tried to work out distance and locality. As my eyes, like a wild animal's, became more accustomed to the darkness, it seemed to me that rising above on my right was a dense wall of heavier substance than air. Miss Augusta's apartments probably, reaching to a point above. Below me, then, must be the flat roof and eventual drop down to the rough moor.

I climbed out cautiously, with an arm still firmly enclosed round the knotted wood. It was easier to find footholds than I'd imagined, but when the branch moved fitfully two feet or so from the granite wall I panicked for a moment. It was too late to turn back. As my left knee swung over the sill my cloak caught on a thorn. I gave a sharp tug and dislodged it, at the same time bringing my two legs together. Fear gradually died into excitement as I realised how thick the greenery was. So long as I could keep close enough to the wall's surface I was comparatively safe. So I continued the descent laboriously, twigs and cobwebs clutching and brushing my face, and eventually reached the flat roof.

I waited for a time, wiped dust and soil from my eyes, and peered ineffectually through the darkness, wishing I'd had some means of a light. Strangely, a sense of location — of dim shapes began vaguely to register. At moments the mist seemed to coil and roll back from any projecting solid surface, and I knew by instinct when the flat man-built surface was coming to an end. I moved more slowly, with extreme caution, and suddenly a cold sharp breath of wind flapped against me, blown up from a gap of boulders below on my left. Boulders only? Or also ruined masonry of the derelict chapel? It was still so dark I couldn't discern any certain outline through the writhing fog.

I'd lost all count of time, but guessed dawn must steadily be creeping up from the east. I waited hesitantly, trying to assess the distance from the base of the wall to the ground, and as though fate was really on my side for once, the foggy air cleared briefly to dim pale grey, revealing that my calculations had been astonishingly correct. Tumbled granite rose in lumps from the moor — high enough for me to land on, if I had luck — and further on, in the same direction, the stark broken mist-wreathed ruin of Merlake's ancient oratory. Beyond that, I guessed, must be the stretch of more even ground that I'd climbed and crossed on the day of my escape from old Thorlock's cave — the hide-out I was now recklessly searching for.

This sense of geography gave me courage. I jumped lightly, before the fog had completely rolled in again, and apart from twisting an ankle slightly, suffered no harm. I perched myself on a rock, rubbed the muscles, and moved the foot from one side to another, then, presently I got up, and found I could walk.

Looking back now, it's difficult to remember quite how I clambered down towards Thorlock's retreat. But I did, arriving near the top of the cave on the opposite side of my former visit.

The mist was lifting slightly again, and already the first signs of blurred dawn gave an unearthly weird glow to the distorted scene of rolling sea, cloud, clawing bushes and humped beast-like shapes of crouched boulders. An occasional gull rose squawking into the sky. Small wild creatures began to stir, creaking the undergrowth through roots of gorse and heather. I recognised then for the first time that I was cold, and with ears alerted heard a tinkle of can or kettle from below. The faint crackle and tang of woodsmoke told me that Thorlock was already astir, and my heart bumped uneasily when I visioned what his reception of me might be.

I was about to make my way down a tortuous steep path, when something surprised — quite shocked — me. Through the milky air on the far side of the chapel, a figure emerged. A woman, wearing a hooded cloak, whose blurred, misted shape could have been some theatrical ghost from one of Shakespeare's plays, but wasn't. No, she was no phantom. With a jolt of nerves I knew beyond any doubt, a second or two later, that it was Lalage. Lalage bent on some strange mission of her own. There was no mistaking her full figure as the cloak drifted back in the wind. The long stream of coarse black hair — the bold profile briefly visible could have belonged to no other.

Quite unaware of my presence she moved deliberately downwards. And it was then, that glancing seawards, following the direction she took, I saw something else huddled against a thrust of cliff — a small craft surely, with a blurred momentary winking of a light that was as quickly swallowed into shadow again. For a few moments the woman's form was taken from view. I rubbed my eyes, straining for clarity. It could have been only seconds before she reappeared — darkness against uncertain grey; and as her feet merged into the furred quivering line of shore and sky, she was met by another — a thin distorted figure who took her briefly and purposefully by the shoulders, making a series of gestures that ended in an embrace.

Their assignation was short. The air thickened once more, dimming everything into mist-blown obscurity. I had a brief glimpse of the seaman returning to his boat, and Lalage hurrying to the shadowed cliff, then all receded into a lonely vista of drifting cloud and sea, of thin blown rain that intensified when at last I found sufficient initiative to move.

When eventually I came to the entrance of Thorlock's cave, he was standing just inside. His wizened ancient face framed by straggling locks, was pushed forward from his bent shoulders, his expression filled with morbid curiosity, that held also a tinge of malevolent triumph.

"So ye're back," he said raspingly. "An' what for? Creepin' 'ere like any witchin' besom, wantin' to pry an' thieve, an' tek what's Thorlock's — "

Knowing I had no right there and that in any case my duty was to go immediately back to the house and report to Ivan what I'd just seen, I nevertheless took another few steps forward.

"I shan't harm you," I said quickly. "Just let me stay here for a time, hide me, and — and — " I fumbled inside my cape for the reticule hanging from my belt, wondering in a moment's panic if I'd lost it. But it was safe. I drew the pouch out, emptied the contents on to one palm, and showed them to the old man, never taking my eyes from his — "you can have these."

Through the damp air, the rubies, sapphires and diamonds glinted — but not more brilliantly than the sudden avarice in the beady eyes which were lit by a leaping glow from the spitting of a log fire at the far end. I noticed Thorlock's old tongue course the withered lips as though savouring the richness of new treasure ready for his claw-like fist.

"Mine?" he said. "F'r me?" His mouth parted in a snarl. "Get me into trouble, would ye? Stolen, are they?"

I shook my head. "They're my own. I'm Sterne's wife. *Ivan* Sterne's — "

The snarl died into a passing look of bewilderment.

"Then why're ye here? — Ha?" As slow comprehension dawned in him, a gnarled fist shot out.

"Give 'em me — "

I drew my hand back quickly.

"Not until I — until you give me

refuge. I — I hate them all as much as you do — those at the big house. I'm on the run, Thorlock. If you help me until — until I can get a boat or some other means of escape, you can have everything I have here — "I waited, breathing quickly, as a number of conflicting emotions crossed his face — suspicion, fear, resentment, greed — most of all greed.

Then suddenly with his eyes narrowed and jaw outthrust, he turned, shuffling towards the far end of the cave, muttering, "C'mon 'ere then. An' bring they jools with 'ee."

Bending, to avoid the brush of hanging weed and wet cobwebs, I followed him down the passageway, past the portrait of the lovely mocking woman in the broken frame, the mildewed relics of former times that once must have been so valuable, coming in the end to the warmer dwelling portion, where a fire glowed casting oddly moving shadows over threadbare ages-old Persian rugs, silver, including tankards, worn silken coverlets, chairs, table and a curious Chinese mask hanging on the far wall. The whole effect was mysterious, macabre, with the dream-like quality of a hidden small world secreted in some legendary sphere forbidden to human feet. Beside the fire's orange gleam, light flickered from tallow burning from tin containers nailed on rock. Shadows from trailing weeds made a delicate tracery of ever changing light and shade over walls and ceiling, quivering over the floor, to the accompaniment of the hollow boom of waves from outside.

The old man went ahead, taking a further corner, with the tail of his tattered greenish-black coat dropping behind over stones and damp earth. The shadows became more massed, but there was sufficient light left to reveal crudely cut granite steps leading to a further chamber. This was small, but roughly furnished with sacking thrown over a bench, and a crude chair hewn from a lump of wood. I had to clamber over a boulder to get inside. Despite his age, old Thorlock was nimble in movement, and said sneeringly as my hand slipped on the granite, "Yer'll have ter use y'r wits an' act quick if you bide heer, wumman. An' if you hear anythin' you jus' stay quiet, see? Or eel be thrown to they fishes in no time."

I shuddered.

"An' now — what about they bawdies o' yours?"

I handed him the jewellery. He stared down at the gems lying bright in his withered palm, spat on them, and rubbed one on his coat sleeve. Then he said gruffly, "S'long as they're yourn t' give, an' you doan say nought of ole Thorlock — " his head poked forward aggressively, 'Y' c'n stay for a night or two. There'll be sumthen' for y'r belly — fish mostly, or mebbe a bit o' frog. Snails too. Snails be rich fare here — " He grinned, showing two fangs of yellowed teeth.

I shuddered. Whether he noticed or not I couldn't tell, but from his air of senile triumph I guessed that he did. Little was said after this. He left me to make the sacking as comfortable as possible, and when he'd gone I had a wild urge to rush out and make a reckless return to the Towers. Anything, I thought momentarily, even to be lost in the wilderness of moor and fog, would be preferable to remaining in this small damp prison. The atmosphere was claustrophobic, frightening.

The impulse was only brief. I controlled the attack of nerves, and decided presently to return to the larger cavern and insist on eating there.

To my surprise Thorlock didn't object. Perhaps he was so bemused and gratified by the jewellery, other matters didn't register, or perhaps after a long period of solitude he even found a little human company rewarding. Whatever the cause, so long as I asked no questions his former aggression gradually quietened to grudging acceptance of my presence, and the food, to my great relief, was fish fried over the fire. Being hungry, I ate with relish, and later sat for a time by the glowing embers before retiring to my dank resting place.

By the changing light I knew by then it was morning, but instead of lifting, the mist fitfully thickened again. Time lost its meaning. I spent a period — it must have been hours — getting my thoughts into some kind of proportion, and coming to the conclusion that I had acted recklessly, without foresight, with no feasible plan for the future. I couldn't stay in Thorlock's cave for ever. If I returned to the house with no satisfactory explanation there'd be further scenes and conflict with Ivan. So far, I'd accomplished nothing in solving the secret of the Towers, nor was I likely to. I'd been an idiot, I told myself wrily — acted just like the rash child Ivan had always accused me of being, and had so proved him right. Unless my rash flight accomplished something positive I'd merely weakened my own ridiculous position.

Ivan. Would our conflict never end?

My thoughts were still in wild confusion when I remembered the many differing facets of his character — how tender he could be, and at other times how fierce and such a bully. And stupid, too. Yes — *stupid*. If he'd confided in me over his numerous women and treated me as an adult demanding respect, how different things could have been between us. Even now a niggling sense of duty told me he should know something of what was going on between Lalage and the unknown seaman. There might be some mischief brewing — a plot endangering my husband's safety. Who could tell? And why was it that the ever-watchful Jed or Marte hadn't spotted the small craft on the beach? Once more envisaging the scene the answer was simple. The fog, of course; and the fact that the boat had been anchored in a hidden spot beneath overhanging cliffs. Something stubborn rose in me as I considered the situation rationally — something that for the time being reduced my anger with Ivan to a minimum. At that point I decided to act.

"Where ye off ter now?" The old man questioned as I pulled my cape on and walked jauntily to the cave's opening.

Deciding to take a strong line I answered, "That's my affair. You'll come to no trouble. I've given my word."

Apart from grumbling under his breath he made no protest, and in a few moments I was outside once more trying to assess the locality. Thinking about it made me wonder how Lalage had managed to escape from view so speedily, and what track she'd taken to get back unseen to the Towers. Obviously there was some other way to the house of which I was unaware.

The realisation spurred me ahead.

I scrambled over slippery rock and wet sand, taking a course south-west from which her figure had appeared. It was rather like moving through a dream. Strange shapes emerged briefly and the next moment were taken back into the writhing grey veil of mist. Once, glancing upwards a gigantic form loomed static and menacingly from above. I stopped, with a lurch of fear, then continued on my way, realising that the shape was simply a standing stone, one of the ancient relics of former times when early primitive Celts worshipped the old gods of earth and sky. The thin wind shuddered from the sea towards the cliffs and moors above.

I rounded a jutting crag, and it was then I saw the hole — an inlet cutting beneath the overhanging rocks. It was smaller than the entrance to Thorlock's dwelling, and much darker. I cut towards it and peered inside. It was obviously a passage leading steadily upwards — a tunnel of some kind, perhaps used for smuggling in earlier days. A vague filter of light from far within trickled towards me beside a thin stream of water.

I hesitated. The prospect of going ahead wasn't inviting. Supposing the inlet formed part of an old mine working — an adit now derelict and dangerous? Suppose movement caused a fall of rock, trapping me there, entombing me until I died. I shuddered, and was about to ignore the challenge when a sudden flash of reason told me the tunnel could easily have been the route used by Lalage for a quick return to the house.

Cautiously at first, then more quickly, as I learned how to negotiate the way, I forced myself on, although I couldn't have said how long, and knew I was right. The dank corridor steepened quite suddenly, coming to rough steps. I waited then, staring up to a blank, dark ceiling. At one side a thin beam of light filtered through, and I thought I heard sounds from above — distant noises that held the hollow echo of feet treading.

Lalage's apartments? And was the barrier some kind of trap door — the secret entrance, perhaps one of many, to the Towers?

Really I had no doubt that it was so, but instinct told me I should go no further at that point, so I turned, and made as hurried an exit as possible to the shore. Once there I rested for some minutes, before turning and retracing my way to Thorlock's retreat. The mist was still quite thick, and showed no signs of properly clearing, which meant that by afternoon it might start to thicken again.

I decided to try and win Thorlock's further co-operation keeping as long as possible to my own temporary quarters, with false promises perhaps of further reward ahead. I'd have to share his fish, avoiding snails and frogs' legs, and refrain from any questioning. At periods, on the pretext of needing air and exercise, I'd venture out and keep a watch on the small boat if it was still there, my eyes ever alert for any sign of Lalage. It wouldn't be easy. The old man's temper was unpredictable, and the blurring mist, though helpful in keeping Jed and Marte away, could make clear vision practically impossible. But if I could obtain a single definite clue of what was going on, I knew Ivan might have cause to thank me. *Might*. Unless he was also in some plot. I didn't think that was so. As I didn't *really* believe he would bother over much about any assignation Miss Dupont had with a strange man. The insidious factor was the *identity* of the seaman, and what he was about beyond a secret tawdry episode with Maurice's decadent aunt.

There must be something.

I had no proof, but deep down I was certain that what I had witnessed heralded some danger to the Sterne family, Ivan perhaps in particular.

With such facts firmly embedded in my mind, I waited for the afternoon.

And when the time arrived something happened.

What hour it was I couldn't tell. A cloying yellowish haze of mist still hugged land and sea. There was still a creeping fitful wind, otherwise everything except for Thorlock's rasping breathing where he crouched by his fire, was silent. Ominously quiet, holding the prediction of storm, or thunder to come. I waited about the cave's entrance, huddled into my cape, and walking to and fro to keep warm. Occasionally a wild bird whirred past, with a gliding flap of wings; the waves broke gently as the tide gradually crept to the rocks. But I sensed their quick rhythmic motion was insidiously gathering strength for onslaught.

At moments, the man's form was visible about the craft. He moved furtively, doing something with ropes and sails. Knowing little about ships or sailing, I had no idea what. Sometimes he brushed his eyes and peered towards the shore. The frail wind freshened and the first signs of actual restlessness seemed to stir the scene to waking life, whipping the waters to breaking foam. With head bent forward from thin shoulders the man left his boat and cut to the cliff side, disappearing round the rocks that had taken Lalage from view. I knew then that my surmise had been correct. He was waiting for her to join him. Cautiously, keeping well hidden in the shadowed portion of rocks, I edged nearer the granite outcrop. The waves were stronger now, the air a blown quivering curtain of spray and thin fog — spindrift. Quite suddenly it was as though wild elemental fury seized the coast. And almost simultaneously Lalage appeared dragging a smaller form with her.

My heart missed a beat.

Maurice.

For seconds I couldn't move. The rising gale beat from the Atlantic driving the woman's cape and streaming black hair in a tossed wild mane of darkness behind her. The fog dissolved into rain. Yet still Lalage and the boy went on.

As the man pulled them on to the deck I put my hands round my mouth and screamed in an ineffectual effort to stop them. Either they didn't hear or preferred not to. Seconds later the boat was adrift, moving relentlessly out to sea.

"Maurice!" I cried, shouting with all the strength of my voice and lungs. "Lalage — wait, come back — "

There was no response. How could there be? All three of them now were at the mercy of their own wild bid to escape. And how could such a small craft endure, especially if the storm increased?

I almost followed a reckless impulse to get back to the house to raise an alarm. But the next moment I realised how futile the attempt would be. By the time I reached the Towers all three might be drowned.

It was then that I heard a frail high cry, and rushing to the water's edge saw hands and a human head momentarily tossed up and taken back again into the sea. Without thought I plunged ahead, thrusting outwards, with the weight of skirts and driving wind against me. I had always been a strong swimmer and it was as well.

A full two minutes must have passed before I managed to grasp the boy's form, and somehow, holding his head above the sucking swirl of waves, got him to shore.

I turned once, before glancing back to the boat.

There was nothing to be seen of it. Visibility by then was again almost nil, and I knew there was little hope for survival in the heavy yellow holocaust of sand, sea, and lashing sweep of rain.

The boy was still unconscious, when,

exhausted myself, and hardly able to crawl, I at length managed to drag him to Thorlock's cave.

The old man was putting logs on the fire. An oil-lamp flickered from a table casting a queer greenish-yellow glow across the hollowed caverns of his face, giving his straggly hair and beard the macabre impression of tangled weed.

"What y'got theer?" he shouted, lifting the stick with which he'd threatened me on the occasion of our first meeting.

My arms suddenly weakened. The boy slipped from them on to the damp floor, and with the breath torn from my lungs, I felt my knees crumple as I collapsed beside him. I didn't faint, and was conscious vaguely of the weapon being pushed away, and of the cracked old voice muttering, "A young un — critter of the sea, eh? Or from up theer? A chile. Weak as a young seal from the look on 'im."

He glared up at me, and I was amazed. Mingled with anger and resentment was also a queer kind of pity in the rheumy eyes. Somehow, with Thorlock's help I got Maurice to better quarters in the more sheltered interior.

Presently, warmed by hot broth and wrapped in dry sacking, I fell into an exhausted sleep. When I woke, the weather had cleared into uneasy twilight. Maurice, I found, was alive and still sleeping.

Further down the passage, nearer the entrance I saw the old man crouched over his treasures.

The greenish light touched them eerily, casting an unearthly radiance on the compelling, taunting beauty of the woman's face in its broken frame.

11

FOR a time Maurice lay inert and half conscious near the fire at the far end of the cave, while I did my best to revive him, with Thorlock's grudging assistance. I was surprised at the old man's comparatively calm acceptance of the situation. I'd expected violent reaction, but he proved of great help in providing a big blanket — liquor which could have been rum or brandy, and throwing numerous of his precious logs onto the flames. I eased the boy into the most comfortable position possible. As far as I could tell cuts and bruises and a wrenched arm seemed the only injuries, but I couldn't be sure.

Thorlock's ancient shrewd eyes glanced at us occasionally with a probing, almost condemnatory expression. I could feel fierce criticism of my attempts at nursing. Presently his claw-like hand gripped my shoulder, and after a series of muttered remarks he snorted:

293

"Have done. Get 'ee off. I'm more used to injured things than thee. Seals, birds, an' all broken critters — I've a knowledge o' such things. Fools women be — mostly."

And as he added the last word his eyes slid momentarily to the portrait up the passage. The flickering light lit it to life and a semblance of movement. I knew in these few seconds that any relationship they might once have had, had been strong — surviving the long years and onslaught of sand, wind, rain and countless storms.

I was jerked to the present again by his rasping voice saying, "Dedn' I say get off? I'll tend this one — " and as I got to my feet giving him the chance to examine the boy, he knelt down and proceeded with his examination, bony knotted fingers showing an expertise and gentleness I wouldn't have thought possible.

Suddenly he looked up. "There's a bone broke here, at th' ankle," he told me. "And he needs proper care. Yu'll have to get back to that theer place an' fetch help."

I stared irresolutely first at Maurice, then at the grey light outside — the sky that was once more cloudy with mist and thin rain blown on the whining wind. "Can't we carry him?" I questioned. "Couldn't we carry him together? You know the way. You must — " I broke off, startled by the rage contorting the ancient countenance.

"Must? *Must?*" he snarled. "This isn' *my* doin' — I didn't want no pryin' woman pokin' her nose in — nor young bodies flung up by the tide. Tisn' for me to seek nobody's help from that there hell's castle — "

"Hell's castle," I echoed. "What on earth do you mean?"

"I'm givin' no answers to such as you. You just git off an' get some sturdy body to take the lad away, or I won't answer for it — not for him either."

Maurice moved and gave a wince of pain.

"Where are they?" he asked. "What's happened?" He tried to sit up, but fell back again.

Thorlock put his hand on the wet forehead, wet not only from sea, but agony of movement.

"It's all right," the old man said, "s'long as you bide and wait a bit. She's goin' now, to git someone as knows you. Jus' rest, boy."

Maurice turned his gaze on me. He flinched slightly, and that hurt me. But his voice held a tinge of its old haughty ring when he said, "*You're* Uncle Ivan's woman."

If he'd not been hurt I'd have slapped him. "I'm your uncle's wife, Maurice. And if it hadn't been for me you'd have drowned."

"*Me?* The heir of Merlake?"

"Yes."

He started to laugh. "You tried to, didn't you? You *tried* to drown me? That's what you did, but you couldn't — because you weren't strong enough. You're a witch, but a silly witch. Look at you, in your torn dress, with your nasty dark hair and white face. There's seaweed round your neck — horrid slimy stuff — "

"Stop it," I said. "How *dare* you talk like that?"

His face suddenly crumpled, the malice

on his lips died, his head fell back, and he became a child again — a frustrated, exhausted child at the mercy of whatever strange circumstances had bred him, and his own thwarted nature.

I knew then I had to go alone to the Towers.

"I'll be off," I told the old man. "I'll get help somehow."

"But not Jed," Thorlock said. "I don't want that bullyin' jailer here. Split his head open I will, if he s'much as shows his ugly face."

And I knew he meant it.

"I'll take the tunnel," I assured him. "But I shall have to get what assistance I can. Jed and Marte are strong. If there's no one else — if I can't find my husband — we'll have to put up with them. Don't worry though — whoever comes I'll see you're well rewarded, Thorlock. There will be more treasures for you when I tell Mr Sterne what a friend you've been. And that's a promise. just look after Maurice until I get back — "

"Treasures?" A sly grin twisted the withered lips. "Like them? The ones you give me? The jools?"

"Just like them," I answered recklessly. "Finer perhaps, so they'll shine brighter than any stars — "

His gaze once more travelled to the painting.

"Aye," he said more quietly, "stars for her neck and her lovely white bosom, an' the sun an' moon for her silky hair — "

His voice had become thin, holding the soughing moan of wind rustling through reeds. Was it safe to leave Maurice in the care of such a 'whisht' creature? I wondered doubtfully. For a moment I paused; then doggedly resolving fear into the necessity of action, I hitched my cape up, by putting a belt round it — one I'd found lying in my cubbyhole — and with my drawers tucked more firmly inside the wet boots, set off on the hazardous journey to the house. Hazardous not because of the physical dangers — but through the frightening prospect of having to divulge the tragedy to Ivan.

Lalage and the man!

I shuddered when I recalled my last sight of their small craft being taken and swallowed in the cold grey vortex of swirling fog and sea, remembering those other defenceless men who had also perished in the former wreck. Was Merlake, as old Thorlock had described it, a place of hell? Some doomed spot of land forever condemned to loneliness and the fury of the elements? By the time I reached the opening to the tunnel I was half prepared to be sucked by unknown dark forces to some waiting dark pool of destruction and death. Only the memory of Maurice and a stubborn decision not to be completely obliterated, forced me on.

As I neared the steps, the light, from darkest dripping grey, turned to insidious green. On either side of me, leaves and black trailing strands of weed coursed the granite. Water dripped with a splashing sound to the stream below on my left. I kept close to the opposite wall, gripping any possible support to prevent a fall. More that once my fingers touched a squelchy living creature. I gave a muffled exclamation and drew back for an instant. It seemed that lurid malevolent faces peered through the darkness, and when

I reached the top something with wings swooped down, brushing my cheek. I was too terrified to cry out. A bat, I told myself. It must be a bat.

I looked up, and was thankful to find that, as I'd previously thought, the ceiling, though narrow, was formed as a kind of trap door. Only a very thin shred of light trickled through a crack. But from above I heard the distant thud of movement. Human movement, it must be. I reached up and pushed the ancient wet wood. At first it didn't move; then, as my hand slid along the surface, it suddenly gave, and I was able to climb through, into a kind of cellar. I stood blinking, unable to discern anything but mist, wet walls, and wan light spreading a feeble glow from an aperture facing me. I moved towards it, and stared. Beyond the barrier was another flight of steps, cutting steeply upwards. Climbing carefully, I negotiated the stairway, and when I reached the top found it opened on to a corridor — a landing. Instinctively I guessed this would eventually lead to Lalage's apartments.

My assessment was correct.

After numerous twists and turns and climbing unexpected odd stairs, I found myself in her small private kitchen. The smell of liquor was strong there; shadows from an oil-lamp, which was quickly flickering out, ran in a distorted fashion over the incredibly untidy interior. The lamp must have been left burning to guide her escape, aided by candles at fitful intervals of the route, which were mostly gutted now, with no life in them.

I sat on a stool for a brief period while I regained strength, breath, and sufficient composure to rouse the household.

How long it was before at last I located Ivan I don't know. By then I was too tired, too apprehensive, and suddenly too weak to say anything but, "Maurice is all right — he's hurt, but safe with Thorlock. Lalage and the man are gone. Drowned, they must be. Maurice, though. Maurice needs help — "

I was aware of consternation, of a pool of faces swimming round me — of Ivan's becoming Jed's, then his own again, and of his voice saying as though from a distance away, "Get her upstairs, see she's attended to, and given warmth and comfort, or you'll be answerable to me. Jed — fetch Marte — there's no time to lose — "

His voice faded then; I thought I heard him murmur, "Oh, Jade-Anna!" before the merciful darkness claimed me and I fainted.

12

I REGAINED consciousness to find myself lying on the bed, with Mrs Traille holding smelling salts to my nose, and something in a glass nearby to drink. Not very long could have passed since I collapsed, and I was instantly amazed to have been so weak. I sat up. She pressed me back saying, "You've got to rest. The Master's orders."

Not wishing for an argument, I didn't resist. Almost immediately a maid entered with a hot bottle for my feet, followed by another with a bowl of soup. The warmth was comforting, and it was only then that I discovered my wet clothes and boots had been removed and exchanged for nightwear and a woollen wrap. A fire burned in the grate.

When the girls had gone Mrs Traille still remained, like a jailer, at my bedside with her arms folded across her plump breast.

"Now you jus' get all that down you,"

303

she said sternly, alluding to the broth. "An' no arguing."

I didn't want to argue. I just wanted to be at peace and left alone, so I did what she said.

Presently, apparently satisfied, the housekeeper left.

I lay for some time, thinking back, getting facts coherent and wondering if Maurice was all right. Later Mrs Traille returned. I noticed that her floppy mob cap, ridiculously, had slipped slightly to one side.

"Hm," she remarked, "glad you're bein' reasonable and not making any foolhardy tries at gettin' away."

"You needn't worry about that," I answered. "I certainly shan't. Where's my husband? He's gone for Maurice, I suppose?"

"Correct," her lips closed with a snap. "Jed and Marte's with him, o' course. A fine to-do you landed yourself in."

"If I hadn't been there, Maurice would have been — would have gone with the others," I retorted sharply. "But of course you don't know anything about that, and probably no one will believe me here."

I sighed.

Her face softened slightly. "I wouldn't say that exactly. You've acted wild an' reckless over many things, but I wouldn't say you went in for lyin'. Trouble is, you doan' act properly to your husband."

"I — "

"You should keep your mouth shut more," she said, "an' realise he isn't the kind of man to defy and fight with." She paused, then added before leaving the room, "If you ask me, he thinks too much of you by half. Sometimes the strong ones are like that — keepin' their thoughts to themselves, and it would be better if you did the same."

I supposed there was some sense in what she'd said. If I'd been the amenable, gentle, obedient type of 'yes woman', content to be subservient always to her husband's whims and commands there'd have been no friction between us; I'd have fitted compliantly with the accepted general pattern of a successful Victorian ménage — been the kind of wife Aunt Clarissa was always adjuring me to be — although Evadne, I'm sure, fell far short of such an ideal. But then Evadne was clever; quite capable of going her own subtle way under a sly show of docility and acceptance of the conventions.

Evadne!

Bother, I thought, why must I so frequently find myself in such odious competition with my cousin? She was married — married to the man I'd once thought myself in love with, and was safe out of my own orbit. She didn't matter any more. Nobody really mattered but Ivan, and most of the time we were at loggerheads, disliking each other rather than loving.

The knowledge jerked me suddenly wide awake. I sat up, put a leg out of bed, and found to my consternation that I ached all over. Steadying myself, I stood up straight, stretched and rubbed one ankle until I could wiggle my toes without pain.

My body was still tired, but after a wash I felt better.

I dressed, wearing my most subdued gown of grey cloth trimmed with tiny black buttons and rows of black braid at the hem, then I sat before the mirror, brushed my hair, and caught it up from the back of my head to a secure dark russet mass, pinned by combs and a velvet ribbon.

By the time I was leaving the bedroom to go downstairs, I heard the tramp of feet from the hall. Glancing down, I saw Ivan and Jed carrying Maurice, who lay on some kind of plank. The boy's face was flushed, a little sullen-looking — but that, of course, could have been due to pain. I wanted to turn and run to the bedroom, but as the little entourage took the turn of the stairs, Ivan looked up and saw me. His face was hard. I stood with my back erect, pressed against the wall until they'd passed, then I went down to the parlour.

There seemed nothing to do but wait. Wait until Ivan condescended to speak to me and perhaps enquire how I was.

It wasn't long. I was standing at the marble mantelpiece staring into the fire, my back to the door, when he came in. There was a pause until he said, "Jade-Anna?"

I turned, apparently languidly, to look at him. Two things momentarily shocked me — the extreme tired look of his face, and how very handsome he was. If I'd obeyed my instinct I'd have rushed to him, flung myself against his chest, cried with relief, and begged him to love me.

But pride held me back. I lifted my chin and said coldly, "Yes? Can I help you? Do anything? How is Maurice? You blame *me*, I expect, for the accident — ?"

My tones were bitter, and the bitterness I felt didn't subside when he said, "What nonsense. All I blame you for is for getting mixed up in such a tragedy. Your pigheadedness — and having no thought for me — "

"*You?*"

"Why not? You're my wife. Suppose — " He took one step towards me, stopped, shrugged his shoulders and continued, as I purposefully drew away from him, "Still, never mind that. I suppose I should be grateful to you on Maurice's account. Yes, he's all right, or will be. I've sent for the doctor. Marte's gone. A good thing the weather's clearing. And the wind's down. It won't be too bad for a crossing."

"And the others?"

"You know as much about them as

me." He spoke curtly. "We may have to wait for a tide or two until their bodies are retrieved — if at all."

I shuddered.

He must have noticed.

"Don't you think you should have stayed in bed?" he asked, still in cool, remote tones. "You're pale. You must be shaken."

"I shall recover," I told him. "In fact, I'm getting used to unpleasant things happening at Merlake. Wrecks and dead bodies seem to be part of the routine here. As for bed — I had more than enough of it before I had to climb out of the window for a little fresh air."

His colour deepened.

"I'm sorry about that. If you'd been more — "

"Amenable and docile, yes I understand perfectly, Ivan. You demonstrated your power and my own subservient position very adequately. But if you ever touch me again — ever raise a hand to me, our marriage will be over — I swear it. You'll be sorry then, because I'll make your name a scandal through all your precious social and business circles."

He smiled grimly. "And you will be a laughing stock, my love. Imagine how your Aunt Clarissa's smug little circles will titter when they hear that rich Mr Ivan Sterne had to put his rebellious wife — her niece — over his knee, to teach her sense — " The grimness on his lips quivered into faint amusement.

Before I could do anything about it, a hand touched my waist, and I knew if I wished, I could end the stupid argument there and then. But the demon of pride in me forced me to jerk myself away, saying contemptuously, "Leave me alone, Ivan. This isn't a game."

"And do you think I don't know it?" He strode angrily to the door, where he paused, turned, and said with his jaw thrust doggedly forward, grey eyes blazing, "You're quite right. Glad you reminded me. At the moment there are far more important and tragic matters to attend to than the wilful tempers and megrims of a selfish woman. Don't worry, Jade-Anna. I've no intention of touching you or coming near you in any foreseeable future. The less I see of you the better. Later, if you wish, you can return to the mainland at any time. Just let me know, and we'll talk about it."

The door snapped to. I stood staring at it for minutes, then I went to the sofa and lay back, with the tears flooding my eyes.

I had only just dried them on a shred of handkerchief when there was a knock, and a maid appeared.

"Mrs Traille told me to ask if there was anything you wanted, ma'am," she said, "Tea or coffee?"

"No, thank you," I told her. "Nothing."

She gave a little bob and left.

Nothing? I thought, what a lie, when I wanted so much — oh, so much. Most of all the love and comfort of Ivan's arms round me, the warmth of his lips on mine, and pressure of his body close. If only he understood. If only we both could.

But it seemed this would never be.

And I wondered, as I had wondered before, how I was going to endure such an impossible situation.

★ ★ ★

Days passed. Officials came from the mainland to investigate the accident. They stayed at the house for three days. Ivan ate with the men; at other times he accompanied them on an inspection of the island or else was closeted in his study or library discussing, I supposed, the tragic business of Lalage Dupont's reckless attempts to escape from the Towers, and probably mysterious business matters of which I knew nothing. Except for a brief introduction I was allowed no contact, although Siri, at Ivan's command, was twice interviewed. I saw her come from the library one morning looking sullen, a little frightened. But when she saw me hesitating by the drawing room door an odd secretive look of triumph flooded her luminous Eastern eyes.

I was irritated, jealous, curious, and emotionally hurt at the same time, that she should be brought into the events when I was now completely left out. After all, if it had not been for me Maurice, Ivan's heir, might be dead. I considered I had at least earned a right to certain confidences from him.

In a fit of depression I wrote to Aunt Clarissa.

Dear Aunt,
I do congratulate Evadne, and of course you and Uncle, for your news about my cousin's 'interesting condition' — isn't that how pregnancy is termed in polite society? How lovely for you to think of baby footsteps pattering about the stately halls and rooms of Mounterrith! And what a lot you must have to talk about and plan. I wish I had the chance to spend a few days with you [strangely this was true]. Everything at Merlake revolves round the Sterne Shipping Line, Ivan's newest venture, or rescuing bodies from the sea. No, I'm not joking. Living on this island is awful sometimes. We've had two wrecks — one a big one, and one just a small boat in which Miss Dupont, some connection of Ivan's I believe, the aunt of his ward, was drowned. At least that is the conclusion so far, as no one has seen her since it happened. You may have read about it in the papers, or perhaps the news hasn't got out

yet. I suppose Ivan would be annoyed at me letting you know. Maybe you think I should keep my mouth shut and be the docile dumb little wife you're always telling me to be. Well, I think even *you* might be shocked at the way I'm treated. Oh, I have everything I want materially, providing my husband thinks it necessary. He's polite, generally, and doesn't beat me — *actually*. But his business deals are incessant, Maurice, his ward, dislikes me, the housekeeper bullies me, and I'm only allowed to walk around certain parts of the grounds. There is no one to talk to. Did you know *anything*, dear Aunt, of what the circumstances might be? Did my marriage to Ivan appeal to you as a rigorous form of discipline that might at last bring me to heel? . . .

I broke off there, suddenly ashamed of betraying my frustration to a woman I so disliked, feeling as well a sense of degrading disloyalty to Ivan.

I ripped the letter into two, then tore the halves into numerous small pieces and threw them into the waste-paper basket.

Ivan entered the room as the last few bits fluttered down.

The beginning of his devastatingly lopsided smile touched his lips.

"A letter?" he queried, "or are you turning into a thwarted poetess?"

Of course, I should have treated his question with humour. But I didn't.

"*Poetess!*" I echoed scathingly. "Don't be ridiculous. What is there poetical here to inspire *anyone*? — especially someone without the gift."

"Oh, I wouldn't be too sure of that. *You* never seem to lack the initiative for bringing drama to any situation — "

I was about to reply in softer vein — somehow bring the conversation to a more genuine personal level, when Mrs Traille rushed into the room unexpectedly.

"Jed and Marte are carrying something — " she gasped out. "Something that looks like a body — "

Ivan turned away from me quickly and followed her through the door and down the hall.

Her assertion was correct. The battered drowned corpse of the tall seaman I had last seen with Lalage aboard the doomed small boat had been washed up on the southern coast of Merlake. Of Miss Dupont there was no sign, nor, as the future was to prove, ever would be.

Later a shred of material and a few unidentifiable remains appeared from time to time, but by then the case was closed, and Lalage written off as just one more unfortunate victim of the sea.

★ ★ ★

During the immediate days following the macabre event, an atmosphere of doom hung over the Towers. I was conscious of a sinister attitude of condemnation that bred a feeling of guilt in me, although common sense told me it was quite undeserved. The servants even were quieter and more subdued than usual, and I fancied a stony glance in Mrs Traille's eyes whenever she met or talked with me. Ivan himself seemed remote, hard and withdrawn. Maurice was daily getting better, but demanded attention with a petulant air of authority that had nothing childlike about it. I found myself disliking him more and more, and for that very reason tried to please him by submitting quietly to his whims, though aware of a sly jubilant sense of triumph about him that was both distasteful and disconcerting.

Christmas came and went almost unnoticed, except for the traditional display of gift-giving, and the usual seasonal fare at mealtimes. And all the time it was a matter of waiting. Waiting for what? I didn't know. But I could feel something in my bones, tense muscles, and repressed emotional conflict that told me a crisis was approaching. Life could not go on for ever under such a cloud. Intimacy between my husband and myself had flagged to a low ebb, and when it occurred held no warmth or mutual passion. It was as though I had become a mere chattel, a need to him that at rare periods had to be satisfied in as cool and clinical a manner as possible.

On such occasions, I had to force myself not to hate him, arguing inwardly that my lot in the marriage bed was that of countless Victorian wives who accepted intercourse as a duty to be born stoically. Not that I ever really disliked contact with Ivan's body — but the manner of his possessing me — yes! this I fiercely detested and deplored. Curiously our easiest moments had become brief conversational episodes when he temporarily appeared to forget our estrangement, and discussed minor affairs of his business ambitions. He referred once or twice to the Chinese war, and his private determination that eventually all trading of opium on the sea should be stamped out and cleared up for ever.

"Of course, that's a pretty big statement to make," he concluded. "Even the smuggling covers a large network, and it will go on for some time to come. But not," his lips tightened, "round Cornish shores. I'll see to that. Or the Sterne line will."

I was stupid in my next remark, which burst from me in a quick rush of resentment.

"Of course. The Sterne Line! — it's

god to you, isn't it, Ivan? All you care about?"

He threw me a furious glance.

"Jealous, Jade-Anna? I should have known. All women are alike. If a man dedicates himself to something that will aid humanity, they become mean and resentful. How petty of you."

He walked sharply away from me. Before the door closed behind him I said loudly and clearly, "I'm not the only jealous one. What about you? Just think back, Ivan."

I didn't know whether he'd heard or not, but I think he did.

That same day I went to the conservatory to cut flowers. The holly and Christmas decorations had withered and I was anxious to have the dusty stuff cleared away. I was about to leave when Claude Lang entered through the garden door. He smiled ironically, saying, "I don't blame you for wanting to freshen things up. You've not been very clever though, have you, Mrs Sterne?"

"What do you mean?"

"By now I would have thought you could have conducted your husband into

319

a gentler mood. He seems more than ever put out this afternoon."

I shrugged, and looked away. "Oh? I don't waste my time studying moods, Mr Lang."

"It might prove worthwhile, and bring you a passport to the mainland."

"I could say the same for you," I answered tartly.

"Ah, but *I* wouldn't get it."

"How do you know?" His words had aroused my curiosity; I glanced at him very directly, noting the sardonic twist of his mouth, the brilliance of his dark eyes which at the same time held a glazed expression. The pupils were very small, like those of an angry cat. Then I heard him saying in deliberate level tones, "Because, my dear, I'm a prisoner. We all are, didn't you know?" He laughed softly, and walked to the inner door, adding, "Except you. You *needn't* have been. But possibly you've left things too late now."

When he'd gone I didn't move for some moments, just stood rigidly looking at the blank door, holding an exotic white blossom in my hand.

The scent and steamy heat seemed to gather an overpowering odour. Not realising what I was doing, I laid the flower on a seat forgetfully, and went through the house, up the stairs to the bedroom. Although a fire was burning in the grate the temperature felt chilly after the conservatory's stuffy warmth. I pulled a wrap round me and went to the wardrobe, wondering what gown I would change into for dinner.

Not the rose pink or lilac, I decided, but something lacy and black, something the might increase my dignity, and emphasise the pallor of my skin, which during recent winter months had lost all trace of summer's glow.

When I went downstairs later I trod majestically as possible, keeping my head high. I'd dressed my hair simply coiled on top, with an artificial gardenia pinned against its darkness.

I was taken aback to find Miss Augusta already seated at the end of the dining room table facing Ivan's chair at the other. She looked more than ever like a flamboyant ancient macaw in her gaudy finery and jewels.

"Hullo, gel," she croaked, "Glad to see you know your place. Black and white, eh? Very proper. Get me the brandy, gel, and be quick about it. Then you can sit — next to me for *once*," she grinned. "All good servants should have a treat sometimes."

Disliking her intensely I did as I was told, wishing after all that I'd chosen to wear my brightest of all gowns.

Crimson velvet.

13

FOLLOWING a stormy January, February turned mild for the time of the year, giving indication of an early spring. Pink thrift and small wild flowers of the island peeped from the short turf, and between rocks. Celandines patterned the ditches, their star shapes glowing gold where violets would soon bloom. The white bloom of blackthorn blossomed foam-like against paper-pale skies veiled by fragile mist.

Young wild animals pushed their noses to the light, and at dawn there was the muted crying and soft trill of birds from their nests.

Everything seemed to be waking up. There was promise everywhere except in my own heart. Perhaps if it had not been for Maurice I might have softened, and my relationship with Ivan become warmer — more reconciled. But Maurice and Siri between them formed a barrier I'd no intention of bridging. Siri, because Ivan was so frequently closeted alone with her — 'purely on business grounds,' he averred, in an attempt to 'obtain certain important information' — an explanation I found hard to accept; Maurice on account of his many devious and unpleasant tricks on me that I supposed I should have reported but didn't.

Why? Because Ivan most probably would not have believed me, and Claude Lang would just have smiled in his malevolent superior way. Possibly I imagined the malevolence. My nerves were certainly keyed up, and I knew I could not go on living forever in such unhappy circumstances.

I was beginning to have giddy spells, and feel at times unwell; my reflection in the mirror showed it, and even Ivan noticed.

"You don't look too bright these days," he commented one day. "Is anything the matter?"

"Nothing you would understand," I answered. "I should have liked a change, that's all. But I suppose you've no idea yet when we are likely to have that protracted holiday?"

He frowned, not with anger, but as though worried — pondering.

"I'm sorry about that, Jade-Anna," he told me. "I really mean it. And don't think I've forgotten. It's just — "

"That the Sterne Line demands your attention. Yes, naturally," I interrupted. I managed to give a brittle smile. "Have no fear, I'm getting used to my position. After all, I shouldn't have expected more."

There was an uncomfortable silence between us until he said thoughtfully, "Would a visit to Mounterrith help? Have you thought of that? You could go for a week — a fortnight — longer if you wished. I'm sure your aunt would show you far more consideration now than she did when you were her — "

"Poor dependant?"

"Exactly. As my wife she'd be proud to show you off."

"Well," I agreed, "it's an idea."

Strangely enough, I'd had a letter that same week from Aunt Clarissa asking if I would care to spend a short time at my old home.

Home, I'd thought scornfully, remembering the indignities and injustices I'd had to suffer in the past, playing second fiddle always to my beautiful cousin. But then my uncle *had* been kind. It would be nice to see him, and what Ivan had said about his wife was quite true, she was such a complete snob I'd probably be welcomed with open arms.

I took the letter from a drawer and re-read it:

I have Evadne here at the moment. Poor child, she is fatigued, and beginning to wilt under the strain of her condition. Christopher spoils her completely, of course — she has *everything* she wants in her own house. But naturally the poor young man can't be with her every moment of the time, as I've done my best to impress on her. Actually, I think he *could* tear himself away from his horses and social circle a little more at such a highly emotional time for his young wife. But men will be men, which all we women have to accept eventually. Your company here would be appreciated, if only for a week. It would cheer your cousin up immensely.

Think about it, my dear.

Your ever affectionate, Aunt Clarissa.

I was mildly amused, feeling very little pity for Evadne. Probably she was being very selfish and perfectly beastly to Christopher now she couldn't make the stir in society she once had. Her figure alone would distress her — she had always been selfishly vain, and I could imagine her throwing her tantrums about at Mounterrith. If I'd liked Aunt Clarissa more I could have been sorry for her. As it was I felt mild triumph at being wanted. Not that I considered seriously spending a whole week at Mounterrith. Two days perhaps, or three, would be the maximum. After that — a wild possibility occurred to me quite suddenly — I could make some pretext of having to visit friends — of Ivan's perhaps — in London, before returning to Merlake, and take off for the city where I could book in at some hotel and have a pleasurable taste of excitement and lead my own life for a bit. I should leave no address, and if Ivan contacted my aunt, or called suddenly to haul me back, she would be quite unable to enlighten him.

He would be angry. Worried to a certain extent, I hoped, but it would pay him out. I hadn't realised until that moment how deeply hurt I still was by his treatment of me, how desperately eager to establish myself as an important factor — *the* most important in his life.

Once the idea had taken root, I determined to make plans accordingly, and when I told Ivan he appeared a little surprised at first, then grudgingly agreeable. Obviously he'd not really anticipated that I'd take up the Mounterrith suggestion.

"And I may wish to do a little shopping somewhere," I told him, when everything was settled, "so could you let me have sufficient money not to appear mean or impoverished, Ivan? After all — I haven't had the — the holiday you promised yet, and I wouldn't want Aunt Clarissa to think you didn't give me a proper allowance."

"Naturally," he answered, coldly polite. "I'll endow you as befitting my position

— and yours — so that you can flaunt your airs and purse most ostentatiously in your smug family's faces."

I winced inwardly, but managed to say quietly, "Thank you, Ivan."

The visit was arranged for early March. Three days before I left something happened that made me more relieved than ever that I was going.

In my bed one afternoon, when I'd gone to put my feet up for a short rest — I'd been feeling inexplicably tired — something cold and clammy leaped out at me from between the eiderdown and spread. I gave a short scream as it touched my neck, and when I glanced towards the foot of the bed saw a frog squatting there, its eyes bulging from its squat head.

As I went towards it, it hopped to the carpet, then to the dressing table. I didn't mind frogs in the normal way; in fact I rather liked them in their proper setting by a pool or stream. But how on earth had it got under my quilt?

With a rush of anger the answer came. Maurice!

I ran to the door, opened it, and

there he was — waiting expectantly, half hiding by a recess in the landing. I ran as quickly as I could towards him and just managed to catch him by the back of his collar before he could make his escape down a side corridor.

Still holding him I forced his eyes to meet mine. The amusement on his face quickly turned to fear when he saw the expression on my face.

"How *dare* you?" I cried, shaking him with more force than I'd meant. "You wicked boy. Why did you do it? That frog? What do you mean by it? It was a shock. Do you realise — " I didn't finish what I was saying, because for a few seconds an attack of faintness threatened. I felt briefly nauseated, almost sick. My grip on his shoulder slackened. I leaned against the wall for a second, and when I looked at him again Ivan, having overheard the scene, was coming towards us from the main landing.

"What's going on?" he demanded in astonished tones. "Anna — " he forgot the Jade " — why the shouting? What has the boy done now? Maurice?"

Maurice hung his head, and then

suddenly, embarrassingly, began to cry.

"I didn't mean it," he gulped. "It was just fun. I thought — I thought — "

"Well? What did you think? And what did you do?"

"He put a frog in our bed," I told Ivan coldly. "He was trying to frighten me. He's always doing something to upset me. If you were more concerned with household affairs and gave more time to him perhaps it wouldn't happen."

Ivan's lips hardened. But his voice wasn't unkind when he turned to the boy.

"Is this true, Maurice? *Did* you try to frighten my — your aunt — ?"

"She's not my aunt. She's a — a sneak. A prying spy. That's what Mr Lang says. Everything's been nasty since she came. You never come now to the schoolroom or ask me things; we never go out together. Once you used to take me down to the pier to see the boats. Now you never do — I hate her."

Ivan's voice was controlled when he said, "Listen to me. I've never whacked you myself, have I? Perhaps I should have done; obviously your education's being neglected. I shall have to have a word with your tutor. Why you're making such a nuisance of yourself, I don't know. Possibly — " he paused before adding, "I haven't shown the care I did when you were smaller. But that's no excuse for rudeness and playing tricks to frighten people. Remember this though, you *are* my charge, and still my heir. I'm fond of you, Maurice. The shock you had recently when your Aunt Lalage drowned has obviously been greater than I thought. I'm sorry about that. But you must remember to consider others. I'm not going to punish you this time; go to your room. I'll see you later; first of all, though, apologise to my wife."

I noticed he didn't refer to me a second time as the boy's aunt.

Maurice bowed his head. His face was very red.

"I'm sorry," he muttered. Then he glanced up at me with wide scared eyes. "I didn't know you hated frogs so, I *didn't*."

I shook my head. "I don't. I just don't want them popping in and out of the sheets."

The incident ended with Maurice walking away towards his bedroom, leaving Ivan and me alone together. His whole stance was dejected, as though he'd been whipped. I had a ridiculous guilty feeling that I might have made much of nothing. Obviously Ivan thought so.

"You haven't much understanding of children, have you?" he said coldly.

"Circumstances here aren't easy for understanding," I answered coolly.

"Oh well — doubtless your Aunt Clarissa will provide a more suitable environment for your present mood," he remarked. "I sincerely hope so. You've shown more than a hint of shrewishness recently, which on top of other things doesn't make for peace in the house."

He didn't soften, or attempt to console me. As he walked away I had a wild desire to run after him and fling myself — somehow — into his arms. But I curbed it.

The feeling of nausea induced by Maurice's unpleasant trick returned. I had just sufficient time to get to the closet before I was violently sick.

I guessed then that what I'd suspected

for the last week, but not admitted even to myself, was probably true. I was going to have a child — a child conceived in moments of intercourse that had held no love. It had been so long since that one precious word had been passed between us, or tenderness shown by the man I'd married.

I wanted him still, but no longer held any illusions about him loving me. Perhaps if I'd been cleverer, or tried more, curbed my wild temper and pretended to be the gentle subservient woman content to be forever dominated by his possessive male presence, we might have formed a warmer relationship. As matters were I knew that the sooner I got away the better — even, ironically — to Aunt Clarissa briefly, whom I'd once so detested.

On the evening before I left, I walked to the bottom of the gardens and stood overlooking the pier to the west. Larger vessels than usual appeared to be anchored near the quay. Everything was very quiet softly hazed under approaching twilight. For a short interlude all sinister speculations faded from my mind. The coast, now in its muted shades of soft greens, pale gold, and pink thrift merging to dusky violet where the granite rocks towered above the fading sea, produced a haunting image of the island that made me loth, for a few moments to go away. Would I ever return? I wondered — or would the parting mean that I was surrendering my marriage, and leaving Merlake for ever? Perhaps I was being stupid — doing something that I'd regret for the rest of my life, in leaving Ivan so completely at the mercies of women like Siri, the dominating Mrs Traille and Lalage — I suddenly remembered that Lalage was dead, and shivered. But supposing she wasn't? Supposing she appeared suddenly in my absence like some wanton spirit to claim her position in the house, as Maurice's mother? But then she'd probably been lying when she told me that. The Towers was a mass of lies! The next moment all regret had faded. I was right to escape when I could. There was no place at present for me at Merlake.

I felt a snuffling at my hand, and looking down saw Ivan's dog, a large spaniel, gazing up at me from mournful eyes. His tail was wagging though, and with a rush of affection I bent down and patted him. His tongue licked my fingers. Stupidly I wanted to cry.

"What do *you* want, Leo?" I said, stroking his silky ears and fine hair above the damp nose. He gave a little bark and ran encouragingly to a stick lying near. I picked it up and threw it. Almost simultaneously I heard a man's voice saying, "He'll miss you."

I glanced up. Impeccably clad as usual, Claude Lang stood a yard or two away. I jumped up quickly, brushing my hands on my skirt. Why did he walk so soundlessly, I wondered. It was as though everyone about the Towers was determined to startle me. My expression must have betrayed me.

"Sorry if I gave you a shock," he apologised casually. "I didn't expect to find you here. I thought your wandering days at Merlake were over."

I gave a light artificial laugh. "I'd hardly call a walk in the gardens wandering."

"No. Of course not; but your heart maybe?"

His wicked Pan's smile had a taunting look.

I lifted my skirts and turned away. "You're being far too personal, Mr Lang."

He didn't reply. As I walked to the house I could feel his eyes following me, boring at my back. As I cut round to the front door a beam of light — a lamp's presumably, filtered down from a window somewhere above.

I glanced up.

Under the fading sky which was now dimmed by the silvered grey of a creeping evening mist, I saw a blurred face silhouetted. No features were visible, but with an absurd lurch of the heart I realised I had been watched, probably all the time, and that the elongated narrow countenance and ridiculously piled high hair could belong to no other but Miss Augusta.

With the dog trotting at my heels I hurried into the hall, and had only taken a few steps when Mrs Traille appeared.

"That dog isn't allowed in the front here," she said disapprovingly, "as you should know by now, Miss Ellan."

"Mrs Sterne," I corrected her quickly, "and please remember it in future."

Without giving her another glance I hurried by and went upstairs. Until I turned the bend in the landing no sound came of footsteps receding along the hall, and I knew she was angry — could imagine the hostile set of her jaw and darting glare of her small fiery eyes.

It was only when I'd closed the bedroom door that I noticed Leo had followed me.

"My goodness!" I said, "you'll be in trouble." I took him by the collar and very gently edged him out.

Funny, I thought idly, as I went to the dressing table, the only true friend I appeared to have at Merlake was a dog.

A moment later there was a knock on the door and a maid appeared carrying a lamp. Candles were already flickering, and the glow, combined with firelight, threw mellow moving shadows round the walls. The ruby and diamond ring given to me by Ivan on our wedding day shone brilliantly — more bright by far than the myriad sparkle from crystal chandeliers.

I remembered guiltily how easily I'd disposed of the rest of my jewellery to old Thorlock. Ivan so far appeared not to have missed seeing me wear it, which was as well. When I returned, if ever, to the Towers, he'd probably have discovered it, and the first awful reaction would be over.

If!

Such a small word, but so vastly important, under the circumstances. Anyway there was no point in making wild conjectures, and presently I turned my attention to the practical business of what clothes I would need to pack for my visit to Mounterrith and afterwards.

Ivan made love to me that night. Beneath his casual air I sensed something else which I judged to be mere male possessiveness tinged with jealousy. I did not respond with warmth — I daren't, for fear of changing my mind. The next morning there was veiled chilly politeness between us when he saw me off from the pier, not in the small lugger manned by Jed and Marte, but in one of his larger ships with a special crew brought in earlier for the purpose.

A short journey indeed. Yet as we set sail, it seemed I might be travelling to the other side of the world, I felt suddenly so desolate and alone.

14

I FOUND Mounterrith itself just the same, although the atmosphere was more highly charged, due to a certain tenseness about Aunt Clarissa which I sensed covered inward irritation caused by Evadne who was in a sullen mood when I arrived.

My uncle was obviously pleased to see me. "It will be comforting having you about for a bit, my dear," he confided when I came downstairs later after a wash and changing my gown. "Things aren't too easy at the moment — because of your cousin's condition, that's what her mother says. I suppose it's understandable at such a — " he coughed " — difficult time, although cows, and dogs and cats, and all the rest of the animal kingdom seem to get through without such a deal of sighing and complaining; still — " he gave one of his rare smiles, and a wink that reminded me suddenly of my father

" — we mustn't relegate Evadne to such a low-down species, must we? Your aunt would swoon or have a fit. Such a fusser she is — "

He broke off there, when Aunt Clarissa sailed into the drawing room, with a bright amiable false smile on her face for me. Ivan had been right, I realised, when he'd prophesied I should be treated very differently as Mrs Ivan Sterne, than I had been as the penniless daughter of Sir Humphrey Ellan's scapegoat brother.

"How very pleasant to have you here, Anna, my dear," she gushed, while I thought how stupid she was to put on such a show, thinking I'd be such an idiot not to see through it.

She gave me a second peck of a kiss on both cheeks, and told me to sit down and make myself comfortable, announcing that she would ring for coffee immediately.

I protested, saying I felt rather sick, which was quite true. Her small bright eyes which had been darting appraisingly over my appearance since I entered, held a knowing look when she questioned evasively, "You're not — surely you and

Evadne aren't both — ?"

"I feel mildly sea-sick," I interrupted quickly. "I'm not fond of sailing."

"Ah — I see." Whether she was disappointed or not I couldn't tell. What I *did* notice was her envious, almost jealous gaze as it fell upon my dress which was of gold velvet, tightly waisted — my figure was still perfect, thank heaven — with a full skirt, and a pointed lace collar tied at the neck by a brown velvet ribbon. My dark russet hair, parted in the middle, was looped over the ears, and drawn into a knot at the back of my head, held by a shred of lace.

Aunt Clarissa, who had put on weight since we'd last met, was tightly corseted into grey satin and wore an ornate apology for a small frilly cap with trailing ribbons falling behind her plump shoulders; the lacy headgear was girlish in design, but on her only emphasised her matronly stature.

As we spoke together she fanned herself constantly. Obviously the stays hurt.

We had five minutes' forced conversation during which my aunt's first effusion

gradually weakened into mild disgruntle-
ment because she could glean little gossip
from me.

"You seem to live very quietly on the
island," she remarked. "Surely *something*
happens? — Don't you receive company?
Are there no parties?"

"Oh, yes," I told her ambiguously,
"business affairs. Ivan's."

"Men only?"

"Mostly." I hesitated before adding
wickedly, "Sometimes, of course, a few
bodies get washed up."

She appeared horrified.

"Bodies? What do you mean?"

"I'm sure I referred in my letters to the
wrecks that happen round the coast."

"You said something once, I believe."
Her voice was chilly, disapproving — the
old 'Aunt Clarissa voice' that I was well
used to, and in the past had foreboded
a lecture, or worse. "But it sounded so
melodramatic. I rather thought — "

What she thought I was spared hearing.
Instead our tête-à-tête was interrupted
by the entrance of Evadne. Except for
a slight thickening round her waist her
figure hadn't altered very perceptibly

344

— it wouldn't of course, I thought — Evadne would probably be able to sail gracefully through her pregnancy without much disfigurement. She was wearing frilly blue — a shade which always emphasised her porcelain features and complexion — but her beautiful mouth had a petulant droop; there was a faint frown between her eyes.

She smiled wanly. "Oh, hello, Anna. You look chic, and so healthy — robust almost." I didn't know whether the last aberration was meant to be a compliment or the reverse. "Oh, I'm so exhausted," she continued in the next breath, "and so utterly, utterly bored."

"Never mind," I said brightly, "when it's all over think how proud you'll be."

"Proud? Why, for God's sake — ?"

"Evadne," Aunt Clarissa said warningly, "*please*. Now Anna's here you two girls will be able to put your heads together and have a nice talk. I'm sure you'll want to know all about Merlake and — "

"Why should I?"

"Well, you can tell her about your life with Christopher. How he spoils you — " she glanced at me briefly " — he does, you know, Anna, she has everything she wants. He's simply devoted to her. Three residences — imagine it! including apartments in London — "

"Oh, mama, not all *that* again. I'm so sick of hearing about the wonderful apartments, my stately home; the devoted husband, and my life in society. And I don't want baby-talk either. Growing fat and ugly, and not being able to do this and that, or go to dances and stop up late. It's horrid. *I* didn't want a baby — "

"Evadne!" Oh, the outrage in Aunt Clarissa's voice!

"Well, I didn't. Not so soon anyway. It's all right for men; they slip out of all the discomfort. And Chris is so *complacent*. A pat on the head, a brotherly kiss, and 'You go and stay with your mama for a time, darling. You'll have peace there and quiet. And a little rest from me, while I get through some business in town.' Business? What business? Entertaining in our London apartments?"

For a moment I felt a fellow feeling, even a little sympathy for my cousin.

"Perhaps a certain amount," I agreed. "Men like Chris and — and Ivan who are involved with companies — and I suppose your husband's no different from mine in that way — generally have club friends they like to see, and then there's the Stock Exchange, and shares — oh, all the stuff we'd both find a terrible chore."

There was a short silence that ended suddenly by Evadne asking more quietly, "Are you happy with Ivan Sterne?"

My throat went dry, and at that point Aunt Clarissa excused herself by saying, "I shall leave you two to your intimate chitchat, I have domestic matters to attend to."

When she'd gone, Evadne quizzed, "Well?"

"Well what?"

"Ivan. Are you two happy?"

"Sometimes," I replied.

"Oh! I *see*." Evadne's voice was knowing, holding a hint of triumph. The petulance and boredom appeared to have vanished as though by magic. "Not *all* the time."

"Who is?"

"I don't see why not; everything was all right with me until this wretched pregnancy business and I really *don't* want the baby, you know, Anna."

"Then perhaps you shouldn't have got married."

"What a thing to say. Why, just because two people fall in love and marry, should a girl be expected to produce an heir on the first opportunity? It's not fair. I can quite understand — " her colour deepened slightly, " — why some girls go to one of those — you know — those women who do things to get rid of it, of the baby, I mean."

Although I agreed with Evadne about producing an heir and the average wife's compliant role in submitting to a husband's demands, my cousin's reference to such an obnoxious method of evading child-birth shocked me.

"You shouldn't think of such a thing," I said, sounding I suppose rather like a schoolmistress. "It's dangerous anyway. *Terribly* dangerous. And if you *love* Chris, really love him, you wouldn't dream of it."

Her glance was speculative, curious

when she remarked, "Love? I'm not romantic like you, Anna. I'm not sure that I *do* believe in it — the romantic stuff. What is it? What's the point of it if it lands a girl with all this — this *burden*?" She patted her stomach and sighed again. "Oh well, I suppose I'll have to make the best of it. It wouldn't have been that way, would it, if *you'd* married Christopher? You'd have revelled in it."

"Don't talk like that," I said shortly.

She shrugged. "I'm sorry. I was a bit mean, I suppose — I knew how you two felt, and it gave me a sort of — of triumph, excitement, grabbing him from under your nose. Oh, but it wasn't only that, of course — he, the whole thing, did wildly thrill me — "

The light manner of her confession, her admittance of pleasure in deliberately stealing the young man I'd once thought so much of, destroyed any brief sympathy I'd felt for her.

"Let's leave the past alone," I said shortly, "shall we? And it's no use brooding, Evadne. It won't be long before you'll delight in showing off your son and heir to your aristocratic friends."

"I hope it's not a boy."

"Why?"

"Because if it is Chris will give all his attention to it, I shall be just its mother — the dutiful spouse who bred it."

"How crude."

She shrugged. "But true. Do you know, Anna, I don't believe Christopher Ferris thinks a damn about me — really. All that matters is to show me off at convenient times to charm his friends, and to use later when he feels like it — " she rolled her eyes heavenwards " — to produce other little Ferrises in his own image. Well — " again the characteristic shrug, " — I'll have to do something about it. Take a lover perhaps — " Her eyes slid to my face slyly, waiting for a reaction.

I gave none outwardly. Whether she meant it or not I neither knew nor cared. Evadne at heart was the same Evadne, out to tease and take the stage, impressing whatever audience was at hand — even if it happened to be merely her cousin.

The conversation after that brief interchange, switched to frivolous matters of clothes or mundane topics concerning the district that really didn't interest either of us. Soon Evadne sighed, drew out her smelling salts, sniffed, and said she really had to have a rest and put her feet up.

When she'd gone I also went upstairs, feeling curiously drained and exhausted.

The few days I spent at Mounterrith gradually began to revert to their old pattern. Evadne claimed all the concern and interest, while signs of resentment to me frequently tinged my aunt's manner. She did her best to control it, but I knew.

"You haven't changed very much after all, Anna," she said acidly once. This was when I'd told her I was leaving the following day. "Why you have to be so restless I don't know. You said nothing about going to London in your last letter to me, neither did Ivan."

"Oh, we didn't know then," I answered coolly, "it all came up very suddenly. We have friends there. Ivan's, of course. And I have shopping to do."

Immediate suspicion flooded her eyes. "It seems extremely curious to me."

"Why?"

"That nothing was said. And that you should be travelling presumably, without a chaperone. Or have I been kept in the dark there, as well? Has your husband arranged for someone to escort you from here?"

"Escort me, Aunt Clarissa? I have two legs and am quite capable of taking care of myself. Part of my journey will be by coach, you know — the rest by train. There are porters for trains you know. And it's no longer necessarily shocking for a married woman to travel privately, providing she holds a first class ticket and the means to pay for attention."

"H'm!" I knew my aunt was not satisfied, and realised also that I should have been more subtle about my departure. Supposing she decided to inflict some steely-eyed guardian on me at the last moment? Her prim sewing maid for instance? Or even the housekeeper.

I needn't have worried; or at least, I *thought* I needn't.

I set off in the family chaise for the travelling coach the next morning, unaccompanied, and filled with guilty excitement. I was fully aware of my reckless action, realised that I hadn't made a single plan except to escape from Merlake for a time, and eventually prove to Ivan that I wasn't prepared any longer to be his 'yes woman', and puppet on a string. A shadow of doubt — a vague passing fear — assailed me — when I had to face the possibility that he might wish to wash his hands of me altogether. Could he divorce me for acting unreasonably, or confine me to some hospital for emotionally disturbed women? The mere idea of it was disconcerting. But I pushed it from me quickly. Until I wished, Ivan would *not* find me. And by then, if he cared for me at all, he would surely be willing to compromise. But then, I didn't really want that. In a moment's soul searching I accepted there was only one thing I *did* want. Ivan and his love — the passionate commitment I'd once savoured and lost.

No half-measures.

No evasion.

If I couldn't have everything of him, I wanted nothing.

How could I live?

Somehow, somewhere, I might perhaps

work in a hotel, or earn money by providing pleasure to some rich gentleman who'd adore me.

What a notion. What a wicked creature I was. But then my father had once said that a spice of wickedness did nobody any harm. 'The aperitif to living,' he'd said, with a twinkle in his eye.

Dear Papa.

A rush of warmth filled me; I almost smiled, and imagined if he knew of my situation he might even do likewise, at the same moment adding, 'But don't belittle yourself, my dear. Be adventurous if you must, but keep your values.'

And that was what I intended to do, in a vague, proud kind of way.

Evadne pouted before waving me goodbye from the house, then gave a display of emotion by rushing to the door, insisting on kissing me, and crying, "I wish *I* was you. I'd do anything — *anything* — to be free and able to show my figure off to society. You must write to me, Anna, tell me if you find any handsome adventurers — "

I was aware of my aunt's disapproving glance, and my uncle gently but forcefully

354

putting his arm round her and pulling her back.

What a relief it was to be able to board the coach at last, and be moving every moment further and further from Mounterrith towards London. I hadn't realised though, how tiring the journey would be, especially the first part, through Cornwall and Devon. There were endless stopping places, which made me impatient and fearful of catching the connecting train the other side of the Tamar. We were a little late. But the guard had obligingly waited, and after the constant clip-clop of horses' hooves, jolting along uneven roads and cramping company, the rhythmic motion of steam-train wheels and comfortable upholstered seating, lulled me at last into a contented doze.

Looking back now my eventual arrival in the city seems blurred and somehow far off, like journeying through a dream. It was not until I stood bewildered on the station platform, my bag and valise beside me that the fact of knowing no hotel to go to fully registered. The atmosphere was smokey and damp, the sombre yellow light filled with a commotion of scurrying passengers, cabs waiting, and porters darting between shadowy crowds laden with trunks and baggage.

I was on the point of asking help of someone — *anyone* — who hesitated to give me sufficient time — when a kindly voice said in my ear, "Can I help you, ma'am? Want to go anywhere particular?"

Startled, yet relieved, I glanced up. The elderly face staring down at me wore a peaked cap, and was obviously a porter's. I told him I had to find a suitable hotel for a few nights, and would be most grateful if he could advise me, and perhaps find transport. He thought a moment, then said, "The Chatsworth, ma'am. That's a respectable place for a lady on her own. Temperance, but comfortable, and good food. Costs quite a bit though — " Through the wan light his expression was slightly doubtful, holding a question. "That sounds exactly what I require," I told him recklessly. I smiled, adding, "I'm not without money." He nodded, and called a cab, and in the matter of minutes we were driving through a maze of London streets, eventually arriving in the area of Kensington, where he deposited me and my baggage at the doors of a square Georgian building overlooking Hyde Park.

Through the dim light which was already thickening with yellow fog, no clear details of The Chatsworth were definable, but once inside the hall a feeling of security encompassed me. Red plush, gilt, soft but clear gas lighting, and the comfortable sensation of treading on thickly piled but inconspicuous carpet, gave a feeling of welcome and unostentatious good taste.

Upstairs it was the same. The bedroom though not large was sufficiently luxurious to give a wonderful sense of being cared for. The colour scheme was deep rose pink and cream, the hangings and upholstery reflecting a warm glow from the fire which had obviously just been lighted. The cream wallpaper was patterned with trailing leaves and pink flowers, and the mahogany furniture gleamed from constant polishing. An aroma of lavender pervaded the air faintly.

I sighed, sank on to the bed, and when the porter had departed after depositing my luggage on the floor, lay back with relief on the pink eiderdown, feeling the feather mattress give cosily beneath my weight.

The sound of approaching footsteps outside warned me in time — but only just — that a maid might be coming. I jumped up quickly, straightened the spread and covers, and when she entered with a bowl and hot water in the ewer, was removing my bonnet before the mirror.

For a time that night I managed to put any lingering misery concerning Ivan, to the back of my mind.

And in the morning the sun was shining.

London in the springtime.

My spirits rose.

After a satisfying and well-served breakfast I decided to go for a stroll in the park. There was no necessity for the time being to worry over the future. Somehow a pattern would emerge. I was young, free, and from sidelong male glances flung my way, not unattractive.

Well, of course, I knew that. But never before in my life had I been free to flaunt myself in new rich clothes, independent of criticism or jealousy.

Had I been able to foresee the future, I might not perhaps have felt quite so secure.

15

ON the third day of my stay at The Chatsworth I visited one of the most select couturiers in London where I purchased a luxurious violet velvet outfit consisting of a tightly waisted gown having a high neckline softened by cream lace and a narrow velvet ribbon, under a warm fully-lined cloak. The cloak had an edging of fur, to match the small bonnet hat that could be tilted at an intriguing angle slightly to one side.

The ensemble was costly, but in my extravagant reactionary mood this didn't worry me in the slightest. Ivan had been extremely generous in what he'd given me to cover expenses and personal pleasures during my stay at Mounterrith. Guilt on his part, possibly, I told myself, rather meanly. Guilt at being free for a bit from my irritating presence which enabled him to indulge his own fancies.

At odd moments I wondered about Siri,

and found to my own self-disgust that the thought of her long sessions closeted with Ivan — for 'business purposes' — still roused a quick sense of jealousy. I managed to subdue such an irrational emotion only through dressing carefully and daringly, quite conscious of my smart appearance, and of admiring male glances when I strolled in the park or through fashionable West End shopping centres. During the first week I visited many of the sights, including Kew, Hampton Court, Vauxhall, Cremorne Gardens, and the Tower. Sometimes I went by cab along the Embankment, and took coffee at a small select place in Chelsea. At that time, the interlaced branches of the trees were feathered by first young green against the spring sky. The weather was kind, and the reflected dark shapes of the squat tugs on the river fascinated me. Romance was in the air, and still angry at Ivan's treatment of me, I frequently allowed my eyes to respond coquettishly in a fleeting glance at any prosperous-looking gentleman who made the first overture. I was, of course, far too proud to indulge in conversation, although I couldn't help noticing that a certain young man of rather artistic appearance *did* happen to loom in my vicinity more frequently than would have been expected by chance. He wore a circular cape with a deep collar, and a felt hat with a very wide brim. After our first meeting, he always gave a slight inclination of his head followed by a doff of the hat and a gentle half-smile. He was handsome in a delicate way, fine featured, with liquid dark brown eyes, sculptured sensitive lips, and rich dark hair that he wore in a narrow beard round his chin, and side-burns.

A poet, I judged, or artist perhaps.

My last deduction proved to be correct.

On a Sunday, as I was sitting on a bench in the park, I was startled but not really surprised when he appeared, moved towards me, and after hesitating for a moment said, in cultured tones, "Madam, mademoiselle — allow me."

He bent down and picked up a shred of lacy handkerchief which I had inadvertently dropped.

"Yours, I think," he said.

I took it, feeling myself redden, although I hadn't misplaced the flimsy article on purpose.

"Thank you. How careless of me."

"Blame the whimsical spring breezes," he said, showing excellent teeth in a sudden wide smile. The smile quite changed him, making him instantly more human, handsome, and just a little mischievous.

I laughed softly, "Yes, of course."

"In any case, I'm grateful for the chance of making your acquaintance, miss — er — ?" He glanced at my left hand, "Ah, you're married."

"I *did* have a husband," I told him. "Once."

Thinking I was a widow presumably, he remarked, "I'm sorry. For *you*, Mrs — ?"

"Ellan," I answered recklessly. "Mrs Anna Ellan."

"And I'm Quentin Darke. So now we've introduced ourselves may I be permitted to join you for a few moments?"

If I'd wished to refuse I couldn't have done. He'd already seated himself beside me.

The discussion that followed consisted mainly of trivialities, far removed from anything political or boring business matters. He had a studio in Kensington, he told me, which he would be delighted for me to visit some time.

"I entertain there occasionally — on a very limited scale," he remarked, with his eyes still flatteringly on my face. "Only for friends, of course. I should be proud to introduce you."

"I don't know much about art," I told him bluntly. "In fact I'm not used to much cultured society. My home's in Cornwall, where the main interests are tin and copper mining, and shipping, of course."

"Cornwall!" a tinge of envy coloured his voice. "Yes, a remote land; Celtic — I always think of it as fey and mysterious."

I laughed. "I can assure you it can be extremely realistic too — savage, and sometimes cruel."

"To you?"

Forcing myself to stare him in the face very directly I said, "Please let us leave me out of it, Mr Darke. I'm not here simply for pleasure, but as a change to help my recovery from a distressing experience."

"I am so sorry. Forgive me."

His tones held such distress I felt quick shame at my duplicity, which, although true in a way, was deliberately misleading.

To make up for the half-lie I consented eventually to make a visit to his flat and studio the next day, where he assured me we should not be alone, but in the company of two acquaintances whom he was sure I should find amusing.

"I will call for you by cab at the Chatsworth, about three o'clock," he said. "You needn't stay long — only so long as you wish. You can give your opinion on my feeble efforts at portraiture, and if I can persuade you to sit for me in the same velvet cloak you're wearing now, I'll take it as an honour — "

"Oh no, please not," I interrupted, "I'm only staying in town for a short time, and really I wouldn't be at all a good subject, I'd fidget, and I'm not beautiful — "

"Now, now, my dear lady, allow me

to be the judge of that. You're too modest — "

"Mr Darke, please don't try and force me, or I won't come at all."

"*That* would be tragic. Then accept my apologies, Mrs Ellan. Although — " his lips twisted whimsically, "tomorrow's another day, and there's no crime in hoping. Very well, at the Chatsworth then — "

"Not that either," I said firmly. "The studio can't be too far from the hotel, and I like walking. If it's a day like this I'll enjoy it."

"And if it isn't? If it rains?"

I glanced at the sky, clear pale blue feathered with frail wisps of mist and baby clouds. "I don't think it will. If it does, I'll call a cab myself."

I got up to leave shortly after arrangements had been completed, saying I had shopping to do, and adding a white lie that I was shortly due back at the Chatsworth to meet an old friend of my childhood.

Whether he believed me or not I don't know, but his gallant gesture of lifting my hand to his lips before we parted was flattering, erasing for the time being the humiliation I'd been forced to endure at Merlake. Once back in my bedroom at the hotel, I studied myself quite critically through the mirror, and was astonished at the change so miraculously wrought by the short interim. Excitement had added colour to my cheeks and a sparkle to my eyes. My hair, even, under the coquettish headgear looked softer and more luxuriant, my lips more tilted and mischievous. How Aunt Clarissa would scold and condemn if she could see me just then. And how haughtily I'd face Ivan if he walked into the room. He could not make a scene at the Chatsworth. If he attempted to I'd tell him coldly I had no intention for the present of returning to him, and if he wished I was quite agreeable for a divorce.

My heart almost stopped beating when I considered the mere suggestion. How would he react? Supposing he agreed? It wouldn't be the end of the world, I told myself staunchly. I was still young — there were other attractive men in the world, like Quentin Darke — men with compliments on their lips who knew how to make a woman feel truly feminine and wanted, and behave in a civilised decorous manner.

The knowledge reimbursed my new sense of independence.

Actually the divorce idea was mere pretence on my part — a play acting fantasy.

Meeting Quentin however, had been a stroke of extreme good luck, and I would certainly go to his studio the following day. There was no knowing who I'd meet there, or what adventurous new course my life might take. His circle of friends might include a theatrical producer who'd fancy me in a play, or perhaps some truly well-known artist — a great man who, like Quentin, would wish to paint me. If so I might agree. A celebrated portrait would be reviewed and discussed by critics in newspapers, creating such publicity that Ivan would be almost certain to hear of it, and then — my ridiculous exaggerated fancies subsided suddenly when memory swept through me of a dark cave in a wind-lashed cliff, of tossed seas lurking under sullen skies, and a woman's face lit to brief clarity, staring tauntingly from a broken frame. I heard, in imagination, old Thorlock's rasping voice merging with the shrill scream of gulls, and envisaged once again the terrible picture of Lalage and the small boat being taken by the tide. Like a malicious ghost's, the senile parrot face of Miss Augusta appeared mockingly through a misted memory of grey turrets and towers, and further back but most vivid of all, the first primitive mating of Ivan and myself — two beings claimed by a passion as wild and wanton as the ruthless elements of the island.

Cornwall.

The memory was only brief, but its impact left me momentarily chilled yet claimed by a terrible aching nostalgia. I sat down, managing presently to force myself to the present. The hotel bedroom began to register; in a few minutes I'd regained composure, and was chiding myself for such weakness.

The rest of the day passed uneventfully, and the following afternoon I set off, on foot, for Quentin's studio.

I hadn't quite known what to expect; studios by tradition I knew, were generally supposed to be picturesque untidy places, smelling of turpentine and paint, with canvasses piled against walls and probably an easel with a half painted work propped upon it. There might be a model — there would certainly be some bearded figure wearing a smock, with tragic-looking haunted eyes.

Actually Quentin Darke's abode was quite different. I noticed, on entering, a frail water colour of a nymph-like creature hanging on one wall, a box of paints on a chair, but the easel had been carefully pushed into a corner, and the furnishing was rich, almost exotic. Instead of the turpentine odour, it was that of wine and perfume. Candle-light flickered over the thick rugs and crystal, and at the far end of the room three young men and a flimsily attired woman were playing cards at a table.

Quentin himself stepped forward and beckoned me in.

"Mrs Ellan," he said, "my *dear* Mrs Ellan, do please come in and be at ease. These are my friends — " He stretched

370

out an arm to introduce me.

I ignored it, for the moment too astonished to move.

My senses froze, as one of the figures ambled forward from the rest, fair hair gleaming, blue eyes speculative, lit by amusement.

"Jade-Anna," he said, "how truly remarkable, and how — how very wonderful."

My fingers felt frozen as Christopher Ferris took my hand in a tightening grasp.

I was conscious of Quentin saying as though from a great distance away, "So you two know each other. Just fancy. My dear fellow, I'm rather devastated, I must say. I'd hoped to have the pleasure of presenting the lady. She's a very special friend of mine — a beauteous addition to our ménage, you must admit."

Christopher gave a little bow. "Beauteous and very rare. Once we saw each other quite frequently, but lately circumstance has curtailed our friendship."

I can't remember what was said after that. All that remains in my mind is of taking a glass of wine, of fashionable, somewhat devious, conversation, with undercurrents of eroticism, and of realising gradually, through my bewilderment and fuddled state, that Chris had no intention of divulging any family conversation between us. The afternoon held a pleasurable intriguing excitement. It was stimulating to be the centre of attention and quite aware of Quentin's concentrated admiration beneath the frothy repartee.

At one point Chris, looking mildly irritated, intercepted the dualogue by planting himself firmly between myself and Quentin, and successfully diverting the subject of classical and romantic schools of painters which my host was doing his best to explain to me.

"Cornwall provides its own art through its natural background," he said, with dry condescension. "We have a culture there that defies boundaries of schools and so-called cultures. Isn't that so, Mrs Ellan?" His lips had a mocking twist, his, blue eyes challenged me. Once my heart would have bounded with delight at his personal interest; my whole being would have responded to the gleam of jealousy underlying the first question. Now I felt indifferent and aloof.

"Oh! you mean the dolmens, quoits and ancient Celtic monuments," I remarked. "Yes, I suppose that's true. But I never see landscapes through an artist's eyes. What I mean is — I prefer the real thing — to enjoy the cliffs and feeling the salt winds on my face, and being able to watch the evening sun fade behind the moors — " I broke off embarrassed.

"How honest and natural," Quentin remarked. "It's true a good deal of high-falutin' stuff is talked by Londoners and the Intelligentsia. Truth, I'm afraid, can very often be the casualty of so-called clever people."

Looking a trifle petulant, Christopher shrugged and turned away. I was secretly and a little triumphantly amused, also curious. Were things wrong between Evadne and himself I wondered, remembering my cousin's bad moods before I left Mounterrith.

Two days later I discovered the answer for myself.

It was following my third visit to the studio and on this occasion Christopher — although he must have been quite aware by then of Quentin's increasing devotion to me — insisted on seeing me back to the Chatsworth.

"I have arranged for a cab to call for Mrs Ellan," Quentin said, with a faint flush mounting his pale face.

"Then cancel it," Chris said abruptly. "Let me have the bill later if you like."

Angered by such rudeness I said hotly, "I'll have the cab, and thank you, Quentin." By then we were on terms of Christian names.

"I think you'd better oblige me by accepting my company," Christopher said in cold unemotional tones that nevertheless seemed to imply a warning. "I have a message for you, from a — mutual acquaintance — " He smiled with brittle arrogance at Quentin. Jade-Anna and I have interests in common, and there is a certain matter we have to discuss.

I bit my lip, feeling an unpleasant sense of rising apprehension, wondering if he had news of Ivan, or if it was Evadne he wished to discuss. On the other hand it could easily be that he simply wanted to be alone with me. Well, if that was so, now was the opportunity to disillusion him, I told myself ruthlessly. So I agreed to his suggestion — or rather command — and managed partially to pacify Quentin by telling him I would meet him in the park the following day.

Twilight was gradually deepening to evening over the city as Chris and I strolled under the spreading trees towards the hotel. There was no wind, the air was mild for late March, and already over the shadowed silhouettes of distant buildings and towers, a film of mist was rising, heralding fog later. Glancing up I saw the glimmer of the first star hanging like a jewel against the luminous greenish sky.

We wandered silently except for occasional commonplace remarks, until Christopher suddenly enquired bluntly, "Why are you here, Jade-Anna?"

"Why are you?" I demanded quickly.

"That's not the point. I'm a man."

"Which puts you in a different category altogether?"

"Yes, I think so. Men have business interests to attend to."

"Oh, certainly. I realise that. A very apt excuse."

He turned his head towards me sharply.

"You seem to have a tart tongue these days," he said. "Why? we used to care for each other quite genuinely I thought, as friends — " oh! how clever he was, " — in the past."

"That was some time ago, Christopher. The past is over. We both have fresh commitments now."

"Exactly." Such a pompous male word. "Which is why I'm asking what are you doing here?"

"The same as you apparently," I told him daringly, "playing about a little. And anyway, you've no right to question me."

His voice was gruff when he said, "I think I have. Not only on your behalf, but Quentin's."

"*Quentin?*" My eyes must have widened in surprise. "What has he to do with it?"

"You know very well. An odd fellow he may be, but I've a warm friendship for him, and you have him on a string."

I laughed outright. "Don't be ridiculous."

He grasped my arm painfully. "You're a fool, Jade-Anna," he said before releasing it. "Quentin, generally, has no place for women in his life except as an occasional model, but he's besotted by you, and I intend to protect him by every means in my power from being hurt."

I was bewildered, and in a strange way disturbed. "But why should you *have* to protect him? And what right have you to try and order me about?"

"None, legally speaking," he said curtly. "Perhaps I made a mistake in not marrying you instead of Evadne — God! she's a damn bore these days, which you certainly never were. On the other hand she'll hopefully produce an heir to our noble house, but afterwards? Do you know the first thing about what a man of my background and type needs? Do you imagine for one moment I'd be content to spend three-quarters of my life solely in the company of a stupid female whose only ambition is for ogling admirers and having me forever at her feet willing to satisfy her every whim for avowals of love and adoration? She's a fool, Jade-Anna.

If I couldn't manage diversions of some kind, and to mix with friends capable of providing some other form of affection, I'd take off to foreign realms or shoot myself. Well — in Quentin Darke I have already found such a relationship. He's clever, sensitive, artistic, and — "

"Yes?"

"Do you know what I'm talking about?"

Very gradually the distasteful truth was vaguely registering through my mind.

"I don't think I want to," I told him.

"No. Probably not, which proves you *do* understand. So in future I take it you'll oblige by refraining from concentrating your charms in that direction."

I was silent for some moments, struggling to recover from the crude shock of Christopher Ferris's statement. I had no knowledge at all of how his sophisticated town friends lived, or the full implication of what he was trying to tell me. It was hard — almost impossible — to believe that the contemptuous worldly voice speaking was that of Chris, the same man who'd bemused me romantically in the past, whose eyes had once been warm on mine, and whose every word to me had been a compliment. And Evadne! what of her? Much as I'd envied her, and in spite of her boring vain ways and mischievous chatter, she was my cousin — a young wife in need of affection, especially at such a time, when pregnancy was tiring and making her ill and depressed. Yet here was her husband already resentful of her looks, her character, and mere presence, leading a bizarre bachelor existence in London, with no thought of her except dislike, and an admittance that her one use to him was in producing an heir. And if the child was a girl? What then?

Poor Evadne.

I had never thought to pity her. But Christopher so disgusted me at that moment, just for a few seconds I did.

A 'damn bore' he'd called her. Maybe she was. But *he*! — with an effort I pulled myself together. Then I heard him remarking casually, "You're shocked. I'm surprised; I'd have thought living with Sterne would have dispelled your maidenly illusions pretty effectively." His hand touched my arm.

"Don't!" I said sharply, jerking myself free. "Keep away from me; I think you're quite — quite horrible."

Even in my own ears, the words sounded childish and naive.

He laughed softly.

"I like you when you're in a temper," he said. "I always did. In fact, I like you in all moods — so long as you steer clear of my own interests. You'd better remember what I've told you, Jade-Anna. Hands off Quentin. You understand?"

"You've made yourself quite clear. And I need no warning. I wouldn't touch either of you with a barge-pole."

"Good. In that case, I'm prepared not to make any trouble for you."

I stopped walking, staring up at him with a queer stab of alarm stiffening me. His face was washed pale from a nearby gas lamp, the eyes enigmatic, the sly half-smile hateful. In that brief interim he reminded me curiously of Maurice's tutor, Claude Lang.

"Trouble?" I echoed. "I don't think you'd be in a position to do that anyway."

"It wouldn't be at all difficult," he said, as we started walking on again. "A naughty young wife on her own in London, and in the company of her previous lover — "

"You were *never* my lover."

"But would the lordly Ivan believe it? In fact — " he paused before adding — "does he know you're here at all? Your explanation to me the other day of being on a mere shopping spree didn't really carry conviction, and you must admit I was extremely co-operative in going along with the young widow idea. We both hold useful cards in our hands, but mine is the strongest. So — " the banter died from his voice " — kindly remove your exotic presence from our amiable personal little group. Quentin at heart is very fond of me. And you — Jade-Anna — would effectively prove to be his downfall."

"I don't need any warning from you, Christopher Ferris," I told him sharply. "As I've already said — "

"You wouldn't touch either of us with a barge-pole. A trite remark, but it will suffice so long as you remember."

Seconds later we had reached the Chatsworth.

Except for a cold good night from both of us, nothing more was said.

When I reached my bedroom rigidity gave place to a fit of shivering. Everything suddenly appeared threatening and sordid. Practical issues began to loom alarmingly. I was not yet out of funds, I had sufficient money left to stay a few more days at the hotel; but so far I'd given no proper thought to what I would do afterwards. The idea of finding some sort of post had now become nebulous and unlikely, unless it was in some very menial capacity — and this no longer held any appeal for me. Deep down I recognised that I'd always half expected Ivan to come looking for me, believing that when I hadn't returned to Merlake, he'd have contacted Aunt Clarissa who'd have divulged the London trip.

But there was no Ivan. Maybe he hadn't known, maybe he didn't care; probably the latter. I felt confused, deflated and for the first time, a little horrified by my reckless flight. The unpleasant fits of nausea were increasing, which meant I could no longer enjoy the excellent menus provided at The Chatsworth. I was in turns depressed or turbulently excited and on edge.

The only peace I had was when I could escape to the garden or park, and seat myself on a bench, letting all thoughts and problems drift for a while like leaves on an idle wind, or shadows skimming the surface of the water.

It was in such a mood, two days following my unpleasant conversation with Christopher, that something happened — something that was irradicably to change the course of my life through events I'd never have dreamed of, even in the wildest nightmare.

The morning was bright and exhilarating with sunlight and shadow dappling the grass which was sprinkled with daisies in the fresh green. A faint, insidious wind stirred the branches of the trees in the park, reminding me of faraway Cornwall, where moors would be glowing with yellow gorse and the thrusting fronds of springing young bracken. Even in London the speared heads of early daffodils were already opening, and flower sellers offering bunches of violets from baskets.

I had bought a paper at the hotel, and was seated on a bench near the Serpentine, idly turning the pages, when a familiar gentle voice accosted me. I looked up and saw Quentin a yard or two away. He doffed his wide brimmed felt hat, came nearer and asked, indicating the seat, "May I?"

I nodded mechanically, taken off my guard knowing he must have been watching for me. I had deliberately made a point of choosing a different place for my brief morning rest, since the unfortunate incident with Christopher.

I was polite, under a façade of indifference, although it was quite obvious to me that Quentin was in an emotional mood.

"How are you, Quentin?" I asked. "A lovely day, isn't it?" I smiled brightly, looking up into his face. His expression was tense, filled with a hungry yearning that I found exceedingly disturbing. Such liquid eyes he had — soulful, and desperate with longing.

A pale long-fingered hand slid onto

one of mine, enclosing the palm gently.

"Oh, Jade-Anna," he said, "why have you been avoiding me?"

"Avoiding you, Quentin?" I echoed, vainly trying to free myself, "whatever do you mean? I saw you only two — no, three days ago. I've had things to do, letters to write, shopping. And you must realise — I told you — I should be returning to Cornwall soon."

He moved closer, trembling violently.

"You mustn't," he said, with his breath warm against my cheek, "you *can't* — I need you. I can't lose you now — "

"Quentin — " I tried to reason with him, as one would have with a child, "you're exaggerating. We're strangers. We hardly know each other — "

"That's ridiculous and untrue. From the first moment we met I knew beyond any doubt at all that we were destined to belong. Never — never in my life — " his voice was rising on the verge of hysteria " — have I wanted a woman before. You must believe that. It's true. Oh, my love, my sweet, exquisite darling — "

With my free arm I managed to force him a few inches away, and when I spoke it was in clear, hard tones.

"You're talking nonsense," I stated coldly. "I'm not your darling, you can't possibly love me, and I'm quite sure I've given you no reason for thinking that. It's ridiculous. Now please pull yourself together, and behave sensibly or people will notice. Already there's a nursemaid coming our way — "

"People! *People!*" he interrupted scornfully, grasping my arm as I somehow managed to struggle to my feet. "What do *people* matter?" The soft eyes had become wide and glaring, his manner was abandoned, theatrical and strange. Yet I knew he was not play-acting. His emotions, though wildly unbalanced, were genuine.

"Listen," he begged with his grip tightening. "I'm rich. We can have a wonderful existence together you and I — travel, exploring the world — creating an existence of the spirit and flesh denied to ordinary mortals — " His breathing was quick and heavy; fear mounted in me. I turned my head helplessly in search of the approaching nursemaid, but she had already receded in another direction, absorbed by her young charge in the pram. There was an old man further away, but as I tried to call out, he settled himself on a distant seat fiddling with something in a paper. Probably food for the ducks, I decided hopelessly. And all the time Quentin was pleading and protesting with ridiculous high-flown declarations of unquenchable passion that alarmed me.

Then I realised in a wave of relief, I still held an answer that might bring him to his senses.

"I'm not a *widow*, Quentin," I told him forcefully. "Do you understand? You're embarrassing me and humiliating yourself. I have a husband. A *husband* — someone I *love*, Quentin, as I could never love anyone else in the world — " Seeing he was at last quietening, and the expression on his face changing from fanatical adoration to slow astonishment, I continued in a rushing flood of words, "You've been wrong about me, I don't care for you at all in the way you're talking about. I don't *love* you, Quentin, I never could. Even if I wasn't married to Ivan, I could never think of you as a husband — never, *never*, I liked you as a friend, until — "

"Well?" his face had paled, become almost white. I thought at first he would faint. Then slowly colour returned as I said bluntly, "I know about your feelings for Christopher Ferris. I didn't at first. Your world was a completely strange one to me. But now I do, and it's no use denying it. Go back to it, Quentin. Find your own life — the one you deliberately chose for yourself. But don't expect me to be a part of it — even as a friend. I just *couldn't* — " I swallowed and went on, "I'm sorry for you, but that's all now; I never want to see or talk to you again. Never, *never*. And now please don't try to delay me. I must go."

His hand fell away from my arm. I didn't look at him, but sensed all life and energy suddenly drain away from his crumpled form. I lifted my head, and in spite of passing giddiness, forced myself to walk erectly from him towards the nearest gate. A thin film of cloud suddenly dimmed the bright sunlight. There was the sound of children's chatter from somewhere ahead, and then a thin high crackle of a shot. I stiffened and glanced back, just in time to see Quentin's figure stagger and fall. For some seconds I couldn't move. When at last mobility returned to my frozen limbs I went back mechanically and stood looking down at him. I didn't touch him, I couldn't. He lay with his eyes staring upwards, empty whites of eyes paler than the pale sky. A lurid trickle of blood coursed down a cheek from one temple and the corner of his mouth. A pistol lay on the ground by a rigid hand that had its fingers outstretched, like a claw.

I knew, without having to be told, that he was dead.

16

THE next few days following Quentin's death were like a bad dream, only worse, because there seemed no end. During the inevitable medical examination and official enquiries I was pulled through further questioning, because, I was told, I was the only witness.

When, asked what my relationship to Mr Darke had been, I replied a slight acquaintance only. The statement was received politely, but with obvious doubt.

"I'd known him only for a few days," I affirmed, "and had visited his studio once or twice to meet his friends and see his work, that was all."

"You mean to say, Madam, that you did not come to London specifically to meet him — on an *artistic* mission, naturally?"

The sly innuendo and emphasis on the 'artistic' angered me. "Of course, I didn't," I told him sharply.

"Yet you were staying alone — an attractive married lady — at a hotel — "

"Here. At The Chatsworth," I interrupted, feeling the perspiration gathering in beads on my forehead.

"And for what purpose, may I enquire — shopping — to see the sights? That's quite understandable — but — " fiery shrewd eyes glamed at me from under bushy brows " — your husband did not accompany you. A little neglectful of him, surely."

"He's very involved with business at the moment, in Cornwall."

"Ah, yes. Sterne. Mr Ivan Sterne. I see from the hotel register you arrived on the — "

"Does it matter when I arrived? Or what my husband's business is? I can tell you no more about — about this awful thing. I didn't know Quentin carried a revolver — I didn't know anything about him, except — "

"Yes, Madam?"

"Well, he turned out to be a friend of my cousin's husband, Mr Ferris, Christopher Ferris."

"So Mr Ferris told us yesterday

evening, Mrs Sterne, and although the gentleman was loyal to you, protective, naturally, he did indicate that you and the deceased had rather quickly become on intimate terms — ”

My cheeks flamed as I declared heatedly, “Nothing of the sort. And if you must know — ”

“We must know everything you can tell us,” the hateful official voice continued, once more persuasive and confidential.

I swallowed. “Well then, I’d told Quentin just before — before it happened — that I didn’t want to see him again, ever. I was walking away when the shot came. I didn’t even *see* it — ” I broke off breathlessly.

“I’m sure it must have been very distressing for you,” the suave tones remarked, “and obviously you’re very shocked. I’m sorry. But there’s one more thing that puzzles me — why did you present yourself to Mr Darke as a widow? Didn’t you wish him to know of your married status as Mrs Ivan Sterne?”

“The question never cropped up,” I answered, “because our — relationship as you put it — didn’t exist.”

"I see." My male tormentor sighed, and started to put away his notes. After a minute he remarked, "That will be all for the present, Madam. My apologies for having had to put you through such an ordeal. But any helpful facts will make proceedings at the inquest easier."

"*Inquest?*"

"Of course, Madam."

"But — I shan't have to be there, shall I? — Not to go through all this again?"

"You'd certainly have to attend. That's inevitable. But no doubt your husband's presence will sustain you — especially if, as you say, Mr Darke was merely a slight acquaintance."

"My husband?" Very briefly the world seemed to spin round me, the words came out only as a whisper.

"Mr Ferris was able to give his address, Madam. No doubt he will be joining you fairly shortly. I have your word, haven't I, that you'll not think of leaving The Chatsworth before his arrival?"

"I shouldn't dream of it," I forced myself to say coldly. "And I'm quite sure he'll be exceedingly annoyed to learn of this — this interrogation — "

I wasn't sure at all, of course. All I was certain of was Ivan's anger and outrage towards me for having got myself into such an unpleasant and embarrassing predicament.

Ivan.

If only he could be made to understand! — if only the past few months of bickering and coldness — jealousy and suspicion could be swept away. If he'd really loved me — but then he hadn't. What he'd wanted me for he'd taken on that wild wanton day of the storm, then married me through a sense of misplaced duty, and for his own convenience by having a wife tucked securely away at Merlake. I no longer held any illusions. Marriage could be a safeguard for him against the conniving ambitions of any mistress he fancied.

Thinking in this bitter way dispelled self-blame and stiffened me resolutely to meet him with assumed confidence, and a determination not to be intimidated.

Nevertheless, when he arrived the following day and was shown into a small private parlour that had been allotted to me for the purpose, my heart was beating uncomfortably quickly, and beneath the dark jade green silk of my gown — one I'd extravagantly purchased since my arrival in London — my legs felt curiously light, and were shaking sufficiently to cause a rustle of the full skirt.

As the door opened I was standing by an oval rosewood table, with one hand on the satin-smooth surface, to steady me. It was a pretty table patterned by a circular design of flowers and leaves in marquetry. Odd to think I noticed such details through the great whirl of emotions that engulfed me. Ivan's clothes also registered, the fashionable bottle green coat and fawn breeches, but only vaguely, as a background to his stern face, stormy grey eyes, set jaw, firm lips pressed condemningly above the cleft chin.

My stomach lurched, and for a moment blurred, taking the firelight and shadows of the room into a grey mist. Then I heard him saying, "Well, Anna? And what do you think you've been playing at? A pretty kettle of fish you've landed yourself into, and no mistake. How *could* you? Oh, I've always recognised you were a firebrand and a rebel. But a cheat?" He laughed shortly. "No. I didn't quite believe that. It didn't remotely occur to me that you could skip so easily from one potential lover to another. It was Claude Lang first, wasn't it? Then this latest conquest — poor dupe."

He sighed, passed me, and went straight to the window where he stood looking out with his hands behind his back.

When he turned there was no softening in his expression, no pity — only condemnation.

"I suppose you realise," he said, coldly as though addressing a stranger, "that you will be required at the inquest, being the only witness?"

"Yes. But I saw nothing, I was walking away."

"You'll have the opportunity to give such information in court." He paused, adding a moment later, "I shall attend with you, naturally, then escort you back to the hotel. You will be returning to Mounterrith, the following day, providing your aunt and uncle will have you, which they probably will, being Sir Humphrey's niece and for the allowance I'm prepared to offer."

The blood seemed to drain from my body. I felt cold, rigid, with all strength in me drained away. Yet the life was still there — the new life in my womb — Ivan's child, though he did not know it.

A whispered question left my lips. "You mean — ?"

"After this episode I'm sure you'll agree our marriage has become farcical. You didn't care for me when you accepted my proposal, and later events have only confirmed the fact that you never will. I don't blame you entirely. The blame initially was mine, for suggesting such a ridiculous union. Still — " he drew a deep breath — "the outcome can be remedied; divorce will take a little time, but in the end you will be free; we both will, and I can assure you that I will behave in as gentlemanly a fashion as possible — meaning, my dear, that you should emerge from the unpleasant business legally — if not morally — without too damaging a stain on your character. Of course — " his cold eyes bored mine with the icy relentless quality of steel swords — "a shadow is bound to linger for a while. There will be whispers in the most select — of drawing rooms, but that won't worry you unduly, will it? With your challenging beautiful presence and handsome allowance to sustain it, I'm sure you'll continue to charm a stream of beaux — "

"Stop!" I cried, unable to bear the supercilious oration any longer. "You're being unfair. You haven't waited for me to explain at all. It's all wrong, what you're saying. There was nothing between Quentin or me — "

"Or Christopher Ferris?"

"Of *course* not. I'm not that kind of woman — "

"To allow Lang liberties you'd denied me for quite a time? To run from a husband to a former lover? To deliberately flaunt yourself so seductively that the besotted poor wretch Quentin shoots himself? — Oh Anna!" The derisive contempt in his voice hurt more than any anger could have done. "Don't act the fool. And for God's sake don't look like that." Just for an instant his whole manner changed. Both hands were clenched at his sides. He took a step towards me, the hard eyes hot with sudden temper. I waited for him to strike me — anything to break the terrible rift between us. But he did not. He simply turned away, picked up his stove hat and strode to the door.

"You'll be notified of the exact time of the inquest," he said, before leaving. "I will pick you up here. In the meantime, I'd be obliged if you'd stay here, and not go out until all formalities are over."

The next moment the door clicked. He had gone.

I existed in a kind of daze for the next few hours, hardly able to accept the import — the finality — of what Ivan had said. Divorce! the ultimate sundering of any connection between us. He couldn't mean it! he just *couldn't*! I told myself desperately time after time. He'd spoken from reaction and shock. He'd been in love with me once. He *must* have been. The day of the storm, and afterwards — he'd not been play-acting! We'd both made mistakes, both misunderstood. I'd been stupid and reckless and wilful, and he'd been overbearing — too secretive to allow me to share as a wife should. Oh, no doubt I'd been stupid to run away to London — but — but, but, but! there were so many 'buts' to consider, and so many 'if onlys'.

I realised miserably that I should have stopped his outburst from the very beginning by telling him about the coming child. The baby — his and mine. But would he have believed me? In his present mood I doubted it, and now anyway, it was too late. I would not demean myself or sink my own pride by making excuses through the plea of pregnancy. If Ivan Sterne didn't want me for myself alone, then he wouldn't have me at all. He could take any measures he liked, I'd profess indifference, and keep my own secret so that when the baby was born I'd deny him the right of access — wasn't that what they called it? — Anyway, I'd by then, probably, be Jade-Anna Ellan again, free of any more obligations to the autocratic Sterne family.

I knew little, practically, of the law,

neither did I wish to.

I determined in those few bitter moments of revelation to think of myself only, and retaining a right to what was mine, ruthlessly steeling myself against personal yearnings or memories of Ivan.

★ ★ ★

The inquest was brief, the strain and questioning far less than I'd anticipated, resulting in a verdict of *felo de se*. When it was over Ivan accompanied me in a cab back to The Chatsworth, informing me that Aunt Clarissa's housekeeper would be arriving two days later to accompany me back to Mounterrith.

"My solicitors will be in contact with you in the not too far off future," he informed me before leaving. "As I've told you, there's no need for you to worry about finance. If any problem arises you have only to contact me through this firm, and it will be attended to."

He placed a card on the table bearing the name of solicitors in Falmouth. I didn't bother to read it, and had not the energy to reply. Tears were thick on my throat. In spite of all my firm resolutions I had never expected to feel so lonely or completely bereft.

17

SO it was over.

Just like that; a death, a court hearing, a curt nod from Ivan after assisting me from the cab at The Chatsworth, and our marriage was dispelled as casually by him, apparently, as the brush of a dead leaf from a tree.

I looked back once from the door, and saw him watching stiff and motionless, until he climbed into the vehicle, and was driven away. I had no impulse to follow him just then. It was as though two strangers had met briefly during an unpleasant incident, and parted as soon as possible.

As I walked through the vestibule and hall I was aware of a few curious heads turned in my direction. I didn't care. The true facts of the unhappy business would never be known; gossip would inevitably brand me as a notorious wicked woman, even though Ivan so nobly — my lips curled derisively — took the blame.

As if it mattered; as if anything mattered.

I was suddenly so tired I had to cling to the banisters of the staircase, pausing a few moments before making my way ahead to the hotel bedroom. Once there, I ordered tea, removed my cloak lifelessly, sat on the bed, and waited. The light was poor. During the afternoon a depressing fog had been slowly rising encompassing the city into dark uniformity. A black and yellow day — with no spring green visible any more — only a damp shroud hugging the river and the lean branches of trees stretching in a blurred network against the lowering sky.

Never had any place seemed more lonely. I thought dimly of Cornwall — of Merlake and great waves pounding the cliffs, and the crying of gulls as they dipped to the moors and sea. Yet the memory had become unreal. All that properly registered was the receding form of Ivan disappearing in the cab through the fog, and the macabre terrifying thought of Quentin lying distorted and spreadeagled on the ground, mouth open, eyes staring glazedly through narrowed lids, with one side of his face bloodied, and the revolver lying only a few inches from one clawing hand.

I would never forget. Never. But every time the memory recurred I managed somehow to turn my mind to more practical things — the impending arrival of Aunt Clarissa's housekeeper, and later the inevitable confrontation with my aunt herself at Mounterrith. She would be aggrieved, condemning, yet secretly triumphant, I was sure, to have her assessment of my character so accurately proved. And when I told her I was enceinte — but this would not at first be necessary. The truth of my condition would probably dawn on her gradually, so that when I admitted it she would no doubt have a humiliating and well-prepared sermon ready. I had no doubt whatever that she would be quick to inform Ivan. From that point I could only surmise and conjecture. Possibly — probably — he would wish to have nothing to do with the child. He might even deny it was his. And perhaps that would be the best attitude for all concerned. I could even put on a dramatic act — just to shame him — stating insultingly that as he obviously considered he'd married a congenital whore, any child I bore could have been sired by any one of my admirers.

Oh yes — that would hurt him. He might not love me, but his pride alone would be shamefully humiliated by an admission from my own lips that indeed he had been so ridiculously cuckolded.

As quickly as the idea flamed, it fluctuated and died in a wave of self-shame. I couldn't lie so despicably. On the other hand, I would fight with all other means I had to keep what was mine. No innocent baby should be condemned to an unnatural lonely existence on Merlake Island with only the macabre Miss Augusta, Ivan, and the frustrated warped boy, Maurice, for company.

The possibility of having an abortion occurred to me, but that could be dangerous, and even in my predicament seemed abhorrent. I wasn't religious in the conventional sense, but already the new life was strengthening in me, assuming a right to have a place in the world and in my own existence.

I hardly slept that first night following the inquest. Questions and answers whirled through my head, lapsing into intermittent periods of exhausted negative wakefulness. The two days passed aimlessly. When at the appointed time Mrs Craddock arrived at The Chatsworth, all emotion seemed drained from me. I was too exhausted to feel much at all. She was an elderly, insignificant-looking woman who had been housekeeper at Mounterrith since I was a child. Her position in the house though subservient to the family, had been authoritative, and quietly efficient. It was the same now. She expressed little surprise at events or my presence there; her manner was composed and emotionless, dealing only with practical issues. In the past I'd found her mouse-like presence boring — sometimes profoundly irritating. Now I was grateful for it. There'd be no quizzing or attempts at gossip; no 'whys'? or subtle questioning. She was in London to perform a duty and escort me, in the capacity of chaperone, to her employer's home.

It was quite late in the evening when we arrived at Mounterrith, following two days of wearing travelling. As I'd expected, there was a secret glint of triumph in Aunt Clarissa's eyes. Her face was flushed, and appeared even larger and broader than I remembered it. Quite obviously she was all agog to question and deliver a moral lecture, but my uncle's presence did not allow it. For once he stood up against his domineering spouse, and insisted that I should be spared any explanations, and allowed to retire in peace.

"You must be tired, my dear," he said. "Egad!" He studied my face with a touch of real concern. "You're pale, and no mistake — Clarissa — " turning to my aunt " — let her meal be taken to the bedroom, and none of your tittle-tattling tonight — "

"*Tittle-tattle?*" The booming voice sounded outraged.

"That's what I said. And see you heed it, my dear."

And she did.

But next morning the interrogations began.

This time, however, the commencement of the tirade was different. She appeared distressed and woeful, and intermittently fiddled with her handkerchief and put smelling salts to her nose.

"Your behaviour, Anna, has not only upset the whole household, but has made me feel that I have failed in some way. You do realise, don't you, that all this unsavoury publicity will reflect on me?" She eyed me with one hand across her plump bosom as though to ease the danger of a possible heart attack.

"No," I answered unfeelingly. "I don't see that it concerns you personally in any way. I'm a married woman — Uncle Humphrey's niece — whom, until my marriage, you very charitably took into your home to treat as your own daughter — " I fancied the barb of sarcasm made its mark. "If I strayed from the straight and narrow path, it was certainly not what you had planned for me. But actually — I *didn't*. The whole thing was just — one of those tragic happenings that probably would have occurred anyway, sooner or later. Quentin was a brilliant, sensitive and clever person, with his life in an emotional tangle. You could say unbalanced, I suppose — "

"In which *you* were involved."

"Well, I didn't realise it. And I do think it's unfair of you to drag the whole thing up again — "

"*Unfair?*" The one word fell like a bomb. "Unfair?" she repeated, and now her first façade of distress had changed to vituperative anger, "When all at Mounterrith — your Uncle and I and poor Evadne, will have to live shamed and cold-shouldered by respectable society because of your disgusting behaviour, and the vulgar business of having our name dragged through the mud."

"I'm sure some of your friends will be quite titillated by the gossip," I said nastily. "And if you don't want me here I can easily tell Ivan and I'm sure he'll agree for me to move to some hotel. In fact, no one has moral jurisdiction over me any more. As a fallen woman I feel quite free to lead my own life how and where I choose. Another thing — " I stared at her very directly. "Has it occurred to you to enquire why Christopher Ferris was on such intimate terms with Quentin's little crowd? I should have thought his place was at Evadne's side during her difficult time."

I had the mean gratification of seeing her wince.

"Please leave my daughter's name out of it. If it was not for your uncle I might have suggested your presence here at such a time under such conditions was not at all desirable for the poor child. And I must request you, Anna — no — " lifting a finger " — *command* you, do you hear, not to refer to him in her hearing, in any derogatory way. Christopher has a right to his own male pleasures from time to time. A man cannot be tied to his wife's apron strings every moment of his life, especially during pregnancy. Indeed, we must be grateful that he was able to be of assistance in helping the police, otherwise you might have carried on in your wilful wicked course, and have landed us in another perhaps worse scandal — " She broke off breathlessly. I realised she was quickly losing control, and if I was not careful would cause such a scene the whole household would hear.

Fortunately, the spate of words was interrupted by the entrance of Evadne, which gave the opportunity for Aunt Clarissa to calm down and pull herself together with a show of mere offended dignity.

"My dear — " her voice was still a little more shrill than usual — "what are you doing down here? You should be resting. You know what the doctor said — "

"Oh bother the doctor!" Evadne gave an impatient wave of her hand pushing her mother's expansive form away. "I'm sick of being fussed and fawned over by that old dodderer. For heaven's sake — " She flopped into a chair. "Can't you leave me alone for a minute?" She glanced towards me, and added more quietly, "I want to talk to Anna."

Trying to appear mollified and understanding, Aunt Clarissa, lifting her head, and shooting a warning glance of fire at me, replied, "Very well, so long as you don't get upset."

She turned to me before leaving. "I

rely on you to show a little discretion, Anna."

After her departure Evadne's temporary show of exhaustion vanished as though by magic.

"*Now!*" she said, turning her lovely eyes on me accusingly, "tell me the truth. Not my mother's version — *yours*. What *really* happened? And why were you with Chris? I always knew you were bent on getting him for yourself — it was clear to everyone. But I didn't imagine you'd go to such beastly underhand means — "

I laughed. "Don't be ridiculous. Christopher wasn't concerned at all. He just happened to be a friend of Quentin's."

"As *you* were, I suppose? It all just *happened*? *You* happened to meet my husband at your lover's studio? And *he* happened to — to — " She broke off, dabbing her eyes and swallowing with such distress I felt almost sorry for her.

"It wasn't at all what you imagine, Evadne. The artistic circle's fairly small and intimate in London, and the two of them, Chris and Quentin were friends. What's more natural that we should run into each other in a friendly fashion?"

"As natural as you showing any interest in art, of course," my cousin agreed sarcastically. "You never have before." She paused then added, "I believe it was all planned. You've just deceived us all — Ivan by pretending you were staying all the time with us, when your whole idea was to slip off to London to try and catch Chris again." Two spots of crimson flamed in her pale cheeks. "Well you can't. You've failed. He despises you — I've a letter here." She drew an envelope from her pocket. "He made excuses for you naturally, because of the family relationship, but it's quite clear what he *really* thinks." She waved the note in front of me. "Read it, if you like. See what it says — "'my most beloved and precious wife' — and the ending, 'your cousin, of course, is to be pitied. I fear for her future. But 'blood will out' my darling. You must remember that and be charitable, because of her parentage'" She got up and came towards me.

When I didn't move she began again, "See? Take it. Read — *read* — "

I thrust her hand away.

"I don't want it. It's your affair. You'll believe what you like, anyway. Whichever way it is, I don't want to know. Sit down, Evadne. There's no point in getting so worked up. Christopher and I are nothing to each other. But there's just one thing — " I steadied myself by resting one hand on the back of a chair because I was beginning to feel giddy, " — Don't ever again sneer at my parents. Don't *dare* — do you understand?"

I must have looked and sounded over-fierce. She opened her mouth to speak, thought better of it, and sank again into the chair. Her hand went to her brow. "Oh dear — I feel so *awful* — " Her eyes closed.

"Do you want brandy or something?" I queried, "or aren't you allowed it? Can I get you a drink?"

"No, thank you." She looked up again, and I saw that her mood had changed. Curiosity for the moment had softened her ill-temper. "Tell me what else happened," she said, "before you left Merlake, and *why*. Have you left

Ivan for good, Anna? Did he beat you or something?"

I smiled bitterly. "Not exactly that. We were shall we say — incompatible. I should never have married him."

"Oh." The short word held disappointment. "Is that all?"

"It's quite sufficient reason when you're living on a remote island surrounded by hostile people."

"Who were these people, Anna?"

I outlined the characters briefly, keeping descriptions on a low key, and minimising the tragedies of the wreck and the boating accident when Lalage had drowned. Evadne was clearly intrigued, and because she was quite aware I hadn't divulged the whole truth, made a number of unsuccessful attempts to get it out of me.

Eventually, realising the futility of further questioning, she remarked disparagingly, "You're thinner in the face, you know. You look rather 'wisht', as mama would say — a little washed out. It doesn't suit you. Me now! However awful I feel inside my looks don't change." She sighed. "I suppose I'm lucky."

"You certainly are," I agreed.

"And I'm having a new gown made for when Chris comes — in about a week. Rose pink, and very full," she actually giggled. "I'll make him fall in love with me all over again." Another sigh, "What a pity about you and Ivan, Anna. Still, perhaps it will all come right in the end. Maybe *I* can help."

"You?"

"Yes, why not? I've cut out an article from a magazine. It's upstairs. You shall see it — all about the art of seduction and how, even if a wife should happen to be with child — she may still be able to retain her husband's whole-hearted devotion. Perfume comes into it, of course, and delicacy of manners — the capacity to make him feel superior — 'the spiritual support, and administration to her ever changeful moods'. That's rather lovely, I think, don't you?"

"For you, I'm sure," I answered ambiguously, although my private opinion was very different.

Shortly after the brief conversation I managed to free myself of my cousin's presence and go upstairs to my Mounterrith bedroom.

It was three times as large as the one I'd previously occupied there, and had a wide view of the hills sloping towards the distant sea. The landscape appeared clear-cut and cold under the slanting rays of the sun. Beyond the grounds of the house moors and hamlets were brilliantly etched, and to the far right from where I was standing the jagged dark shape of Carn Carron rose like a giant's head beyond the estuary — thrusting in everlasting conflict against the hungry ocean. The same Atlantic I thought with a stab of despondency, that battered its force against Merlake. And I recalled the boats that had been taken, the helpless bodies swallowed by the sea and tossed like children's toys or so much flotsam on the ruthless rocks.

Lalage.

I had a sudden vivid mental picture of her voluptuous figure and frightened hungry eyes. Yes — beneath their heavy-lidded mockery there'd been fear; I hadn't recognised or accepted it before, but she was like all the rest on that bleak doomed island — caught up in some macabre mystery from which only death had given release. It was as though her existence had been played out under a cloak of deception which could explain her varying moods and capacity to be at one moment a lewd-tongued accusing virago, then shortly afterwards a statuesque supercilious lady of fashion walking with her young nephew Maurice in the garden of the Towers. Which one had been the true Lalage? Or had either? I recalled the time when the red roots of her hair had shown distinctly beneath the luxurious black locks, and I tried to envisage how she would appear as her natural self. Striking in an exotic way, obviously, and probably when she was young and more slender, extremely beautiful. Her complexion would be clear then, and the full lips dazzling when she smiled. Such a taunting smile.

The image conjured in my imagination reminded me of someone, but I couldn't think who. The face in old Thorlock's portrait, perhaps? But no. They were different in type and bone structure. Then *who*? And how could I remember even faintly, someone I'd never met and who probably did not exist or ever had. Possibly I was recalling a picture seen in childhood, or a portrait like that of Lady Hamilton? Youthful impressions could be vivid and enduring.

Yes, this was the likeliest explanation. Nevertheless, the puzzling conundrum still remained at the back of my mind, although I knew it would probably never be solved because in any case it was unlikely I would ever see Merlake Island again.

How wrong I was.

And how tragic, eventually, events were to be leading to the conclusion of its long bitter history.

* * *

A week passed. A period of grim supercilious acceptance of my presence at Mounterrith, during which my aunt never missed a chance of making some barbed comment or displaying a tightening of lips and narrowed hard glance of her eyes whenever they fell upon me. Had it not been for my uncle's determination to make me feel one of the family again,

I'm sure I'd have had to eat in my room alone, like any unwanted creature of alien race banished to purdah.

Of course, I wouldn't have been alone — *quite*. I was becoming daily more aware of the developing life in my womb — that small part of Ivan, which whatever he might say or do, would remain and eventually develop as a separate entity provided everything proceeded normally. And there was no reason why it shouldn't. I was young and strong and quite competent to bring a healthy child into the world. The vague unease and depression I'd felt at first, gradually began to lift. There were despairing moments when I longed for Ivan so desperately I thought my heart must break. But such times passed, because I willed them to. If one was sufficiently determined, I told myself, no man had to be essential in any woman's life, providing she'd something of her own to care for.

So I set myself against him with every ounce of spare energy I had, and tried to plan for the future. The problem was that I just couldn't *foresee* any practical plan.

Life at Mounterrith would be unbearable under Aunt Clarissa's domination, and the thought of a young child — mine — having to bear it, unthinkable.

I had read in a book that there was a pattern to every life, but in my own case I doubted it. All that had happened to me so far, had mostly been of my doing, and it was hard to imagine Fate giving me a push now. But perhaps Fate was stranger than human will. Or perhaps there was no Fate at all — just a sequence of unexpected occurrences capable of changing everything with one sweeping terrible blow. Whatever the answer I was caught up one early April afternoon in drama so acute that it seemed at first my own life must end.

The morning had been calm, with skies paper-pale under a clear rising sun, the scene so vivid it could have been a painting on glass. There was no wind at all until the midday meal was over, when a faint insidious breeze rose from the west, rustling the spring undergrowth in the garden to uneasy movement. Yes, everything gradually seemed to herald approaching disaster. I tried to believe the sensation was nerves, due to my condition; but by three o'clock thin clouds were mounting the sky. The sun faded first to a mere shadowed radiance, then presently was darkened as though extinguished by a giant hand.

I had been gathering a few daffodils for the house and went in when the first drops of rain fell. Soon one of the wild unpredictable Cornish storms was raging, similar to those I'd so tragically witnessed at Merlake. A spreading well of fear encompassed me. Most of that day I paced about Mounterrith, staring through different windows, trying vainly to recognise details of the landscape through the dripping rain-soaked glass. It was impossible. Nothing registered but the driving sweep of water and wind, and the constant moan and lash of trees beating the walls of the house.

"Why can't you rest a little, or find something to do?" my aunt complained. "What's the matter with you, Anna? You have sewing to do, haven't you? What about the new wool and canvas you got the other day for a tapestry? Or if you don't feel like needlework perhaps you could help amuse Evadne a little? If thunder should come she'll be nervous, poor child. You know how lightning always upset her — "

"I don't think it will thunder," I said. "But the tides will be high."

"Well, what about it? We're not exactly on the coast here. The sea doesn't affect us at all."

"Merlake will be in the thick of it."

My aunt laughed scornfully. "So you still think of Merlake. I don't see that it concerns you any more. By the way — " her glance and voice darkened ominously " — I had a letter from an acquaintance of mine this morning — one can hardly call her a *friend* for imparting such unsavoury gossip — stating she'd heard Ivan is going to *divorce* you. That's not true is it? A separation, well — " she sighed " — unfortunately one can't deny *that*. But *divorce*!"

For a brief interim I forgot the storm and all its sinister implications as I answered my aunt defiantly, "It's quite true. I already thought you'd know. But I can assure you Ivan's going to protect my good name, so you needn't worry.

424

Ivan will be the bête-noir, and I shall appear as the wronged woman. No one will dare cast a stone at the noble name of Ellan."

Aunt Clarissa regarded me silently for a second or two with such dislike on her face, I instinctively turned away.

"No one will be deceived for one moment," she said with a tremor of anger in her thick throaty voice. "You should be *ashamed* for bringing such disgrace upon your uncle's name."

"I thought my father had already done that," I answered coldly. "Oh, for heaven's sake — "

"Anna! you forget yourself. I will not have heaven or the Deity brought into such a reprehensible conversation. More than enough has already been said on this completely degrading situation. I shall leave you now, hoping you will learn to recognise your own shortcomings and show a little gratitude to your uncle and myself for accepting you once more into the bosom of the family."

Bosom of the family! I almost laughed. But when she'd gone misery once more engulfed me — misery and the strange gnawing fear of tragedy looming. As a child I'd experienced an unexplainable capacity for sensing disaster ahead which adults had put down to coincidence. But it was more than that as the years had proved. 'A rare gift,' my father had told me before we'd been parted. 'Your mother had it. Generally she was right, so take heed when that inner voice of yours is urgent enough. It may be a warning, child.'

This time it certainly was.

The following morning I heard from one of the servants that tragedy had hit Merlake. The girl's husband, a sea-faring man, had arrived at the mainland with the news that a conflict between some sort of foreign vessel — a private boat or a smuggler, he wasn't sure quite what, had been driven to the coast of the island in the storm, causing a skirmish with firearms. One or two had been drowned, although the 'furriner' had been captured and taken into custody.

"They say it was a real terrible sight," the girl added. "Jest think of et."

"Was the — was Mr Sterne there himself?" I interrupted, trying to ward

426

off a rush of nausea and trembling.

The girl lowered her eyes.

"I don't rightly know, ma'am. But — "
She hesitated.

I gripped her shoulder.

"But *what*? Tell me. *Tell* me, I want
to know. I have a right — "

She shook her head. "'Tisn't for me
to say ma' am. You see — "

"It *is* your right. I *demand* it. I'm his
wife — " I started shaking her. "Tell me
instantly, or you'll regret it. I'll have you
dismissed — "

My threat appeared to frighten her.

"No one *knows* anything," she said,
"not for certain. But Joe — he's my
husband, said Mr Sterne could'n be
found. Oh yes — yes, he was there,
ma'am. Right on the scene. But the
light was so bad, an' there was so
much screamin' an' fightin', an' them
guns boomin' — I know nuthen else,
ma'am, honest I don't — but I expect
it'll be all right. He's sure to turn up.

I let her arm go, and turned away
shuddering. I wasn't sure at all. But
I already knew what to do. I must
leave Mounterrith at the earliest moment

possible and find out the truth for myself. It was still raining, thin rain now, driven like a shroud over the landscape. The sea might still be rough, and the light poor. Possibly there would be a fog later. But somehow I must find a boat with someone willing to take me.

No large vessels would be sailing until the weather lifted. My course, therefore, must be to locate a man sufficiently courageous who would consider the risk worth what I was willing to pay.

For myself I cared not. Without Ivan, life, anyway, would be worth little — or even that of my unborn child. All that mattered was to find my husband, if he was alive.

And if he wasn't?

Then I would want to die.

18

FOLLOWING the news about Ivan, the terrible implication that he'd not survived the sea skirmish, I immediately found my uncle in his study and asked for his permission to be driven in the chaise to Penzance. Mercifully he was alone, and although surprised, didn't attempt too strongly to dissuade me.

"But, my dear girl," he said, shaking his head, "what good can you do there? There'll be no positive or accurate news yet. Don't you think — "

"I *must* go," I interrupted vehemently. "There'll be sailors about — someone will have heard more than we have. Even if it's not true, I can't wait here doing nothing. Don't you *see*? — he's my *husband*. If anything happened — " I broke off, with the tears choking my throat. His face softened. "Very well," he said, "if it matters that much, you have my permission. Only don't do anything stupid, my dear — "

"Thank you — " I planted a quick grateful kiss on his cheek, feeling comfort somehow from the friendly cigar smell of him, and rough contact of his beard.

When I reached the door I bumped into Aunt Clarissa.

"What's happening now?" she said.

Uncle Humphrey coughed. I didn't wait to hear his answer, but rushed away to get ready for the journey, sensing that whatever his explanation, his wife wouldn't agree. It didn't matter. Once my uncle had given his word he very seldom broke it, and I knew that on this occasion his sympathies were with me.

I didn't bother changing my gown, but pulled on a pair of boots, my plainest cape, and a bonnet under which I could push my hair to keep it tidy from wind and rain. My uncle had already sent word to the stables when I went downstairs. I didn't like deceiving him. But if I'd divulged the whole truth — told him 'by hook or crook' — what a stupid saying — I was somehow getting across to the island, he'd have withdrawn permission or I'd have had to find other means of transport — a farm cart or a carrier's van perhaps — which would have meant loss of time, and probably wouldn't have worked, with my aunt constantly suspicious and watching me.

The thick misty quality of the rain was increasing when we set off. The high moors were submerged by it, and hardly visible. At times a horse reared when some distorted shape or monolith emerged fitfully and disappeared again giving a strange impression of movement.

"Please be as quick as possible," I urged the man, "it's so important — " He mumbled a word or two that sounded like "Can't do the impossible, Madam. Not a day for travelling, this isn't."

I sat back impatiently, ribs tense, with my heart thudding in a wild tattoo. A wind was rising again, beating the branches of bushes and crouched trees in a sweeping motion across the road. How long it took to reach Penzance I couldn't tell. But at last we were there. The coachman would have stopped at an inn near the square, but I ordered him to cut down to the harbour. He was disgruntled, arguing that refreshment for the horses and myself — also for him

— would be advisable. "Folks talk in this place," he said. "You'll be more likely to hear something inside than down there; with this rain, and what seamen there are about, in a bad temper — "

"Take me to the harbour," I insisted again. "I know what I'm doing."

I knew he was extremely annoyed, and would be more so when he heard he'd have to return to Mounterrith without me. Probably there'd be trouble for him when he got back, and I was sorry for it. But nothing in the world mattered to me any more except the necessity to be on my way — however hazardous the sea crossing — to the island.

There were more grumbles when I left the chaise and told the man to wait by the quay, while I made enquiries. "A boat's just berthed," I told him, although I wasn't at all sure of it. "I shouldn't be too long — " through the rain I saw him frown — a frown of worry as well as irritation. On a sudden impulse I came out with the truth. "Listen, Oaks, wait for half an hour, not more. If I'm not back by that time, return to Mounterrith, and tell them I *insisted* on finding a boat to take me to Merlake — "

"*Merlake?* Now look here, madam, I can't do that. What d'you think the master will say? And the mistress — "

"They know *me*. You won't be blamed. If you like just say I never came back to the chaise. But I think the first explanation would be best. Anyway — *she* won't mind, not my aunt. Tell my uncle I'll be all right — "

By then he was quite bemused. "You see you come back — " he shouted as I stepped away. "There'll be no craft will sail in this murky weather — be careful now — "

I heard no more but a horse's neigh. The grey foggy rain swirled round me as I sped over the wet shingle to the shore. In spite of Oaks' certainty there'd be no activity there, there was plenty. My prediction that a boat had arrived was correct, and cargo was already being unloaded. There was intermittent muttering as I pushed my way through the labouring blurred forms of tired — seamen. One clutched my skirt with a lewd remark on his mouth, but I steered clear of him, pushing on, head thrust forward, bonnet pushed onto the back of my cape. The tide was fairly high, but not yet full. A small group of men — two or three — were making their way to an inn near the pier. I stopped then, and one turned. His face was bearded, rough, but not unkind. Something about my manner must have impressed him when I blurted out my urgency for a craft to take me to Merlake. He stood still allowing the other two to go on.

"But you won't find anyone now, miss," he said. "No one in his senses would take a woman across that treacherous bit o' water unless he was wanting the death of both of 'em."

"Oh come now — it's not so bad as that. I'll pay you well — or anyone — who'll do it. It's so urgent. You see — my husband — Mr Sterne — I'm Mrs Sterne, his wife — may be drowned. There was trouble. A fight or something — " I broke off, as his manner changed, became thoughtful, speculative.

"Aye. I've heard on it."

"You *have*?"

"Nothing for sure, ma'am, about his death I mean. But reckon if you go you could do nothin' 'bout it, nothin' at all. Far better for you to go back where you came from — "

"I'm *going*," I said fiercely, foolishly and recklessly, "and if I can't find anyone to take me I'll *swim*."

The statement was mere bravado, of course, but it was sufficient to change his mind.

"I'll see what I can do," he said. "Th' only one I c'n think of is Black Heron. A wild ugly chap in some ways, but a master at rowin' and sailin'. An' what he won't do for cash isn' worth talkin' about. You wait here. I'll go'n find out."

I stood against the wet granite wall making myself as inconspicuous as possible, with the cape drawn tightly under my chin, and the dark hood pulled well over my face. Realising it had been unnecessary and a burden to wear the bonnet I took it off, and let it fall to the damp sand at my feet, where it lay a foolish useless relic of my flight. I was shivering. Every minute the mist and rain were thickening. My skirts were already sodden at the hem.

If only I could have worn breeches and high men's boots! But to have attempted to set off in the chaise as a boy would have meant I'd have been stopped and held at Mounterrith. So I started moving to keep my circulation alive. Occasionally, as the fitful light of a lamp or lantern quivered in the wind, the masts of ships and hunched figures emerged briefly like distorted ghosts through the grey air. From out at sea a siren sounded. Gulls screamed as they dipped down to decks, scavenging among sand and pebbles. The minutes dragged. I wondered if the man had given up his search for Black Heron, and had not bothered to come back and tell me.

At last, however, he appeared, and with him a gigantic thick set form wearing seaman's attire and a cap pulled to the side over one ear. When he drew close I felt a quick stab of apprehension. 'An unpleasant-looking character,' my uncle would have said — black-whiskered, with a scar running from one temple to chin, and a hard mouth, puckered upwards where the wound had healed badly over his cheek, giving the impression of a permanent sneer.

"Here he is," the other friendlier man said. "Black Heron as I was tellin' you about. He says he's willin' to risk the sea providing there's enough to make it worth it."

Under Black Heron's suspicious mean eyes I searched for my reticule, found it in a pocket of my damp gown, and took several sovereigns out. When I'd handed the gold over he said, "That all? Tedn' much for riskin' me life an boat, an' all I've got, lady."

I fiddled frenziedly for more and gave him another coin.

"I've no more," I said stubbornly. "If you're not satisfied hand it back, and I'll find someone else."

He grinned nastily, although the grin was more of a snarl. "You'll get nought back, woman. An' you'll be findin' no one else to take 'ee on such a fool trip. So stop argufyin' an' foller me."

After a nod to the first seaman he cocked a finger and strode ahead, cutting away from the pier. I went after him, half running, lifting my skirts and petticoats well up over my small boots. The rain blew against me, sending rivulets of water running from my eyes down my face. The bobble at the end of the man's cap bobbed up and down in the wind like a small malicious spirit luring me to my doom. Yet I wasn't frightened — just desperate and heedless of danger for myself — only for Ivan.

At last we reached his small craft which was lying roped, half on its side, near the edge of the waves. No sail was apparent, and when I questioned him about it, he snorted, "Sail? In this mucky stuff — doan' be a — " I shut my ears to the offensive word and decided at that point to have no conversation with him at all.

It would have been impossible anyway. The journey across to Merlake was a nightmare of elemental fury — of lashing wind and beating waves that several times sent floods of water breaking over the deck. There was a tiny cramped cabin below. Once Black Heron shouted to me — "Why don' 'ee get below — go on, scram."

But frightened at the thought of being trapped in such a small space if the craft sank — which at times I thought it surely must — I refused to move, and sat clinging to the side of the vessel, until the man's voice roared, "Get f'ward then. Bail, wumman — tek that can an' do a bit o' work."

So while Black Heron's massive muscles and arms struggled with the oars, I did my puny best to deal with the superfluous water.

How we endured and eventually reached the island I don't know. But eventually Black Heron's strength and skill brought us — half driven in on a great wave to a sandy inlet lying west of Merlake pier.

I could hardly stand when he pulled me ashore, and for a moment I thought I'd faint. I put my hand to my stomach involuntarily, and was violently sick.

"I'm sorry," I gasped. "I — "

Even through the distorted light I sensed a knowing look on Black Heron's face.

"Sea-sick?" he shouted. "Or carryin'? Is that it? A brat in your belly?" He guffawed, and I could have hit him. But I hadn't the strength. He drew a large hand over his eyes to wash the rain away, then swept me up as though I was a kitten into his arms, and started climbing. "Let me go — " I cried, giving a muffled scream.

"Shut up," he shouted. "I gotter get you to the house, an't I — which way?"

I tried to think, but all I was aware of was the offensive hot wet smell of him — the wind tearing my breath away, and the sweeping misted cloud of rain lashing against my face. I made an effort to push a knee into his great stomach, and it was then that a figure came scrambling down the rocks from above. There was shouting and confusion. A moment later I was dropped unceremoniously on to a patch of earth. For a few seconds before losing consciousness I had a blurred glimpse of two men struggling. Then there was a crack of a shot followed by the tumbled form of the seaman rolling and bumping over boulders into the grey sea of nothingness below.

★ ★ ★

Darkness came. A deep well of nothingness that could have lasted for minutes or

440

eternity. I never knew. Time died. And from the limbo of mist and shadows a quivering small light penetrated the sea of gloom urging me to movement. I got up, trying to wipe the cobwebbed blur from my eyes. But nothing was clear — only the pin-point of jigging brilliance that danced and jumped ahead like a macabre imp of wickedness — pulling and drawing me as though by an invisible thread.

I followed, pushing through obstructing bushes and brambles, forcing limbs along, although at times my feet wouldn't move and I stood for moments glued to the ground. Then the thing — the light, or dwarf, or whatever it was, paused too. It looked round, grimacing yet featureless with its round head gleaming luminously through nightmare shadows. The string tightened round my body, and I went on again. Gradually the undergrowth fell away, and I found myself in a dank land, alone except for the 'thing' — with great mounds of blackness rising from a high plateau. They were mushroom shaped of tremendous height, monstrous and incredibly menacing.

The light flickered, and in an elongated form, made a beckoning gesture which took me round the base of the looming erections in a circular direction. At the foot of the tallest hill immense boulders were heaped — slithery slimy glittering humps of evil. There was no sound but a hollow moaning that could have been the wind or crying of the countless drowned. Nothing lived. Nothing was human. There was nothing visible to be seen but the leaping gyrations of the 'thing' — the thing I had to follow.

The loneliness was terrible. Never before could there have been such an awful negative void of lifelessness. Just the inky mushroom mountains looming and the fingered glow ever leaping ahead, luring me to the great hell of complete emptiness. Round the base of the largest erection we went, until the mocking figment of evil paused and waited, diminishing one moment, expanding the next, without form, without end. And then I saw the hole. It was a hungry black circle cut deep into the mountainside, quivering for a second — sucking me avidly into entering. The thing now was only a pin-prick of light far away, hovering and jumping — leaping by boulders and over cavernous holes.

I clung desperately to spikes of rock, slipping and slithering, pausing at moments, when my feet refused to move. And on every side of me I fancied faces leered — ugly vile faces, lit occasionally to a vicious wild beauty. I closed my eyes pressing on as a blind person might, until I slipped and fell, and had to make the monstrous journey again.

At last I reached black granite steps. I climbed them automatically, compelled by a shuddering darkness of spirit and the bobbing creature in front. When I reached the top, the void spread into a green radiance that gradually absorbed 'the thing'.

I glanced down.

From a deep stygian well of curdling water, a face stared up at me — a dead face like that of some ancient legendary kind or warrior — ageless, someone or something I couldn't recognise, but seemed to have known since the first wild moment of the earth's conception.

I shuddered, stifling a desire to fall and be one with the terrible silence and chill of death. Did a voice call from the bottomless pit? Did a ghost hand pull me back from extinction, and was the shrill wave of laughter that followed real, or a figment of my own imagination brought to momentary life by some instinct greater than fear? Madness? Was that it? The mockery and leaping light? The quivering distorted thing that had brought me there, to the very brink of hell?

Involuntarily, I stepped back. The greenish pale face receded as the pit closed, taken into the ever enclosing walls of the hole.

I struggled helplessly for air, both hands grappling in darkness. And as I fell, toppling down the cumbrous steps, I screamed.

My own scream dimmed everything else, and was still echoing round walls and ceiling, through water and the rushing of air, when consciousness returned, and I became aware of a mask-like countenance bent towards my own face. I tried to heave myself up, but a hand restrained me.

"Rest, girl," a familiar voice said. "An' drink this — " Sight focussed then. It was a woman's face, broad, with dark eyes and black hair under a lace cap. I tried to think of her name but couldn't. When I'd taken a sip of something from a glass, I blinked and looked round. I was in a bedroom, but had no idea where. There was something familiar about it, that was all. Memory registered no further. I closed my eyes again.

"You'll be all right, Mrs Sterne," the thick familiar voice said. "You had a tumble, but the doctor's been sent for. The weather's clearin' a bit, he'll soon be here."

And even then I didn't know what she was talking about.

I sighed and tried to get up. But a wave of giddiness forced me back again.

"You lie still now," the gruff tones commanded. "Don't try and think. Just rest."

Suddenly everything — or part of it — came back, on a wave of horror. "There were steps," I cried, "and a pit. I had to go on, but everything was dead.

And then I saw it — the face — it was — it was — "

"It was a nightmare you had. Nuthen' else — just a bad dream. Forget it. It'll pass. Here — take a nip more o' this."

She handed me the glass again, and I took it gratefully. The sting of spirits warmed me, and presently, seeing I was better, the woman turned, after telling me she'd soon be back with something on a tray to eat.

Minutes ticked by. There was a little gold clock on a small table at the bedside. I began to count each rhythmic sound — one, two, three, while the other part of my mind searched desperately for coherence. After a while warmth returned to my limbs, giving me energy to go to the window and look out.

The scene stretched grey and desolate under a yellow brooding sky. Rocks and moors sloped down to the leaden sea, where a short pier curved like a giant's knobbly finger. I knew instinctively I should recognise the place — already familiarity was stirring, in an effort to bring coherence from confusion. But it was not until figures moved round the curve of the hill that the sudden truth hit me. They were carrying something, something lying still and stiff on a plank or board; face turned to the sky just as the lifeless countenance had done in my dreadful dream.

"Ivan," I cried, and turning quickly, rushed to the door. Once there however, I could get no further. Sickness rose in me; I had to cling to the knob until faintness passed, enabling me to reach the bed. I dropped myself upon it, and lay back exhausted.

Slowly, my numbed brain cleared, and one by one the happenings of the last few days slipped into place. My flight from Mounterrith, the frightening sea journey, and the suffocating feeling of Black Heron's arms pressing my body against him. Then the fall, and now this.

When Mrs Traille came in a few moments later, she started to speak, but I wouldn't listen, I couldn't. Because I knew what she was going to say. I pressed my hands to my ears turning my face to the wall.

Ivan was dead.

I knew it. Everything in my nightmare must have foretold the truth. The dark pit had been my own despair and loss, the face staring up from the green water had been that of my husband.

Then it was, that I wished, myself, to die.

19

I LAY for some time in a kind of coma, half wanting to rise and face reality, the other part of me trying to shut out the truth.

But at last I forced myself from the bed, automatically reached for a bell, and rang it shrilly. Presently I heard firm footsteps approaching. The door opened. Mrs Traille stood there. She looked annoyed and anxious and before I could speak said sharply, "Get back into bed. I'm responsible for what goes on now, an' if you collapse agen there'll be trouble. I've enough to do — more'n enough, without having to make useless journeys up all them stairs — "

"I shan't collapse," I told her defiantly, and indeed, her short tirade had fanned all the obstinacy I had, which made me feel instantly stronger. "What's happened to my husband? I must know. They brought him back, didn't they? On a stretcher?"

Taken unawares by my blunt questioning the housekeeper was silenced for some moments, with her mouth slightly open in a round button of astonishment. Then she said:

"How did *you* know? That's not your — "

"Business?" I interrupted, "but it is. Of *course* it is. And I wish to see him — *immediately!*"

"You can't."

"Why?" I rushed at her, gripping her muscular shoulders. "Why? Why? Why? I'm his wife. I have every right. Now tell me. Where is he? Downstairs, or here somewhere?"

Taken aback by my manner, she shook herself free, and answered truculently, "The small room — the yellow one. It's quieter there, an' the doctor'll want him peaceful without any talk or emotional goings on when he comes. Now try'n be reasonable, Mrs Sterne." Her attitude softened. I noticed for the first time how tired and strained she appeared without the bombast and scolding. "Can't you leave it for just a bit? 'Tisn't as though you was fit now, is it?" Her glance was probing, filled with a secret knowledge that swept my belligerence away. "You're with child, aren't you? And in shock as well. Mr Ivan wouldn't thank me for lettin' you see him as he is."

"As he *is*? What does that mean?" My voice rose again shrilly. "Is he wounded? Dying?"

"Nothin' of the sort. But — "

"Yes?"

"He wouldn' know you anyways. Not yet. Had a rough time the master has — "

Ignoring her commands and pleading I made a sudden rush past her and on bare feet ran down the main landing to the turn of a smaller corridor where the yellow room was. The door was shut. I opened it quietly and looked in. The curtains were closed so I guessed it was late-evening — or early morning? — what did it matter? Time and place counted for nothing. All that mattered or properly registered to me was the sight of the silent recumbent figure lying on the bed. The side drapes had been pulled back, to give air probably, and a small oil lamp stood nearby on a round table. All trace outside of wind had now died. The silence and complete stillness were more frightening and awesome than any murmuring or argument could have been, and I shivered, recalling the lonely silence of my dream.

I tip-toed over the carpet and looked down. Ivan's head — the proud noble head above the arrogant profile and finely carved features — was bandaged. The lids were closed over the clear grey eyes that had once, in the past, so long ago, now it seemed — been warm with desire for me. The firm yet sensuous lips, were pale and unmoving, like those of some effigy carved in marble. Only the very faint rhythmic movement of breathing indicated any sign of life at all.

"Ivan — " I whispered. "Ivan — " There was no response. As I moved closer the lamplight flickered, lighting momentarily each small line etching the parchment pale skin — accentuating the shadowed hollows beneath the high cheek bones.

Unable any longer to remain so completely aloof, I stretched out an arm, and with one finger lightly touched a cheek. For seconds nothing happened; then, slowly, miraculously, the eyes opened. At first they simply stared. I was afraid; terribly afraid, because I thought he didn't know me. The waiting seemed interminable. I drew back a little and rested my face on the quilt, filled with a dreadful unhappiness and sense of rejection.

Although the room seemed cold, a fire was burning in the grate at the far end. I was about to drag myself away and warm my hands, when movement stirred the bedclothes. I glanced up fearfully, and then, slowly, miraculously, Ivan smiled.

I held my breath, hardly able to believe the smile could be for me. But when he lifted a finger, beckoning, I knew.

I drew near again. The smile had deepened; the eyes were so warm and welcoming, so lit by joy, it was as though a flood of sunlight had dispelled a long winter. Radiance suffused me. All the months of tenseness and bitterness fell away. Summer — summer! My heart thrilled, as his hand enclosed mine.

We were together.

Never before had I sensed the truth

or full awareness of loving. Perhaps I never would, quite so completely again. But this one moment was sufficient to endure for a lifetime.

Presently, still with my hand in his — Ivan slept. And later the doctor came.

★ ★ ★

Ivan's recuperation from his injuries was slow but steady, and during those long summer months until late July, I learned many things — not at first as a dramatic story, told in succeeding instalments, but through odd remarks and explanations which eventually fitted into place like a jigsaw. There were as well lonely periods when he relapsed into himself, and was unforthcoming, and brusque, speaking to me in the old arrogant way, conveying that he wished to be left completely on his own. These times were hard to bear. Often my self-restraint and temper were near breaking point; then I had to remind myself that his moods were not personally directed towards me, but were caused through pain — he had a badly broken leg and head-wounds, and it must have been frustrating, also, for a man of his tremendous energy to be confined in his room, at the mercy of women's care and attention.

One day he said to me, "Don't expect me to be a saint when I recover, Jade-Anna. Once I'm on my feet again I'll have order and obedience at Merlake once more."

"I hope you manage it," I said once, sweetly, "and with more success than before."

"I will — I will. There'd have been no disorder here in the first place if I'd had my way. Well — " He gave a little smile and whimsical lift of one eyebrow, "not much, anyway — except for you, of course. And I'll wager it'll be quite a task getting *you* under control."

When I didn't answer he beckoned with one finger. "Come here."

He was sitting in a chair by the window of our bedroom.

I went over to him obediently. He pulled me down and kissed me.

"I walked across the room this afternoon," he said, "without assistance."

"You *did*?"

"Shall I demonstrate again?"

I set my mouth firmly.

"*No.* You just stay there, or I'll leave."

He still had his hand on my wrist. "You won't, my love. Here you are, and here you'll remain until I give permission."

He was half laughing, and I tried to smile, but somehow I couldn't. There was a long pause. Then he said, "Don't look so serious. Although," he sighed, "you've reason to, God knows. It's not been easy at Merlake, has it? And maybe it'll never be entirely peaceful with you and me — "

"There's more in life than peace," I interrupted. "As for Merlake — "

"Yes?"

"I'm growing used to it."

"And Thorlock? And Jed? Aunt Augusta, and Maurice — "

"I can put up with Aunt Augusta and Maurice."

"I don't know that I want you just to put up with things — especially with the child coming."

I felt the warm colour stain my cheeks. Since I'd told him about the baby, he'd been curiously reticent and appeared unwilling to discuss its future.

"Oh, but the island's a lovely place for young things — or could be," I said, "especially with some of the mysteries and barriers done away with."

"Such as Thorlock?"

I was startled by the abrupt question. Before, Ivan had always managed to steer clear of any deliberate reference to the old man.

"I wasn't only thinking of Thorlock. Of course, I've wondered a good deal about him. He's never seemed quite to belong to the real world. But then," I spoke more practically, "he was real enough to keep you there, in that strange cave, until Jed found you. So I think we should be grateful."

"I suppose so."

"Why does he live there, like that?" I couldn't help asking. "It's damp, so cut off that no one could possibly find him in a mist, and the way down the cliff is so dangerous; it was only by chance I discovered him."

"Which you'd no right to do," Ivan told me sternly. "You could have been killed.

However, I'll admit the old bounder has his uses, and there'd be no point in uprooting him now."

"But why is he *there*, Ivan? And those ancient relics he keeps. Where did he get them? and that — that old portrait?"

Ivan paused before answering.

"So you saw that."

"I could hardly have missed it. She was so very beautiful."

"Yes. My grandfather's wife."

"Do you mean your own grandmother?"

"No. He married twice. She was very young when he met her on the mainland. Ambitious, lovely, and I'm afraid quite amoral. The restricted life at Merlake drove her to seek diversion elsewhere. Hence Thorlock."

"Who was he?"

"A servant here, part-time gardener and partner in devious deeds. He was very good-looking in those days apparently — consequently the secret passion and unfortunate liaison that was inevitably spotted by my jealous grandsire."

"What happened?"

"My grandfather threw her out, both of them with a few possessions, told them

458

to keep out of his sight, anywhere on Merlake, but if they attempted to leave he'd have them shot on sight. I guess he would, too. From any remaining records and stories handed down by word of mouth, Veryan Sterne was a ruthless determined character."

"How were they expected to live?"

Ivan gave a short laugh.

"Old Veryan wouldn't care a damn. And if they hadn't survived — " he shrugged " — well then, that was just a distasteful episode conveniently got out of the way."

"It sounds horrible."

"It probably was. When Veryan died of course, things changed. My own father was of a different calibre altogether. Studious, eccentric. Victor and I were both abroad in the army, fighting the numerous wars for which Britain has become so famous. We were twins. Victor the elder by half an hour. There was an older brother, Richard, but he had a fall from a horse and died. This left my father near-demented, and of course Victor was heir. Then — "

I waited.

Suddenly Ivan appeared to have lost all interest.

"What's the point of going over old history?" he said. "Creating past images and dreams? It's been — " he hesitated " — quite pleasant talking things over in a friendly fashion for once. But the basic facts are going to be quite a different kettle of fish, aren't they? Legally speaking."

My heart sank. It was as though a knife had at one swoop cut through the warmth of our new developing relationship into two parts. His eyes now held a faint calculating bitterness.

"I don't know what you mean," I said dully.

"Oh, yes, you do. Don't prevaricate. Even if we both attempted to gloss over what's happened — it wouldn't work would it? My neglect, your London escapade — our mutual failure to come to terms. Now — " holding up a hand as I started to speak. "Just be sensible. Listen to me. I'm grateful for all the concern you've shown on my behalf, although it was quite mad of you to get mixed up with Black Heron in such a wild sea dash. Just now — when I opened my eyes and saw you here looking so young and stubborn and desirable, it was though a whole new future opened — but — "

"And with me — with me," I interrupted.

"*You*, yes. You're an impossible romantic. But, Anna — Jade-Anna — I can't *live* in such a highly charged atmosphere. I have work to do still — man's work. Another thing — " His expression darkened.

"Yes?"

"The baby. When you told me first, I was — well, I accepted the wonder of it because in my weak befuddled state I so wanted to. But how do I know it's mine? *How*, Jade-Anna? God knows I'd like to. But I'm a practical man — "

His words so cut me I stiffened with contempt and anger — rage and pain so fierce that all the fury I felt burst from me in a wild spate of words.

"*No* — You *don't* know, do you? You never will, because I can't prove it, and because you can take nothing on trust.

Everything in this house is the same — filled with doubt and malice and shame! — yes, *shame*. Well," I almost choked trying to hold my tears back, "you can keep it all, Ivan Sterne. I want none of it — nothing at all, or of you. You're right, quite right, we could never live together, especially after this. You're insufferable — "

I rushed from the room, not bearing to look at him again, and started running along corridors and down the stairs to the hall. There was a cape hanging from a peg. I flung it on, and ran out through the front doors, along the terrace to the drive, cutting round the side of the house upwards, towards the track that led eventually past the ruined chapel and down again by boulders and through rough tangled undergrowth to Thorlock's cave.

It was like scrambling in my dream again, sometimes rushing, at moments pausing with my feet glued to the ground. When I reached the projecting earth and rock that so effectively hid Thorlock's retreat from any watchers from moors or sea, there was a shuddering of the ground followed by a spatter of tumbled stones and soil.

Then I fell.

I didn't faint, neither was I hurt much, except for a twisted arm. At first, as the bent figure of the old man came towards me, my instinctive terror was for the baby. If I lost it — then indeed everything concerning Merlake, for me would be completely over; and perhaps after all, this would be for the best. Through the following hours of that long day I half wished it to be so. But life is strong, and somehow, under Thorlock's careful administrations, the baby within me lived.

As the afternoon closed in towards evening, the old man became reflective, and talking half to himself, let out many things which before had been secret and wrapt in mystery.

"It was the war," he said, poking at the embers of the fire he'd lighted for my comfort. "The war that did it."

"Did what?" I queried.

"Kep me here. Me an' her — " he said, still in the same faraway tones. His eyes travelled momentarily to the broken-framed portrait. "A lovely wumman she was — beautiful, rich with life an' lovin'. The kind o' loving that ole devil Veryan was slowly killin', like one as watches a caged bird sicken' an' perish. But he — " he spat, " — he hadn' a spot o' softness in him — carin' for nuthen but gettin' the stuff here or Cardiff or Bristol, an' makin' a fortune of it. I *knowed* it y'see, an' that's why he wouldn' let us leave. Cos of me tellin'. So I w'd've if I'd got a chance. But there warn't any. Shot we'd bin, so we stayed, like all them others up at that theer big house — "

"What stuff do you mean, Thorlock?" I'd already heard Ivan's version of the story, and wondered if Thorlock's tallied.

"*Opium*." The word came out like the crack of a pistol. "The ole master Veryan Sterne wasn' above doin' anythin' — smugglin', wreckin', even — so he could get isself richer an' richer. When he died the son was different — but — " he touched his head, "odd — funny like in the upper storey. Studyin' so I've heard from that there nasty Jed — turnin' a blind eye. He didn' live many years

464

though, an' I do b'lieve this other one — what do they call him?"

"Ivan?"

"Ivan. That's right." The shadow of the ancient head was emphasized to macabre gigantic stature from the spurting flames of firelight, against the rocky walls.

"I've heard," he went on, "that he's doin' all to stop it. There's ships that calls here secretly as a — what d'they call it — base — an' sometimes those makin' for cities like Bristol an' Liverpool gets blown off course — "

"How do you know this?"

"Jed, an' that miserable nasty son o' his, Marte. But I kip watch, an' tells 'em what I knows, an' gets paid well in a kind o' way — " His voice died into a vague monotone. "Food an' the like. What else do I need — without her?" Again that fleeting glance to the portrait. "She was the real life to me. Sometimes I do think at evenin' time, a time like this, wi' th' sun dyin' and the red shadders leapin', that her soft feet treads from th' sea, an' the wind sighin's her hair brushin' me face. Oh a beauty she was — wi' the kind o' lush rare softness the wild

465

critters has, as roams the coast — "

He drew deeply on his long clay pipe.

"I think I understand, Thorlock," I said. "The trouble is that other people never seem to."

After that there was silence.

Hours later Jed arrived, and I was carried back to the Towers.

20

ORDERS were given to me to stay in bed for three days. I was glad to comply. I had no wish at all to see Ivan or any others of Merlake's macabre domineering characters. I was told by Mrs Traille that Ivan was now comparatively active, although he found stairs difficult, and that he would be along to see me sometime.

"Tell him I've no wish to talk with him," I replied coldly. "I've a headache and want to rest."

She eyed me shrewdly.

"Sure?"

"*Quite* sure."

She left, muttering something under her breath. About an hour later there was a knock on the door, which I had already locked.

"Let me in, Anna," Ivan called dictatorially.

I didn't reply.

He repeated the order.

"Go away. There's no point."

He tried the knob. I wondered if he would attempt to free the lock, or perhaps use a master key. He did neither and a moment later went away.

The next day the doctor called, and told me he was delighted by Ivan's condition.

"Oh? How good of you to make the trip," I remarked tritely.

He looked puzzled, then forcing a bright practical note into his voice said, "And now it's a good idea, don't you think, to take a look at you, Mrs Sterne."

"Why?"

"Because of your condition naturally. Any young wife expecting her first child should have periodic examinations."

"There's nothing wrong with me," I said bluntly.

"All the same, you've been through considerable strain, and I must insist. Your husband specifically mentioned it."

"I really don't know why. I'm strong as a horse, as my aunt used to tell me."

"Even young horses and foals sometimes require a little attention," he said with a quirky look of humour round his lips and in his eyes.

I gave in.

When the tapping and prodding and tests were over, he said, smiling broadly, "Excellent. I have a good report for Mr Sterne."

I almost said, 'Don't bother. There's no need. He's simply wanting to appear the correct concerned husband, but he doesn't care two hoots really. We're nothing to each other.' However, I stifled the impulse, and presently, after putting his instruments into his bag, the doctor bid me farewell 'for the time being', adding that the following day I could go downstairs and take a little 'gentle exercise'.

Gentle exercise! What a farce, I thought. All I wanted was to rush and run from the conflicting atmosphere of the Towers, away from tormenting memories and the insults hurled at me by the man I had once cared for so passionately and deeply. Logically, I supposed he'd had some reason to doubt me. But our relationship should have extended beyond logic and the *appearance* of things. With me it had. Oh, I'd doubted him at times, of course I had. But the touch of his lips on mine, a certain warm glance of his grey eyes had been sufficient to erase everything except the knowledge of my need, and love for him, dispelling the past as just an absurd shadow.

This time though he had gone too far. What was it he'd called me — liar? Cheat? I couldn't quite remember. Only that he'd seen me in the guise of any cheap whore wanting to pass off another man's child as his own.

Quite contemptible.

However, until I once more left Merlake, which I was determined to do on the first convenient opportunity, I would obviously have to keep up some façade in front of the servants. So before going downstairs I rehearsed how I would speak and move when Ivan was about and even practised before the mirror. Aunt Clarissa had frequently suggested sneeringly that I had all the qualities of being a competent actress — 'on a certain level' — meaning, I supposed, of the melodramatic or despised music-hall type, in this way subtly alluding to my father in the same breath.

She was probably right, which was a good thing. So I cultivated an air of icy politeness and good manners, and as I seated myself at the table for luncheon on my first day downstairs, I felt confident the servants could notice nothing amiss. I wore lilac silk, which emphasised my russet hair and contrasting pale skin. The bodice was fittingly decorous but dignified, with a narrow froth of lace at the neck. Ivan was attired in a black velvet jacket, pin-striped breeches, and a cream silk shirt and neck-scarf, over which his finely carved firm features were set unsmilingly. He looked paler than usual, but showed no trace of weakness. During the meal very little was said. I ate mechanically, but with a strange unwanted restlessness churning my inside. I tried not to look at him, but could feel his eyes on me much of the time. Condemning still? Or was he planning something? I didn't know, and this disturbed me.

When the meal was over I told him coolly that the doctor had ordered I should rest each afternoon.

He gave a slight inclination of his head.

"Naturally. Then do as your physician orders. We can always talk later."

"I hardly think there's anything more to talk about," I said cuttingly. "I don't wish to alter any plan you have, Ivan, but now you're better I would really like to return to Mounterrith when it can be arranged." I was standing at the door, with my hand on the knob.

"And if it *can't* be arranged?" he said.

"But — " I floundered in confusion. "Why shouldn't it be? I mean — "

"Haven't you discovered yet, Jade-Anna, that no one leaves Merlake unless I specifically wish it? You've done quite a bit of hopping to and fro between here and the mainland recently, and the fact I'm sure is becoming noticed."

"Does that matter? When we're divorced — "

"*If* we're divorced," he said meaningfully.

"But — "

Before I could move he strode towards me, gripped my wrist and pulled me back into the room, past the table and fireplace, and through into the conservatory. The door closed sharply with a snap.

I stood facing him, chin lifted, determined not to be put at a disadvantage. There was a brief silence before he remarked, "You look very — picturesque — today."

"Thank you."

"Can't you smile?"

"What is there to smile about? Really, Ivan. We're surely beyond play-acting and meaningless compliments."

"Are we?"

Irritated to feel the tell-tale blush staining my cheeks I turned away, to go to my room. The conservatory had somehow become oppressively hot. The sweet heady scent of hot-house and tropical plants brought a threat of approaching giddiness that I knew could turn to nausea.

As I lifted a hand to push a damp curl from my cheek, a strong arm was suddenly round my waist, forcing me to face him.

"My God!" he said, "You're not doing

that to me. Not getting away this time."

I made a feeble attempt to escape, then waited, quite rigid, and uncompliant until his grip relaxed and he stood taut and unsmiling, staring at me challengingly. There was a slight tightening of his upper lip, a narrowing of his gaze, and an increased pounding of my heart. Unable to stand the tension any longer I turned my head away. A hand enclosed my skull and forced it round again. His arms suddenly were tight about me, pressing me close, while his mouth sought and found mine, and he was kissing me cruelly, with such hunger and desire, that equal passion rose in me and we were interlocked in an embrace so wild and violent the world swam, taking me to temporary darkness.

Measured in terms of time, the contact could only have been brief. With his hands encircling my shoulders he half released me, and asked, "Was that so terrible? You wanted it, didn't you?"

"Why should I? What made you think so?"

I knew the remark cut him, and felt a contrary pleasure in the knowledge. At the same time, I could have bitten my tongue for being so mean.

He drew a hand over his damp forehead, went to a cabinet and brought out the brandy and glasses. "Take this," he said, handing me a small one. "Drink it up. Just for once I don't think it will impair your delicate state — if you *are* delicate. But you're not, are you, Jade-Anna? We both know you're strong as a horse, as you've often asserted. Headstrong, wicked and wilful as a — a — "

"Well? As a what?"

The grey of his eyes darkened to the smoky glow of embers lit by fiery sparks.

"Heaven only knows," he said, "but it's quite clear that nothing obviously is going to change you. I'll have to accept you as you are."

"But I thought we'd decided otherwise."

"We'd decided nothing, Jade-Anna. At first, yes, following the Quentin episode. Under those circumstances, I'd do the same all over again. I'm no saint or fool. And was never prepared to play the cuckold — "

"There, you see. You didn't believe me at the time and you don't now. Oh, stop this, Ivan. What's the use? *I* have my pride too — " I broke off breathless.

He smiled.

"Of course you have. You're stuffed with it. As for believing you — maybe I do, now." His voice had changed, become quieter, almost gentle. "In turn, though, you should make an attempt to believe me. Don't you agree?"

I didn't know what to think. Thought was quickly receding into such a wave of longing I was speechless.

"Do you love me?" I heard him say after a pause. "The other day before this last — misunderstanding, I almost thought you did."

"I — I — " suddenly all resistance died in me. Tears struggled and broke from me like a fresh rain spilled from a summer sky. He lifted me up, and my arms were round his neck. My damp cheeks and tumbled hair close against his jacket. It seemed to me, just for a second, that the whole world sang.

Then, firmly, but trembling himself, he carried me up to bed.

★ ★ ★

It was some time before the story, history and mysteries of Merlake were gradually unfolded, making a pattern at first, as bewildering and fitful as the ever-changing moods of Cornwall's remote and wildest territory.

Yet when I looked back, later, everything appeared quite logical and believable, although of course only Ivan himself had held the key to the island's most carefully guarded secret.

"My chief mission of recent years," Ivan told me one day, "until I met *you* of course, when my interests became somewhat divided, shall we say — " he smiled fleetingly " — was concerned with my private struggle to control the spread of opium, despite official policy. This meant there were occasions when ruthless methods had to be used against the smuggling activities of certain merchants determined to import vast quantities of the deadly drug — even to these islands. Hence Jed — Marte — the fortification of Merlake, and the constant watch that had to be kept, in case any lawless boat

477

invaded our shores. I didn't want to see men wrecked or die in combat, God knows. But better that, than the insidious decay, corruption and death from smoking the vile poppy. Oh yes — it had slowly been infiltrating our own islands. On a small scale, of course — but very subtly contrived. I was determined no Sterne boat any more should be involved. It made me sick to realise what had been going on for so long."

"You mean your father was concerned?"

"No. As I've told you before, Jade-Anna, he was a recluse and scholar, and his reign at Merlake was brief. I was referring to wicked old Veryan, my grandfather. During his lifetime my twin brother Victor and I were in the army out east. Our elder brother, Richard, was alive then in residence at the Towers as heir. Doubtless he took part in the vicious practice. Following Richard's fatal accident, Victor prepared to return home, but unfortunately he contracted fever and succumbed to it." Ivan paused, then added quietly, "So there remained only me."

"I see."

"No, Jade-Anna, you don't completely. Unless you'd witnessed personally the demoralising effects of that pernicious weed you'd find it difficult to understand my obsession in trying to stamp the thing out, or for that matter — my recent involvement in purchasing the new line. With full control I'll have the power now to bring the smugglers to heel. And by God, I'm already succeeding. Doing just that. Anyway — to continue with the story — before he died, and my own departure for Merlake, Victor made a strange confession, with a request to me that I felt forced to honour. During his last leave, he told me, he'd fallen in love with a young woman in Plymouth and married her secretly, knowing his family might not approve. He'd meant to break the news gently, a little later. Shortly after the ceremony he'd been recalled unexpectedly to his Regiment and his next leave had had to be cancelled due to some flare-up in Eastern affairs. Then he fell sick, and it was at that time he learned, by letter, that his wife had borne a child — a boy, whom he never doubted was his. He begged me to do all

I could for her and the young baby. An address was given to me, and following the burial I sailed for England and made my way as soon as possible to the place mentioned."

He frowned. There was a pause.

"Yes, Ivan?" I prompted.

"I found it," he continued. "A couple of filthy rooms in a disreputable locality of dockland."

"What a shock for you."

"In more ways than one. After making enquiries on the ground floor I was told by a macabre looking old crone that Mrs Sterne — or 'her who called herself Mrs Sterne', lived at the top of the rickety staircase, but that she had 'a friend' with her at the moment. I went up. Before I reached the top a burly lascivious-looking fellow lurched down, and blundered past me into the street. There was an oil lamp hanging nearby so I caught a clear glimpse of his face. It was an ugly countenance — lewd-eyed, red-cheeked, holding a look of cunning mixed with a furtive kind of fear that told me something was very wrong. 'I'm off, mister, to the police,' he muttered as he passed. 'The murderin' bitch.'"

"A minute later I knew what he meant. My new sister-in-law — " a note of contempt, of renewed horror emphasised the last few words " — was crouched on the floor with her breasts bare, and her red hair loose on her shoulders. *That* — the woman my brother had married. It was revolting. She had a knife in her hand, and was staring down on the corpse of a man. I knew he was dead; his throat was cut from ear to ear, and Marcella — that was what she called herself — looked like some horror out of a waxwork show. I didn't doubt she'd killed him; blood dripped from the knife and had spattered her dress and arms. There was blood everywhere — it was still trickling down the man's chin. I thought at first she was mad. Her mouth was open, her eyes glazed and empty-looking. But when I spoke she pulled herself together and had an explanation ready of course. Victor had been away too long. He'd left her without the means to live, and she'd had to exist somehow — for his sake — pointing to a young child in a wooden crib, Victor's son. There'd been a fight, and somehow this 'friend' of hers — Luke — had got killed. It was an accident, she'd insisted. 'An *accident*. Will they say it was *me*?'"

"I told her to wash and when she'd cleaned herself speedily at the sink I took a good look at her and knew she'd been lying, as she must have lied to Victor during his first infatuation for her. Oh she was beautiful in a lush way, but older than I'd expected from my brother's description. The rooms she'd taken could have had a certain exotic elegance about them before deterioration set in. But any pretence of dignity had vanished. She looked what she was — a conscienceless whore making what livelihood she could from her body's assets. It was only the baby — Victor's son, that decided me to help her. And there was no time to delay. I picked up the baby, told the woman to get something on, and minutes later we'd left and were making for the harbour. Luckily there was a fog, and it was evening, quickly growing dark. The stranger who'd passed me on the stairs had not yet had time to get any police

482

alert properly arranged — that he'd do so I had no doubts whatever — to save his own face. Soon a description of the woman would be circulating, and her name given. The first thing to do therefore was to get her and the child to Merlake."

"I had plenty of gold in my pocket and managed to charter a craft manned only by the captain, his wife, and a deck-hand. The journey to the island was the worst I'd ever known. There was a freak storm. Just off the coast of Merlake the boat overturned and three drowned — the captain, his wife and the seaman. Somehow I managed to get the child and his mother to safety. The rest of the story — well it sounds fantastic now, but the plot worked. The woman evolved a new name for herself — a name you know, Lalage Dupont. The boy Maurice became her nephew and my heir. Victor's son, I was determined, should have every chance to inherit Merlake without dishonour to his name. I knew very well that Marcella's description would be issued on the mainland as the woman wanted for murder. So every device was used to change her appearance — including the dyed hair."

"From red to black. Yes, I'd discovered it was dyed," I said.

"Of course I had to report the wreck," Ivan continued, "and when the body, presumably of the captain's wife, was eventually washed up, I identified her falsely as my sister-in-law. She was quite unrecognisable by then, but was wearing a bangle of the type fashionable at that time, which I stated had been given to her by my brother. My word was not doubted, no intimidating questions were asked. Neither was there ever any trace found of the other victims. Marcella's death was accepted, so no case of murder against Maurice's mother was followed up. An open verdict had been recorded on the death of the man she'd stabbed. However, care had to be taken that she never ventured on the mainland. Someone, somewhere might have recognised her, and for this reason, as well as the opium business, the inhabitants of the island were forbidden — except under certain exceptional circumstances — to leave. Oh, there are many details yet to be explained, but I think enough's been said now to give the outline, except — "

"Yes?"

"I've been making enquiries through the years, searching for indisputable proof that Maurice was truly Victor's son. And at last I have the answer. From dates, records, gossip, and delving into old history, I've discovered the child had been conceived *before* the woman's relationship with Victor ever started. He's not my heir. But naturally he'll still have every chance in life that I can give him — a good home, education and an opportunity to follow some worthwhile career."

There was a pause.

"But Ivan," I queried, "how can you *prove* he's not your nephew, after so long?"

"I have found the father," Ivan told me. "It's taken years, but I've done it, and everything fits."

It took me some time to get sequences into order and from time to time during the days following Ivan's narrative, small points cropped up including a query about Siri, which I had to put to Ivan.

"Why were you so concerned about her?" I asked.

"Jealous?"

"I was at the time," I admitted.

"My dear love, if you could have conjured up a *little* trust in me, or used that pretty head of yours more effectively you'd surely have guessed she was to me, merely, a matter of business. She was far cleverer than she appeared to be, and had a pretty good knowledge of the shipping company's plans — the line now under my control — for continuing their dirty trading methods. You see the drug traffic round our coast, though comparatively small, brought in a tidy sum, and was run under coverage of respectable large cargoes and then generally delivered casually by smaller boats to hidden secret bases. Merlake in the past had been a godsend — or rather devil's hidey-hole for such nasty work. Now never again, thank heaven. But Siri, remember, has been of great use — under duress — in giving guidance concerning when to expect a smuggler's approach — what type of boat, and under whose control. And by the way, the seaman who'd got enamoured of Lalage and attempted to get her to the mainland, had been a survivor, with Siri, of the wreck you witnessed."

His voice changed.

"You should never have been there. And I should have walloped you soundly. Know that?"

I smiled up at him, "I don't know yet quite *what* to think of you, Ivan."

"Good. A high-spirited wife needs to retain a little awe of her own husband. It's the way of things. Natural."

He drew me to him, and warmth flooded me, with such radiance and awareness of countless summer times ahead together, that all the questioning and mysteries of the past were suddenly unimportant. Nothing in the world mattered but Ivan and me, and a future salvaged at last from the miasma of doubt and misunderstanding.

Conclusion

From the 'Daily Clarion'

YESTERDAY Mr Ivan Sterne was honoured by Her Majesty Queen Victoria at Buckingham Palace. A Knighthood was conferred for his gift to the nation of Merlake Island as a beauty resort for visitors wishing to inspect the grandeur and wild life of this unique spot of British terrain, and for his great services in stamping out illegal trading by shipping companies. He was accompanied by his wife, who was formerly Miss Jade-Anna Ellan, a well-known member of an old Cornish family, and their eldest son, Mark, now eight years old.

Sir Ivan and Lady Sterne appeared a most striking couple as they left the Palace, and later, when asked the secret of her enduring beauty and youthful appearance, Lady Sterne remarked with an amused glance at her husband,

'Perhaps you had better ask Sir Ivan that. He's a better judge of character than I am.'

The couple recently acquired a new gracious residence outside Falmouth, Carcroft Hall, which will be their permanent home.

NURSE ALICE IN LOVE
Theresa Charles

Accepting the post of nurse to little Fernie Sherrod, Alice Everton could not guess at the romance, suspense and danger which lay ahead at the Sherrod's isolated estate.

POIROT INVESTIGATES
Agatha Christie

Two things bind these eleven stories together — the brilliance and uncanny skill of the diminutive Belgian detective, and the stupidity of his Watson-like partner, Captain Hastings.

LET LOOSE THE TIGERS
Josephine Cox

Queenie promised to find the long-lost son of the frail, elderly murderess, Hannah Jason. But her enquiries threatened to unlock the cage where crucial secrets had long been held captive.

TIGER TIGER
Frank Ryan

A young man involved in drugs is found murdered. This is the first event which will draw Detective Inspector Sandy Woodings into a whirlpool of murder and deceit.

CAROLINE MINUSCULE
Andrew Taylor

Caroline Minuscule, a medieval script, is the first clue to the whereabouts of a cache of diamonds. The search becomes a deadly kind of fairy story in which several murders have an other-worldly quality.

LONG CHAIN OF DEATH
Sarah Wolf

During the Second World War four American teenagers from the same town join the Army together. Forty-two years later, the son of one of the soldiers realises that someone is systematically wiping out the families of the four men.

THE LISTERDALE MYSTERY
Agatha Christie

Twelve short stories ranging from the light-hearted to the macabre, diverse mysteries ingeniously and plausibly contrived and convincingly unravelled.

TO BE LOVED
Lynne Collins

Andrew married the woman he had always loved despite the knowledge that Sarah married him for reasons of her own. So much heartache could have been avoided if only he had known how vital it was to be loved.

ACCUSED NURSE
Jane Converse

Paula found herself accused of a crime which could cost her her job, her nurse's reputation, and even the man she loved, unless the truth came to light.

THE PLEASURES OF AGE
Robert Morley

The author, British stage and screen star, now eighty, is enjoying the pleasures of age. He has drawn on his experiences to write this witty, entertaining and informative book.

THE VINEGAR SEED
Maureen Peters

The first book in a trilogy which follows the exploits of two sisters who leave Ireland in 1861 to seek their fortune in England.

A VERY PAROCHIAL MURDER
John Wainwright

A mugging in the genteel seaside town turned to murder when the victim died. Then the body of a young tearaway is washed ashore and Detective Inspector Lyle is determined that a second killing will not go unpunished.

DEATH ON A
HOT SUMMER NIGHT
Anne Infante

Micky Douglas is either accident-prone or someone is trying to kill him. He finds himself caught in a desperate race to save his ex-wife and others from a ruthless gang.

HOLD DOWN A SHADOW
Geoffrey Jenkins

Maluti Rider, with the help of four of the world's most wanted men, is determined to destroy the Katse Dam and release a killer flood.

THAT NICE MISS SMITH
Nigel Morland

A reconstruction and reassessment of the trial in 1857 of Madeleine Smith, who was acquitted by a verdict of Not Proven of poisoning her lover, Emile L'Angelier.

SEASONS OF MY LIFE
Hannah Hauxwell
and Barry Cockcroft

The story of Hannah Hauxwell's struggle to survive on a desolate farm in the Yorkshire Dales with little money, no electricity and no running water.

TAKING OVER
Shirley Lowe and Angela Ince

A witty insight into what happens when women take over in the boardroom and their husbands take over chores, children and chickenpox.

AFTER MIDNIGHT STORIES,
The Fourth Book Of

A collection of sixteen of the best of today's ghost stories, all different in style and approach but all combining to give the reader that special midnight shiver.

DEATH TRAIN
Robert Byrne

The tale of a freight train out of control and leaking a paralytic nerve gas that turns America's West into a scene of chemical catastrophe in which whole towns are rendered helpless.

THE ADVENTURE OF THE CHRISTMAS PUDDING
Agatha Christie

In the introduction to this short story collection the author wrote "This book of Christmas fare may be described as 'The Chef's Selection'. I am the Chef!"

RETURN TO BALANDRA
Grace Driver

Returning to her Caribbean island home, Suzanne looks forward to being with her parents again, but most of all she longs to see Wim van Branden, a coffee planter she has known all her life.

SKINWALKERS
Tony Hillerman

The peace of the land between the sacred mountains is shattered by three murders. Is a 'skinwalker', one who has rejected the harmony of the Navajo way, the murderer?

A PARTICULAR PLACE
Mary Hocking

How is Michael Hoath, newly arrived vicar of St. Hilary's, to meet the demands of his flock and his strained marriage? Further complications follow when he falls hopelessly in love with a married parishioner.

A MATTER OF MISCHIEF
Evelyn Hood

A saga of the weaving folk in 18th century Scotland. Physician Gavin Knox was desperately seeking a cure for the pox that ravaged the slums of Glasgow and Paisley, but his adored wife, Margaret, stood in the way.

DEAD SPIT
Janet Edmonds

Government vet Linus Rintoul attempts to solve a mystery which plunges him into the esoteric world of pedigree dogs, murder and terrorism, and Crufts Dog Show proves to be far more exciting than he had bargained for . . .

A BARROW IN THE BROADWAY
Pamela Evans

Adopted by the Gordillo family, Rosie Goodson watched their business grow from a street barrow to a chain of supermarkets. But passion, bitterness and her unhappy marriage aliented her from them.

THE GOLD AND THE DROSS
Eleanor Farnes

Lorna found it hard to make ends meet for herself and her mother and then by chance she met two men — one a famous author and one a rich banker. But could she really expect to be happy with either man?

THE SONG OF THE PINES
Christina Green

Taken to a Greek island as substitute for David Nicholas's secretary, Annie quickly falls prey to the island's charms and to the charms of both Marcus, the Greek, and David himself.

GOODBYE DOCTOR GARLAND
Marjorie Harte

The story of a woman doctor who gave too much to her profession and almost lost her personal happiness.

DIGBY
Pamela Hill

Welcomed at courts throughout Europe, Kenelm Digby was the particular favourite of the Queen of France, who wanted him to be her lover, but the beautiful Venetia was the mainspring of his life.

PREJUDICED WITNESS
Dilys Gater

Fleur Rowley finds when she leaves London for her 'author's retreat' in the wilds of North Wales that she is drawn, in spite of herself, into an old tragedy.

GENTLE TYRANT
Lucy Gillen

Working as Ross McAdam's secretary, Laura couldn't imagine why his bitchy ex-wife should see her as a rival.

DEAR CAPRICE
Juliet Gray

Clifford Fortune married Caprice but his brother, Luke, knew the marriage was a mistake. He could allow himself to love Caprice blindly but that would be betraying his own brother.

IN PALE BATTALIONS
Robert Goddard

Leonora Galloway has waited all her life to learn the truth about her father, slain on the Somme before she was born, the truth about the death of her mother and the mystery of an unsolved wartime murder.

A DREAM FOR TOMORROW
Grace Goodwin

In her new position as resident nurse at Coombe Magna, Karen Stevens has to bear the emnity of the beautiful Lisa, secretary to the doctor-on-call.

AFTER EMMA
Sheila Hocken

Following the author's previous auto-biographies — EMMA & I, and EMMA & Co., she relates more of the hilarious (and sometimes despairing) antics of her guide dogs.

LEAVE IT TO THE HANGMAN
Bill Knox

Dope, dynamite, guns, currency — whatever it was John Kilburn and his son Pat had known how to get it in or out of England, if the price was right. But their luck changed when one of them killed a cop.

A VIOLENT END
Emma Page

To Chief Inspector Kelsey there was no shortage of suspects when Karen Boland was murdered, and that was before he discovered that she stood to inherit substantially at twenty-one.

SILENCE IN HANOVER CLOSE
Anne Perry

In 1884 Robert York is found brutally murdered at his home in Hanover Close. When, three years later, Inspector Pitt is asked to investigate, the murder remains unsolved.

A RARE BENEDICTINE
Ellis Peters

Three vintage tales of medieval intrigue and treachery featuring the author's monastic sleuth Brother Cadfael.

POIROT'S EARLY CASES
Agatha Christie

In this collection of eighteen stories, Hercule Poirot begins his celebrated career in crime.

THE SILVER LINK
— THE SILKEN LIE
Lynn Granger

Elspeth is determined to preserve her Scottish heritage and the Elliot name, but running Everanlea, a large hill farm, presents problems.